Praise for *Rascal on the Run*

This vivid, sure-voiced page-turner is a compelling murder mystery and so much more. Deftly weaving together two murder cases and their subsequent trials with colorful dialogue and a generous measure of sly humor, it unpacks the personal demons of its father-and-son lawyer protagonists, and the painful history of the American South. A retired lawyer himself, Howard Scott clearly knows well the terrain he writes about—the courtroom antics, the family dramas, the blatant racism that still flourishes in mid-twentieth-century Athens, Georgia—delivering it all as smoothly as his characters deliver their closing arguments. Here's hoping that we'll see more of Critter Stillwell, his quirky siblings, and his buck-the-status-quo Southern belle mother in the future.

—Ann Vanderhoof, author of *An Embarrassment of Mangoes* and *The Spice Necklace*

The genial style of Rick Bragg meets the pathos of Pat Conroy in this touching, often laugh-out-loud tale brimming with wry language and knee-slapping metaphors. The novel could have stayed in the shallows of humor and succeeded, but the story becomes noteworthy, even enduring, because it delves deeper. A correction of Harper Lee's view of the South instead of an homage, *Rascal on the Run* persistently questions how a person, community, and region can recover from a haunted past. It's in these explorations and the answers offered that it shines. Fans of Southern stories and historical fiction are sure to love this insightful, unforgettable debut.

—Blueink Review

D0912173

Rascal on the Run

RASCAL
ON
THE RUN

HOWARD TATE SCOTT

Paperback: 978-1-7362118-0-9
Hardcover: 978-1-7362118-2-3
Ebook: 978-1-7362118-1-6
LCCN: 2021900578

*This is a work of fiction. Names, characters, places, and incidents
either are the product of the author's imagination or are used
fictitiously, and any resemblance to actual persons, living or dead,
businesses, companies, or locales is entirely coincidental.*

Cover design by Kapo Ng
Interior design by Liz Schreiter
Editing and book production by Reading List Editorial:
readinglisteditorial.com

*TO ALL THOSE WHO HAVE TAKEN
THE ROAD LESS TRAVELED.*

- *1* -

I am my father's son, inside and out. I have his angular shoulders and long arms, and I've tried to use them with the same fearless work ethic. As I grow older, his prominent jaw defines my face the way an escarpment emerges to define glaciated rock. His chin was there all along, I see, and Vivienne, my longtime cruising companion, tells me I have the same habit of bracketing it with my hand when pondering legal principle or the market price of Georgia white shrimp. I walk the earth with my father's lanky gait and see the world through his egalitarian gray eyes. I am the third in my family to bear the name August Guilford Stillwell, and my father is the second. Granddaddy, the son of a Georgia sharecropper, never allowed himself to be less than Mr. Stillwell, but people called my father Guy, and anyone who noticed me standing in his long shadow called me Critter.

My father was an old-school, rare-back-and-give-'em-hell lawyer with a stentorian voice that thundered from somewhere deep in his chest and rattled the ear bones of everyone else at the table. He could speak Latin, quote the King James Bible, and tell a dirty joke, all in one impassioned jury summation. He was a zealous litigator, infamous for closing arguments that left the whole courtroom laughing through tears, but I believe it was his unshakable belief in justice that won jurors over in the end. Guy Stillwell made a name for himself defending those less fortunate: people of low means, people of color, people slipping through the cracks of moral ambiguity. He discriminated against no one—as long as they could scrape up the money to hire him. There was endless forbearance about a client's predicament, but seldom any forgiveness of the fee.

Working as a sort of glorified gofer at the law office during the summer of 1963, I went with Guy to the county jail to visit with a prospective client who'd been charged with robbing a bank over in Madison but swore up, down, and sideways that he was innocent.

Guy asked him, "Do you have money for a defense attorney?"

"I can get five hundred dollars from my mama," said this fella, who was not much older than me at the time. His name was Mott Loebel.

My father perused the arrest report. "Says here the robbers absconded with a little over three thousand dollars. I'll need half of that."

"Yeah, but . . . whoever did that robbery—not me, understand, but whoever that might be . . . well, they probably only got half," said Mott. "And probably their partner told 'em not to spend it right away or they'd look suspicious."

"Probably so." Guy folded his hands on the steel table, contemplating. "Sounds to me, friend, like you need a fifteen-hundred-dollar lawyer, but if all you're able to spend is five, I can refer you to a greenhorn who'll handle your case for that. You could take your chances. Accept that you might find yourself leg-ironed at the end of the day. Have you ever felt the cold of a leg iron, son?"

"No, sir."

"It's a peculiar kind of cold," said Guy. "An implacable, icy despair that goes to the bone and leaves the skin as raw as frostbite."

Mott swallowed hard and said, "What do you think I oughta do?"

Guy leaned forward, elbows on his knees, the way he did when he wanted the client to know he was fully engaged in their dilemma.

"Pony up the fifteen hundred," he said. "Once we've taken care of the fee, I'll work out a plea deal with D.A. Ruckels. Come clean. Be a man and take responsibility for what got done. If you roll over on your partner and divulge the whereabouts of the money, maybe the State of Georgia sees fit to reward your cooperation. With time off for good behavior, you're home with your mama next Christmas."

"I ain't no ratfuck snitch," said Mott. "I ain't doin' that to Early. He's my friend."

"That's admirable, son, but I guaran-damn-tee Early's having this very conversation with his own lawyer right now. One or the other of you is gonna be the first man to write down a confession. Somebody's lawyer is going to be the first one in the door to make that deal with Ruckels. Early's lawyer or yours. Unless he's such a good friend, he'd rather sit in jail and watch you go home next Christmas. Is that the kind of friend Early is?"

Mott glanced right and left, looking for a way out, tears in his eyes. Guy set a Big Chief tablet on the table in front of him and placed a pen next to it.

"Good news is, nobody got hurt," said Guy. "You're young. We all make mistakes when we're young. Everybody understands that. You could walk away from this and rebuild a life on the right side of things."

That summer, following Guy and his partner, King Hodges, from case to case—juggling paperwork, running up and down the courthouse steps with writs, briefs, and motions—I came to understand that good lawyering is more about solving problems than it is about winning cases at all costs.

"The objective is not to dive into litigation at the drop of a hat," Guy said as we drove away from the jailhouse. "Solve the problem in the most efficacious way possible for everybody involved."

"What if the other party doesn't want it solved?" I asked.

"Then you go to court and kick his ass up to his shoulder blades."

That summer, *To Kill a Mockingbird* was playing at the Alps Drive-In theater out at the end of Baxter Street. I saw the movie eight times with eight different girls, and every one of them called out the obvious comparison of my father to Atticus Finch. I smiled and nodded, but the truth is, Finch didn't drink hard enough to keep up with Guy Stillwell, who was what people would come to describe as a "high-functioning alcoholic"—no pun intended. Instead of the humble front porch occupied by Gregory Peck, my father saw to it that our family home had a grand wraparound portico with tall white columns and rattan peacock chairs. He'd spent years diligently stewarding every dollar he made. I knew of cases where he accepted goods in trade—a couple of country hams or a few bushels of corn—in lieu of cash, but he never aspired to be seen as a do-gooder. He was a hold-nothing-sacred shit-disturber who earned every dollar of his fortune and every inch of his bigger-than-life reputation.

Guy spent most of his life at the law office, a refurbished antebellum mansion down on Hancock Avenue, close to the courthouse in downtown Athens, and because I always wanted to be near him, from the time I was walking, I spent a lot of my time there too—after school, on rainy Saturdays, and most of the summer. When I was too little to do much else, I slid down the grand staircase banister, made file-box forts in the attic, and fetched cigarettes from the dime store. When I was bigger, I helped Guy's law clerks review investigation files, sorted and labeled crime scene photos, and fetched bourbon and Binaca from the liquor store.

When I turned fifteen, King Hodges hooked me up with a brand-spanking-new provisional driver's license, so I could chauffeur him and Guy wherever they needed to go. Neither of them wanted to risk an accident or the embarrassment of a DUI, and they knew they'd already pressed their luck far beyond what was prudent. My father was still able to get through the early part of the day without a drink, but if King didn't have his "hair of the dog" with breakfast, he started shaking as soon as the previous evening's bender was metabolized. Without asking incommodious questions, I happily took the wheel of "the land yacht"—a Cadillac Eldorado Brougham upon which King had gotten a lien to secure the retainer for a client who subsequently went to jail for tax fraud—or "tax avoidance," as my daddy would say.

From that summer on, I was as much a fixture in the law office as the towering bookshelves on both sides of the grand staircase that rose from the marble floor in the foyer to an open catwalk that circled the second floor. At the top of this very *Gone with the Wind* "This is one night you're not turning me out!" sort of staircase, the imposing double doors of my father's office stood open or slammed shut accordingly.

Inside the sanctum sanctorum, he sat behind an English Chippendale desk the size of a coal barge and paced a well-worn path on a Persian rug. On the wall opposite the windows was a gallery of framed photos and newspaper clippings—sensational cases, political players, and industrial magnates—but I was more fascinated by the wide trophy case below.

This barrister bookcase was about six feet wide and four feet high and had glass doors that lifted up and slid back. Inside, there was a bizarre collection of household, industrial, and agricultural implements, large and small: an ice pick, a carburetor, a can of Campbell's tomato soup, a pack of Black Jack chewing gum, a crowbar, an old flintlock and several other handguns, assorted cordage, poisons, and blades of varying length and serration. According to a quaint Southern custom that would never fly in the current century, if a murder trial ended with an acquittal, the prosecutor was obliged to award the murder weapon to the defense attorney as a trophy. My father's trophy case was crowded with stories, and I never tired of hearing the gruesome details, which amounted to a master class in legal stratagem.

Guy's reputation for fierce and wily defense went back to the 1940s and outlived his larger-than-life career. When King retired, he joked that I ought to rename the firm "Stillwell & Boy." Even after my father died, when folks called the offices of Stillwell & Hodges Attorneys at Law, my father's secretary Mary-Louise (whom I was also blessed to inherit) would say, "Attorney Stillwell is indisposed. You can speak to his boy if you like." It didn't even occur to her that when they asked for Attorney Stillwell, they were asking for me. Thus was my father's colossal standing in the community that encompassed Athens and all the surrounding counties.

If I had inherited my father's driven ambition, I might feel slighted by all that, but I was born to privilege, like my mother, Theodora Marblesmith Stillwell, who just the other day reminded me, "We can afford to let that sort of thing go."

My mother has perfected the art and science of letting things go. She's had a lot of practice. She talks about the past, about politics, and about my father in particular, applying a gauzy mental mosquito net, the way a cinematographer does when he films an aging starlet. My baby sister, Tatum, who tends to the computational, calls this "the Instagram filter of dementia." My older sister, Bootsy, ever the romantic, says it's "the sweetest possible application of abject denial." Vivvy, with the benefit of distance and clean sea air, calls it love.

"I speak from experience," Vivvy says. "Stillwell men are hard to quit."

I'd like to think that's true, but my mother found a way. One muggy night in 1988, after investing thirty-some years in the arduous mission of their marriage, which had become a slog as joyless as the march to Golgotha, she decided she'd had enough of his drunken invective and turned him out in the middle of a substantial downpour. My father showed up at my door, soaked and dispirited. The deluge came down in torrents typical of the region, which is subtropical, and the season, approaching fall. Big, warm raindrops saturated my father's white linen shirt and mingled with genuine tears in his eyes. I never saw a sorrier man.

"She's done with me, Critter," he said. "She gave me the shank of her adult life, and I gave her mine. Now it's all over but the paperwork. I'm relieved, mostly, and she's earned whatever her lawyer wrings out of me in the settlement, but goddammit, she could have waited for the sun to come up."

"What happened?" I asked, but he shook his head.

"I'm unwell," he murmured, "unwell" being our family's time-honored euphemism for shit-faced. "I need a place to lay my head."

I was not happy to see him in this condition, but it never crossed my mind to turn him away. My father and I had invested in each other too, you see. Nine-tenths of everything I knew about practicing law I'd learned from him, starting out as a studious and well-behaved youth of thirteen. So studious and well behaved was I, in fact, that my parents sent me to military school the following year. Had I not been expelled for running bootlegged alcohol from Athens to a dry county sixty miles away, I might be a brigadier general by now, but that's another story.

Guy took hold of my arm and made the spread-eagle step from the dock to the houseboat I kept moored to a piling on the Oconee River behind a model home that anchored a budding subdivision being developed by myself and a small cadre of thoughtful investors. The boat was a shallow-water pontoon with about as much square footage as a modern RV, remarkably urbane, with a nice front porch, compact but hospitable living area, kitchen, judiciously situated water closet, and a queen-size owner's bunk. A covered rooftop deck was furnished with bamboo seating, a wet bar and gas grill, and scrim curtains for mosquito control.

The Oconee is a ponderous, brown river, too low and slow to navigate half the year, so the boat couldn't actually go anywhere, but still, boat life suited me. Every now and then I was startled from sleep when my boudoir bumped up against the boathouse where my development cohorts kept an aluminum skiff and fishing gear. Other than that, I was as comfortable as a baby in a sling.

The structure rocked a little when Guy stepped on board. He turned gray around the gills and vomited into the dark water, then lingered at the rail, groaning that he felt like he was dying and feared he might not, until the rain eased off, replaced by evening mist. I went to the galley kitchen and made scrambled eggs with ketchup and cayenne pepper to ease the drumbeat in his head. Over the past year, as his arms and legs dwindled, his belly had distended to that tight half globe that signals advancing cirrhosis of the liver. There wasn't much in the way of food he could keep down anymore, but he liked the way I cooked his eggs.

While I waited for the pan to heat up, I dialed the old home, and my mother picked up, calling off to the side, "That's all right, Doralee, I got it. No, I got it up here, Doralee. That's fine. Thank you."

"Hey, Mother."

"Critter! What a joy. I was just saying to Doralee that we haven't heard from you in I don't know how long."

"I just wanted to let you know I've got Guy over here."

"Oh. Goodness. I told the taxi driver to take him home. To the apartment. You know."

I did know—had known since I was fifteen—that my father kept an upstairs apartment in an old mansion on Hill Street where he enjoyed the company of a series of lady friends. Every one of them, so far as I know, was a girl of good character, usually a grad student working on her law degree or a PhD in psychology or English literature. It was an equitable arrangement: the young lady had a lovely Edwardian apartment in which to study without the distraction of a day job, and my father had the pleasure of her company. Expectations were clear from the start, so there was never any drama.

"Good fences make good neighbors," Guy said in reference to any contract negotiation. My father weathered each transition unperturbed. When one of these young women passed the bar and went on her way, another moved in to replace her, but the idea that any of them could replace my mother was patently ridiculous. Never once had I heard my father refer to the place as "home," and I had never heard my mother refer to it at all.

"Truly, I was hoping he'd marry this one," said Mother. "She's good people. Comes from the Savannah Pankhursts on her daddy's side."

"Be that as it may—"

"August," she cut me off, "I need you to be full-grown about this. The man is on a downward spiral. We cannot have him end up with some Arkansas traveler who's gonna sink her claws into family money that rightfully belongs to you and your sisters after I'm gone."

"Well, last time I checked, you're still here, and he's still married to you, so that's not an issue."

"Critter, honey, I love your daddy, and I always will, but you've handled enough of these cases to know exactly what I'm talking about."

"Have you had him served?" I asked.

"Earlier this evening. Honestly, I thought he'd be pleased, but it seems to have set him off. Doesn't take much these days. King's preaching the gospel of AA, trying to get him to make another attempt at rehab. Maybe that'll stick this time."

"I try not to make it my business."

"Critter, honey, sooner or later it'll be your business, like it or not. I worry that you're in denial about that."

"He's due in court tomorrow," I said. "He'll need a fresh suit of clothes and his lucky Ferragamos."

"Bootsy's on her way over with a bag for him."

"What about you?"

"What about me?"

"Are you okay?"

"Of course." She laughed, and it sounded as happy as a collie off its leash. There was no bravely heartbroken "fiddle-dee-dee, I'll think about it tomorrow" inflection that might have imparted a little poignance to the occasion. "But aren't you sweet for asking," she added.

We said goodbye, and I split a cathead biscuit and scraped the scrambled eggs onto it. Guy had made his way up to the roof with a bottle of Johnnie Walker Black Label I'd recently received as a thank-you gift from a client. Not an accomplished criminal. Someone caught up in a case of murder by mishap and charged with negligent homicide. This particular gentleman could ill afford the Scotch.

"I guess he figured it was a bargain," said Guy, "compared to the prison years he might have endured had he not engaged an attorney with such a flair for closing arguments."

I set his egg biscuit on the coffee table, took a clean highball glass from the bar, and rescued an ounce or two for myself.

"That's it. Hair of the dog." He clapped his hands on his thighs. "What have you heard about State versus Farringer?"

"Prosecution is still trying to get the DNA admitted into evidence. Nothing I can't handle."

"And that—that land deal with the—the Whatchamacallits . . ."

"Letting some dust settle."

"Abernathy versus Abernathy?"

"Tatum's doing some digging. Seems like there might be some hidden assets involved."

Guy rumbled his disapproval. "You need to onboard a proper PI. Someone who can testify in court and not come off like a golldamn wraith under cross-examination."

Rather than revisit this particular disagreement with our father, I just said the requisite "yes, sir" and lit a citronella candle to fend off the persistent mosquitoes. I had my reasons for keeping Tatum on the payroll, and my father's attention to detail had slipped somewhat, so it wasn't difficult to quietly do as I pleased at the law office, as long as I kept my mouth shut about it. Mary-Louise was a willing accomplice to whatever kept the peace. She knew as much about law as any modern paralegal and was particularly helpful on any divorce case that put a well-heeled gentleman back on the market. She had a bubbly Dolly Parton personality with an hourglass figure and mile-high hair to match, and she was dedicated to my daddy. A series of deftly handled divorces had left her with plenty of money to retire on, but there was never any question: as long as Guy kept practicing, she'd be his Girl Friday.

"An old friend reached out to me regarding a possible criminal matter," said Guy. "He's strapped for cash, but we should be able to secure a lien on his yacht for the retainer." He handed me a hastily scribbled note with the name of the boat, *Rascal*, followed by a serial number, make, and model.

"Does this old friend have a name?"

"Several," said Guy. "But technically, the yacht is the property of a shadow corporation out of the Cayman Islands. Do a registration search and get the lien. We'll cross additional bridges as they need crossing."

"Got it."

"I know I can count on you to do what needs doing."

"Yes, sir."

He nodded an appreciative nod. "You were raised right. I'll say that for myself."

I sipped my Scotch and let that go by. When I was a boy, the division of labor in our home was typical of an affluent family in the midcentury South, a stately plantation-era home veiled by dogwood blossoms and day-drinking. My parents, each at the center of their own universe, were pillars of the community, political movers and shakers. My sisters and I often felt like an afterthought, but we were also living proof that their love was hearty and intimate in the early years.

Their relationship fostered my own belief in love when I was not yet a man, but eventually, it started to sink in that somewhere outside my understanding, the robust partnership had thinned to pretense, little more than a smoke screen that maintained their place in Athens society but occupied no real estate in their hearts.

"I spoke with Mother. She seems to be taking all things in stride."

"Good." Guy accepted this with a philosophical nod. "I don't wish her any more trouble."

"I know."

"Don't tell her I was weak."

"Were you? I didn't notice."

"That's my boy." He grinned and knuckled my jawbone.

"She says she loves you and always will."

"Yeah, she told me," he huffed. "Right before she put me out in the monsoon."

The crickets came alive as the clouds broke up, revealing a few bright stars. Erelong, we saw headlights turn off the paved driveway, and Bootsy's bright yellow Thunderbird eased down the dirt path, gleaming under the yard lights that flanked the model home. The top was down, so she was obliged to hop out and fetch a package from the back seat without opening the car door.

"Hullo the house!" she called, and I waved.

"Up here, Boots."

She breezed up the steps and set a white pastry box on the table, singing, "Who wants peach cobbler?"

Guy waved the suggestion aside, but I hitched up my chair and opened the box, ready to tuck into this time-honored Southern delicacy. On top of the sugared crust was a thick envelope with my name on it.

"Mr. August Stillwell, attorney-at-law, you are *served*," Bootsy declared and then went off in gales of laughter. "Yes, sir, I served you! You have been served, well and truly!"

"What the hell . . ." Guy seized the envelope and perused the deposition subpoena from Mother's lawyer, who hailed from some high-dollar firm in Atlanta.

"Mama's lawyer wanted to have the sheriff serve you at the law office tomorrow," said Bootsy, "but I begged him—I said, *No, no, please, you gotta let me*—because I knew the look on your face—" She all but collapsed laughing about it.

"Hilarious," I said.

"Oh, come on now. You always got such a kick out of Daddy sending me to serve papers—knocking on doors like I was selling Girl Scout cookies, dancing with some poor sap at the Daughters of the American Revolution gala—oh! Daddy, remember the one where he thought he was gonna be my French tutor?" Bootsy giggled, wiping tears. "Priceless."

"I'm glad you find the dissolution of our family so entertaining," said Guy.

"Don't be dramatic," said Bootsy. "We'll always be family, in our way. It's just paperwork."

"Spoken like a serial divorcée."

"Exactly. Having been through it several times, I can promise you, it ain't nuthin' but a thang."

"Words cannot express the comfort that brings me," he glowered.

"Nine p.m. and we're still sober enough for irony. What's wrong with this picture?"

She fetched herself a glass along with two forks and parked next to me on the sofa so she and I could share the cobbler. When we propped our feet on the coffee table, her legs were almost as long as mine. Longer, if you took her platform wedge sandals into consideration. My big sister liked being tall. She liked to brag that she'd inherited her mama's décolletage and her daddy's incorrigibility. She liked to sign her full legal name on checks and Christmas cards: Belinda Marblesmith Stillwell-Buck-Biddle. More than any of that, she liked to get under Guy's skin and devil him with smart talk that reminded him how good a lawyer she could have been if she'd chosen to go to law school instead of running away from home the summer of 1963. She was intelligent and tart-mouthed, fully in command of her sexuality, which made our father profoundly uncomfortable. She enjoyed poking him in the eye about that and their ever-opposing political views.

Still, there was no denying, for my father, the sun rose and set on his elder daughter. She was the sugar to life's bitter lime. She could get around him in a way nobody else could, so Mother and Tatum and I had come to depend on her to defuse his anger during his worst moments, ask the questions he didn't want to answer, and maintain his equilibrium when needed. Mother could have easily sent the houseman over with a bag for father, and I could have been served at the law office without fanfare, as per routine. This was all theater for Guy's benefit, and Bootsy played the Tennessee Williams belle with big-haired joie de vivre.

"So, Daddy," she said, setting aside the empty cobbler box, "inquiring minds want to know: Are you gonna marry Miss Pankhurst?"

"I have no idea what you're talking about," Guy said, because any lawyer worth his salt offers a knee-jerk denial of transgression. "I see no reason to disrupt the status quo. Divorce at our age is a goddamn waste of money. She's always been able to see that in the past. Critter, I expect you to go on over there tomorrow and talk some sense into her."

"You'll do no such thing." Bootsy delivered a preemptive slug to my upper arm. "Did it ever occur to you that Mama has her own romantic prospects? She deserves some happiness, and she's too Catholic to run around as a married woman."

"Then she oughta be too goddamn Catholic for a divorce," Guy argued. "Anyway, she's gotten as wide as a double-sided barn door. I don't see a lot of legitimate comers lining up, and she's too smart to let some Lothario get his meat hooks on the family silver."

"Well, I don't know about all that," said Bootsy. "I've seen District Attorney Doolittle Redstone on her calendar more than once this week."

"Redstone," Guy scoffed. "She wouldn't glance over one shoulder at that poncy SOB."

I was inclined to agree. I'd gone up against Red in enough trials to know he was not just your average SOB; he was a first-class revolving SOB who lined people up like pawns in a chess game and used the law to spin the board whichever direction served him.

"He asked Mama to write a position paper for his upcoming campaign," said Bootsy. "It seems to require a great deal of tête-à-tête and so forth."

"Campaign?" I said. "He's not up for reelection for another two years."

"He's running for Congress," said Bootsy. "Georgia Tenth. Same seat Daddy ran for back in the day."

Our father sank back into his chair, deflated. The unsuccessful congressional run was a sore point for him. He was uncharacteristically quiet as we sat, sipping whiskey. Bootsy was good at bogarting the bottle, making sure he was just drunk enough for nostalgia but not so hammered as to hurt himself.

"If Redstone thinks he can handle her, he's welcome to try," said Guy. "He might just discover she ain't the sugar and spice he's been dreaming about all these years. He had his chance with her when we were all in law school. He went off to the war thinking she'd sit home waiting for him, keeping her lamp lit like a vestal virgin." He chuckled softly. "Turns out ol' Doolittle was a whole lotta little and not much do."

Bootsy and I rested our heads on the back of the bamboo sofa and stared up at the sky over the Oconee. We'd heard all Guy's anecdotes so many times, he didn't really have to tell them anymore. As he rambled on, the stars became paper lanterns strung tree to tree in the old oaks behind the Kappa Alpha fraternity house haunted by Robert E. Lee and eight generations of proud Southern sons that followed his footsteps. The sound of the water gave way to the whisper of the breeze through the river birch leaves. Old stories of love and envy hung in the humid air, stinging the backs of our throats along with the acrid scent of citronella.

"Repetition is the iron forge of religious tradition," Vivvy says. "Stories. Parables. It's the same with family mythology."

I don't disagree, but as a lawyer, I have learned that there are two possible reasons why a person tells the same stories over and over again. Most likely, it's because they're lying, and a good lie wants practice. But sometimes, it's because the storyteller feels the full truth has not been heard. Some vital piece of the story is still trying to make its way out.

– 2 –

The heart of Athens, Georgia, beats warm and steady beneath the lush grass on the University of Georgia campus and the long driveways on Milledge and Prince Avenues. Stately homes, once inhabited by antebellum aristocrats, were sold off during the Great Depression, divvied up into apartments or retooled as frat houses, but never ceded one iota of decorum. Fluted columns of the Doric order reflect the architecture of the city's Greek namesake. The original constitution of the Confederate States of America is preserved in UGA's main library and brought out for display every year on Confederate Memorial Day. In the Athens I know and love, a deep reverence for history is tempered by the sass and rascality you hear in the music of her famous offspring: REM, the B-52s, and Widespread Panic.

Putting himself through law school in the 1940s, Guy always felt like a square peg in a round hole. Most of his high school friends and college fellows were off fighting World War II, and Guy would have willingly joined them, but he was sidelined by night blindness and flat feet, a solid 4-F—"not acceptable for service"—by draft board standards. He put himself through law school at the University of Georgia, working as a stringer for the *Atlanta Constitution*. He graduated top of his class and passed the bar exam on his first try. On all counts, my father might have been considered a great success, but he was dogged by the stigma of that failure to serve in a war that had cost so many families so dearly. The shame of it lingered in the minds of the community pillars and, worse yet, in his own mind. The shame of it festered like a splinter under a thumbnail. Ignominy drove him to distinguish himself in good ways and bad.

He was president of Kappa Alpha, a fraternity founded by Robert E. Lee and housed in a crumbling antebellum mansion—a grand architectural relic of the Old South with tall white columns on the front porch and a Civil War cannon perched on a cement slab in the yard. Every year to this day, as far as I know, the Kappa Alpha Order hosts its annual Convivium: a formal weekend-long event during which fraternity brothers and their much-envied dates dress up in antebellum costumes, attend a solemn ceremony honoring General Lee and the fallen Confederates, and party from dusk to dawn.

Guy loved to tell the story of the 1945 Convivium, which was apparently more convivial than most. If one did the math, it would appear that this may be the weekend Bootsy was conceived.

Miss Theodora Marblesmith arrived on the arm of Doolittle "Red" Redstone. Instead of the traditional Rebel gray, Red was decked out in his dress whites, all in the guise of conquering hero, home from the Pacific Theater, where he had killed some ungodly number of Japanese and lost the pinkie, ring, and "fuck you" fingers on his right hand while changing the front left tire on a Jeep. The injury wasn't as serious as the physical and mental mutilation suffered by some others, but it was enough to bring him home and set the stage for a political career built on righteous indignation. The maimed hand was good for not much but pointing out the failings of others. When Red raised it to gesticulate, it looked like a child pretending to fire a pistol, so my father, who liked to brand everybody with clever nicknames, called him "Bang Bang" behind his back.

Theodora—called Teddi by her sorority sisters—presented in full India Wilkes regalia, hoopskirt swaying, waist cinched to a tight hourglass, chestnut hair piled high and sprinkled with primroses. The bodice of her dress was cut low enough to inspire the appreciative gaze but substantial enough to accommodate a secret stash of Lucky Strikes tucked into her cleavage. As she danced, the lacy edge of a hot pink petticoat peeped from below the sweep of her hoopskirt.

Teddi was a Catholic Republican in an overwhelmingly Protestant Democrat South, progressive in her politics but staunch in the traditions of her faith. In a time when girls were allowed only the narrowest aspirations, she was in her first year of law school and intended to dedicate herself to the betterment of the world. She was a whip-smart, unconventional beauty who came from old money, a damsel in no distress whatsoever.

"You shoulda seen her," Guy used to crow. "That girl coulda spit on walls."

I understand now that he was talking about audacity, a quality uniquely co-opted by Southern belles and serial killers, shoplifters, and those who run for political office—people for whom conviction comes naturally and self-doubt is an afterthought. Teddi carried herself with a buoyancy born of entitlement, an innate self-confidence that was flatly unfathomable to Guy, who'd clawed his way over from the wrong side of the tracks. He saw her dancing beneath the paper lanterns, and for an extraordinary instant, he had to believe he was good enough for her, simply because he wanted her so desperately; there was no room in his imagination for a world in which he could not have her.

"May I cut in?" Guy tapped Redstone's broad shoulder. Red blustered an objection, but Teddi said, "Certainly!" and gracefully pivoted into the arms of her new partner. Mother says she took pity on Guy because Redstone and some others had been bullying him about his 4-F status, and she never could abide a bully. She says they talked about the war at first, because that was what everyone talked about at the time, but they discovered the rebel thread they had in common.

When Guy remarked on President Roosevelt's failing health, Teddi said, "Bless his heart, but I lost my love for FDR when he dropped Henry Wallace as vice president last year. As far as I'm concerned, Eleanor is now his only redeeming feature, and our best hope of advancing desegregation is voting Republican in the down-ticket midterm elections."

Guy laughed. "Miss Marblesmith, I was not expecting to hear liberal talk from a woman in a hoopskirt."

"What were you expecting? 'Fiddle-dee-dee' and 'Mammy, fetch me another brandy'?"

"No, I assumed we'd be gazing into each other's eyes, dumbstruck with desire."

"Oh, really," she said, raising an eyebrow.

"The most ardent male fantasies involve very little conversation."

"Maybe if you were a better dancer."

"Oh! Woman, you've wounded me." Guy clutched his chest, pantomiming a shot to the heart. "It's these goddamn hobnail boots. These are the very boots worn by my granddaddy, Lieutenant Colonel Farish Stillwell, as he followed General Forrest over the bridge at West Chickamauga Creek. Feels like they were hammered on by a farrier. No wonder the Rebels trudged back to Georgia in agony."

"And yet I see you trying to dance in them every year," she said. "Why is that?"

"What is one man's agony compared to the glory of a just war?"

"Which war are we talking about?" said Teddi. "I've lost track."

He drew back to look her in the eye and determined that she'd said this without sarcasm, keenly aware that they were surrounded by men who'd trudged home shell-shocked and missing limbs.

"Miss Marblesmith, you are truly full of surprises."

"Oh," she assured him, "you have no idea."

Three months later, FDR was dead, Truman was in office, America ended the war by raining holy hell on Hiroshima and Nagasaki, and Guy and Teddi were married at city hall. Guy's parents were long dead, his father from a heart attack and his mother from a broken heart. Teddi's parents sat on a wooden bench in the gallery, as somber as Ash Wednesday.

Mrs. Marblesmith was an heiress, a Daughter of the American Revolution, granddaughter of a lumber and marble baron, wife to the mayor of Athens, and niece to more than one congressman. Her family had owned the lion's share of North Georgia since the first settlers wrested it from the Cherokee. This wretch who'd glommed on to Teddi, taking advantage of her tenderness—he was no better than a carpetbagger, and Teddi's mother told him so to his face. The Marblesmith name had been dragged through the mud. Everybody who mattered in Athens knew there was only one way they'd give their only daughter to this low-born white striver from Armpit, Georgia, and all that evil gossip was confirmed six months later when Teddi gave birth to a nine-pound baby girl. "*Prematurely* gave birth," Mrs. Marblesmith maintained, but Junior Leaguers know their way around a calendar.

Guy passed the bar and joined forces with King Hodges, who was also low-born and ambitious, a heavy drinker and jovial man-about-town. Stillwell & Hodges was the antithesis of a silk-stocking law firm. No one who wished to remain on the Marblesmith Christmas card list would darken the door, so they scrounged clients from the county jail, from barroom brawls, from eviction notices and car accidents—anywhere and everywhere two lawyers could insert themselves into the troubles of others. They turned no one away, so they got a lot of calls from black people and others who were accustomed to being turned away as a matter of course.

Guy made a big name for himself in the late 1950s when the GBI (Georgia Bureau of Investigation) launched a series of undercover ops that culminated in one major raid that swept the city of Athens. A slew of charges collectively known as the "Sin City Cases" were filed against restaurants, bars, and clubs who'd been hosting backroom slot machines and selling liquor by the drink, which was illegal in a dry jurisdiction. Guy and King were up to their ears in the Sin City Cases, and Guy cut a dashing figure, front and center, as network television crews rolled in from Atlanta and newspaper coverage went statewide and wider.

The illicit activity was going on under the nose of Sheriff T. Tom Heck, who'd been letting it slide for years. They never proved he was being paid off, and Guy argued it was nothing so sinister as that. The sheriff may have gotten a favor or two—an occasional dinner at the country club, a few beers at the Moose Lodge—but the whole arrangement was more like a wink and a shrug to get around the Puritanical biddies who wanted a dry county and lickspittle politicians who needed old money on their side.

Guy represented Sheriff Heck for free. The essence of Southern justice back then was one hand washing the other, and that took an evil turn in some counties, but Sheriff Heck was a decent fella, by and large. At a pretrial hearing, Guy made a motion to dismiss and pointed out that Sheriff Heck had been an equal opportunity scofflaw, allowing the black VFW and the juke joint by the river and a cinder block social club in the woods to flourish right along with the white establishments—all in the cause of keeping the peace.

Blacks had their clubs, whites had their clubs, and as long as they all operated quietly with no stabbings or shootings, everything was copacetic. The sheriff stayed out of it, for the sake of expediency, recognizing that his was an elected position. Once every four years, he had to declare himself a candidate, drag a stack of "Give 'em Heck!" yard signs down from the attic over his garage, and do whatever glad-handing needed to be done in order to keep his job. He knew his constituents and was happy to mete out the sort of commonsense justice they were used to. They didn't appreciate these GBI outsiders barging into their quiet little city, throwing their weight around.

Guy's eloquent closing argument made for good television. As his notoriety spread, his fees burgeoned, and he reinvested the proceeds in a variety of entrepreneurial exploits, including a small oil company and a small record label that released two 45s for a rising star named Whispering Bill Anderson. He bought up several small farms, leasing some to white families who'd lost their land during the Great Depression and others to black families whose forebears had worked those same fields as slaves.

He also partnered in a Carling Black Label beer distributorship with his friend Newt Ballerini, the golden son of a grand old Georgia family, who'd returned from Europe a war hero and set the gossips buzzing by bringing a beautiful Italian wife home with him.

By the time I was in grammar school, my father was a wealthy man, but the shame that had dogged him through law school persisted. He couldn't leave the shadows behind.

"Don't tell me those old ghosts drove him to drink," Vivvy says. "Alcoholism is a disease."

But I grew up among the ghosts, so I know different. When I was in elementary school, Guy up and bought the old KA fraternity house with the cannon out front and had it remodeled to house his growing family. He invited Doc, the aging KA houseman, to stay on and continue tending the grounds, living in a little shack called "the quarters" down by the creek on the far side of the property. Every summer, my parents hosted a big ol' formal party beneath the expansive old oaks. Until the summer of 1963, Guy always took perverse delight in inviting Red Redstone.

"Keep friends close," said Guy. "Enemies closer."

– 3 –

Tatum was a mere sprout in 1963, a disturbingly canny child of five, as skinny as a mosquito's leg and no taller than the slide-out cutting board in the kitchen. Beneath a prominent forehead, her eyes were the color of sharpened pencil lead, wideset, and underscored with blue half circles.

"Milk allergy," said Othella, who cultivated Mother's vegetable garden and was tasked with watching Tatum until Tatum was big enough for elementary school. "Child oughta be drinkin' goat's milk."

Mother always accepted Othella's word as gospel, so she instructed Doralee to acquire the goat's milk and slip a teaspoon of brandy in it if Tatum resisted the taste, but the blue circles persisted, imparting a vaguely haunted quality to her already intense gaze. She always studied people a little too hard when they stood by her and Othella in line at the drugstore or sat near them on a bench in the courthouse, where folks gathered on summer days to watch my father duke it out with District Attorney Ruckels—or A.D.A. Redstone, depending on how big a case it was. A murder trial was a big event in our little town, a rare occurrence, but there was plenty of other malfeasance and the occasional high society divorce, all of which provided good entertainment, especially if my father was heading up the defense or advocating for the downtrodden spouse. When folks wanted a no-holds-barred fighter for a lawyer, they hired Guy Stillwell, so everybody knew there would be plenty of blood and bare-knuckle rhetoric on display. Guy could lay a perjury trap better than any other lawyer in Georgia.

Othella packed sandwiches and potato chips so they could make a day of it, and Tatum never expressed any objection, so far as I know. Everybody knew Tatum was Guy Stillwell's kid, so there was a lot of looky-loo. She didn't know enough to look away when they caught her staring back at them, so they'd shuffle, avert their eyes, and finally glare and say, "Why don't you take a picture? It'll last longer."

Tatum took this to heart, apparently, and excavated an old Kodak Brownie camera from a shed behind the carriage house. She liberated the works from its Bakelite shell, cleaned the bits and pieces, and reassembled it. Tatum took her Brownie everywhere. When she raised it to snap a photo, people smiled and assumed someone had given her this old piece of junk as a toy, but goddang if that thing didn't work. One day I went looking for her in the attic and found an eerie collage of snapshots that looked like they were taken from the perspective of a bulldog.

Twenty-five years later, a number of these were still thumbtacked to the slanted rafters.

"I always wondered how you got the film developed," I said from the doorway of her attic lair.

"I had a darkroom in the root cellar," said Tatum, as if that didn't raise more questions than it answered. Her delicate fingers flew in rhythm over a keyboard, and a photograph began loading, line by line, on the screen in front of her.

"What's that?" I asked.

"I found your yacht."

Tinkering away beneath the gimlet-eyed gallery, she had cobbled together an array of bulky monitors, exposed motherboards, and switch boxes to form some sort of oracle, a doorway beyond which lay the answer to any question I presented to her. I did not pretend to understand this secret world Tatum called Arpanet—the Advanced Research Projects Agency Network—an antediluvian version of the internet.

Remember, this was 1988. I considered myself to be on the cutting edge with my QWERTY keyboard pager and a Motorola mobile phone, which was the size of a red brick and hosted approximately one hour of talk time, during which I was obliged to mention at least twice that I was taking the call in my car. Guy would have nothing to do with any of this nonsense. "I don't want to be that easy to get ahold of," he'd say with a wink, and it wasn't necessary for him to elaborate.

"There will come a time," Tatum assured me, "when secrecy, privacy, and the ability to hide one's assets will be the stuff of nostalgia. Money and information will be exchanged via ether."

"So you're saying, a person could be, for example, on a boat," I said, "and they could be connected to communications via the computer to fax, telephone, and all that?"

"Faxing will be obsolete," she said. "So will lawyering as we know it. The technology is evolving. It's the investment opportunity of the century."

Long before my colleagues began to grapple with the legal ramifications of such a world, she and her unseen cohorts were knitting science and science fiction in ways my father found unfathomable. He had no interest in "all that Aldous Huxley gabblecrap" and would never become a willing participant in it. When Tatum talked about *email* and *virtual reality*, he dismissed her out of hand. In his mind, she'd grown up to be that crazy lady without whom no Southern family's attic was complete.

The computer image continued its snail's pace download, and Tatum studied it with that unsparing blue-rimmed gaze. In the brittle light of the computer monitor, she did look like a specter, a little too wise for a girl just turned thirty. She was still as thin as a matchstick, and she kept her hair cropped short. I couldn't remember the last time I'd seen her wearing something other than black jeans and motorcycle boots, even in the oppressive heat of a Georgia summer.

When the photo had filled in enough to hazard a guess, I leaned in and said, "That looks like it."

Tatum tore a stretch of perforated paper from her dot-matrix printer and handed it to me. The vessel appeared sporty and grand, even in the grainy gray-scale images, and the name *Rascal* was plainly legible on the prow.

"Where is it?" I asked.

"Thunderbolt Marina down by Savannah."

Thunderbolt, Georgia, was a known hotbed of Klan activities in the 1960s and a convenient port of call for the Dixie Mafia.

"Interesting." I folded the printout and tucked it in my shirt pocket. "I don't suppose your Magic 8 Ball there can tell me who's behind the shell corporation in the Cayman Islands."

"I'll see what I can come up with."

"Thanks, Tate. Check's in the mail."

"Whatever."

Downstairs, Mother was in the kitchen with Bootsy and Doralee, boxing up fried chicken, corn dodgers, and fried green tomatoes in Tupperware containers for Othella, who was in her eighties now and had taken a nasty spill earlier that week.

"She's bound and determined to stay on at her house," said Bootsy, "but the chemotherapy's been rough on her, and Poppy hasn't been able to find a daily caregiver who can handle her."

I reached for a fried chicken leg but wasn't fast enough. Mother smacked the back of my hand with an oven mitt and said, "You don't need that cholesterol, Critter. Doralee baked some for you with the skin off."

"Great. Thank you, Doralee."

"Do I detect a note of sarcasm?" said Mother.

"Not at all."

"I've been trying to call Daddy all afternoon," said Bootsy. "Have you seen him?"

"I was down in Augusta interviewing witnesses," I said. "I'll stop by the apartment and check on him this evening."

"Oh, he's not there," said Mother. "He's decamped to the Regent. Sleeping on King's sofa for a few days."

"We're not privy to the details," said Bootsy, "but whatever he said to Miss Pankhurst, it did not go over well."

"Here we go." Mother piled the Tupperware containers in a quilted tote and looped the handle over my wrist. "Give Miss Othella a squeeze for me."

"Will do." I kissed her cheek and palmed one of Doralee's corn dodgers for the road.

This sort of errand running had filled most of my free time ever since that summer I got my driver's license, and before that, I performed many of the same tasks on my bicycle with quilted casserole totes swinging from the handlebars. Thus occupied, I was always part of the action, in the know and on the go.

Working at the law office, I was always in the middle of things, a fly on the wall, eavesdropping on all the adult gossip, gawking at the gruesome crime scene photos, and sneaking an occasional nip from the globe-style bar cart next to the leather sofa in my father's office. You'd unlatch a hidden hasp at the equator and lift up the northern hemisphere to reveal sunken bottles of bourbon and vodka and a rack of shot glasses with flags of all the nations.

The good stuff was in his lower left desk drawer, but I knew not to mess with that. I knew the difference between white liquor, such as the moonshine they sold down by the river, and red liquor, which meant proper distillery-bonded bourbons, Scotches, and whatnot. That stuff in the desk drawer was an ass-kicking in itself, setting aside the hell I'd catch from my mother if she smelled it on me.

King kept an apartment on Prince Avenue, similar to the arrangement at my father's Hill Street place. Sometimes I dropped him off there and slept on the mile-wide front seat of the land yacht until he came out an hour later. Other times, he'd tell me to drive around town so his wife would see the distinctive vehicle cruise by when she was shopping in the department store or sitting at the soda counter at Woolworth's. If she dashed out to her own car and started following me, I was to lead her on a grand tour of asphalt and gravel backroads, chicken farms, and cotton fields until I managed to shake her.

Every summer, King and Guy hired a rising second- or third-year law student to clerk for them, and the summer of 1963, that person was

Othella's grown daughter, Olympia Sterling, whom I'd known as Poppy from the earliest days I can remember. Poppy was the first female they'd ever hired for the position, one of the very few women in law school. Bootsy had dated the previous two male clerks, distracting them from their duties by crushing their souls to a fine powder, so Guy saw the light of feminist truth and decided to give girl clerks a chance.

The University of Georgia had been integrated only two years earlier, so Poppy was also the first black UGA law school student to clerk for the firm. This raised some issues, because Poppy wasn't allowed to sit at the Woolworth's soda counter or drink from certain water fountains, and she couldn't get served by the waitresses at Tony's Café, where all the old-timey lawyers, superior court judges, bailiffs, and oftentimes even juries all went for lunch.

Poppy lifted an imperious chin toward the bald glares of the white male clerks in the records office. She showed up fifteen minutes early every morning, impeccably dressed and coifed, and went about her daily business with an air of implacable efficiency, preferring to rise above rather than confront. While everyone was eating lunch at Tony's, she sat in the park across the street, intently studying for the bar exam, which she was scheduled to take that August.

Guy wasn't eager to alienate anyone, but he was equally unwilling to let this injustice slide. With Poppy in tow, he muscled through his day the same as he would have with anybody else at his side. If he heard someone mutter under their breath, he called them out and shamed them in his hail-fellow-well-met way. I saw tears in his eyes when she passed the bar that summer and again, many years later, when she was sworn in as a superior court judge.

When I pulled up in front of the Sterling house to deliver the fried chicken and fixings, Poppy was out on the front porch smoking a cigarette.

"Evening, Counselor," she said.

"Evening, Judge."

I didn't feel as comfortable calling her Poppy anymore; I hardly ever saw her outside the courtroom, and inside the courtroom, she scared the bejesus out of everybody. She was only two years older than Bootsy, but they wore their forties differently. Bootsy kept her hair colored and practiced the Jane Fonda fitness religion. Poppy's close-cropped Afro was heavily salted with silver, and her girth added to her gravitas. Judge Olympia Sterling's presence on the bench was more than the sum of her weight and height. Her voice made mundane things sound like pearls of wisdom. Her authority was not questioned because it was buttressed by an unparalleled knowledge of the law and genuine passion for justice, and oddly enough, that's where I'd occasionally catch a glimpse of the Poppy I'd known when we were kids.

"Hope you're hungry," I said, setting the tote on the porch swing. "Mother and Doralee cooked enough for the French Foreign Legion."

"Y'all are too sweet."

"How's Miss Othella?"

"Sleeping," said the judge. "She's been confused. Can't remember why everything hurts."

"Sorry to hear it."

"It's not easy to see a tower of strength fall apart like that." She took a deep drag on her cigarette. "Your daddy didn't show up in court this morning. His law clerk shuffled in forty-five minutes late, trying to make some bullshit excuse for him."

I sighed, chin to chest. "Oh, great."

"I worry he's approaching the point of no return. And I see you drowning your sorrows the same way he did back in the sixties."

"I appreciate your concern, Your Honor, but—"

"Don't you *Your Honor* me up in here, Critter. I'm on my mama's front porch, talking to you as a friend, as somebody who cares about that old man and owes him a debt of gratitude."

"I hear ya."

"I granted a continuance, but it seems like I've been doing that a lot lately where he's concerned."

"I understand," I said, "and I'm trying to help him work through a backlog of cases that need attention, but I have my own caseload to deal with."

"I can't in good conscience act like there's one set of rules for him and another set of rules for everybody else."

"Yes, Poppy. I hear you. I don't know what else you want me to say."

"Maybe you ought not to be out of town on days when he's supposed to be in court."

"Maybe so," I said tightly. "I'll take it under advisement."

She stubbed her cigarette in a potted plant. "What was it he used to say? That thing about three universal truths?"

"Gospel according to Guy Stillwell," I recited. "You can't drink yourself sober, you can't make water run uphill, and you can't borrow yourself out of debt."

The judge smiled, remembering.

"Trouble is," she said, "he's trying to do all three."

"I'll talk to him," I said. "I'm on my way over there right now."

Arriving at the Regent, I called Guy's room from the front desk.

"Wait for me in the club," he said. "King's up here giving me the come-to-Jesus."

I took from his tone that King's effort was meeting with the same brick wall as always. King had been sober for twenty-five years. Seems like he wasn't on the wagon five minutes before he was trying to get Guy on with him, a twelve-step evangelist, having moved on to a healthier addiction: proselytizing.

I'd been a member at a private club on the second floor at the Regent for a good many years, so I expected to see a stately old black man named Rory tending bar. Rory knew his way around a proper pour, and he'd been a client of Guy's for one thing and another over the years, so I knew I could leave Guy there drinking by himself and count on Rory to confiscate his car keys and call a cab when the time came. The fair-skinned redhead behind the bar wore the same white tuxedo shirt and red cummerbund Rory always wore, but she gave it a very different contour. Standing behind the bar with her chin propped on one fist, she tapped a pen absently next to her elbow, glaring down at the crossword puzzle in the *Atlanta Journal-Constitution*.

"Where's Rory?" I asked.

She flashed a ten-thousand-watt smile and pointed to the breast pocket of her tuxedo shirt. Pinned to it was the little etched brass RORY nametag that used to be on the old man's shirt.

"It's my pleasure to be your Rory this evening," she said. "What'll it be?"

"Johnnie Walker. Neat. But seriously. Where is he?"

"He had a heart attack and went to live with his daughter in Florida."

"Dang. He'll be missed."

"That he will."

"He was good people."

"So I hear."

"I'm August Stillwell," I said. "Friends call me Critter."

"Well, try not to take it personally."

The bartender set up the shot and placed a glass of ice water next to it. The way she did this without asking, or being asked, irritated me for reasons I didn't fully understand and was obliged to forget when she flashed that dazzling smile again, and I noticed that her eyes were the same kind of unearthly violet blue as Elizabeth Taylor's.

The TV above the bar was tuned to *Unsolved Mysteries*. Robert Stack droned humorlessly about a case involving a real estate developer who killed his wife in what was supposed to be a murder-suicide pact, only instead of the suicide part, he hoofed it after placing her body in a chest-style freezer in the basement of a model home.

"Maybe you could change the channel to something a little less grim," I suggested.

"No, I'm watching this," she said. "There's a thing about Athens coming up after the commercials."

"Athens, Georgia?"

"No, Athens, Greece. Robert Stack is investigating a case where the victim was submerged in olive oil. Hence my fascination."

"Good ol' Rory," I sighed. "I sure do miss him."

"You and me both," said the redhead.

I sipped my whiskey and studied the printout from Tatum's computer. I'd secured the lien easily enough. Most of the arrangements had already been made, and now I had a firm grasp on the whereabouts of the asset. The value of the eighty-two-foot motor yacht was in excess of $650,000, and the shadow corporation in the Caymans appeared to have no other debts or liabilities. The craft featured a fully customized cockpit extension, three staterooms—each with an en suite head—and a host of aftermarket features that would allow a person or persons to live at large for an extended period of time.

I'd done a good bit of homework on this sort of thing. My plan was to get rich enough to buy a yacht similar to that someday, leave Georgia behind, and spend the rest of my days sailing exotic seas. This was not a pipe dream; it was a strategy in which I had invested a lot of self-discipline and legwork. It was going to happen. I just had to bide my time, keep towing the barge at the law firm, and resist the temptation to spend money trying to impress members of the fairer sex.

"Seven-letter word for *tenacity*," said the bartender.

"Excuse me?"

"Tenacity." She tapped her pen on the crossword puzzle. "Seven letters."

"Let's see. *Persistence . . . doggedness . . . resolve?*"

"That'll work." She filled in R-E-S-O-L-V-E and nodded to my empty glass. "Go again?"

"Sure. Thank you, um . . . what's your real name?"

"Let's stick with Rory. Save on the nametag budget." She set up the shot and tapped the nametag. "You don't know if this was his real name, either. Maybe he got it from his predecessor. Or maybe RORY stands for Registered Occupational Risk Yeoman."

"Or maybe it stands for Rockin' Opulent Refreshment Yogi."

She laughed an unfairly musical laugh. "Well played, sir."

"Anyway, that is his name. I was his attorney."

"Another attorney," she said dryly. "Can't swing a cat in here without smacking somebody's lawyer."

"When I was a pup, Tony's was the place where all the lawyers went to wheel and deal. It was like a rite of passage for law clerks. When you passed the bar, you'd take all the partners to lunch at Tony's."

"And all the bartenders would feign interest." She batted big doe eyes at me.

That cracked me up, and suddenly, I'll confess, I was somewhat smitten. What is it about a woman who can make you laugh? To my mind, there's nothing more seductive. "Because it makes you breathe differently," Vivvy says. "There's that little loss of composure."

"So, Rory," I ventured, "what are you doing after work tonight?"

"Wishing lawyers tipped better."

"Well, if you'd like to grab a bite to eat—" I started, but she pointed the remote at the television, turning up the volume.

"Hush! I think this is it," she said. "Oh, look, there's the covered bridge. And there's the Regent! What about that? I'm on television. Sort of."

"That looks like it was shot in the 1960s," I said. "You probably weren't even born yet."

She slid me a wry side-glance. "Nice try."

"Dateline: Athens, Georgia, June 1963," Robert Stack intoned. "The tranquility of a sleepy college town in the Deep South is shattered when local restauranteur Brinkman Pollard, a local football hero and World War II veteran, is found dead in an upstairs room at a local house of ill repute."

"Wait . . ." I stared up at the TV, shot glass poised in front of my chin. "I know this case."

"A hit man eventually confesses to the murder," said Stack, "claiming that he was hired by Edward 'Newt' Ballerini, a wealthy entrepreneur and sole heir to one of Georgia's most venerable family dynasties."

The montage of crime scene photos and mug shots cut to a clip of my father standing outside the courthouse in 1963, looking impossibly young. Poppy stood behind him, holding his briefcase while he addressed the curious gaggle on the courthouse steps: "Mr. Ballerini vehemently denies any involvement in this tragic affair. He is innocent of all charges and looks forward to his day in court."

"While awaiting trial," said Stack, "Ballerini skips out on his $200,000 bond and vanishes without a trace."

Newt's mug shot appeared and then dissolved with a dramatic trill of noir jazz.

"Left behind," said Stack, "was Ballerini's wife, Fernanda."

"All these years," Fernanda sobbed, clutching a framed portrait of Newt to her ample bosom. "I just want to know what happened. I just want to know *why*."

Stack delivered the standard "if you've seen this man" plea, standing with Red in the Athens-Clarke County D.A.'s office, strategically positioned between the American flag and a Redstone for Congress poster.

"He was actually here in Athens?" The bartender slapped her hand on the bar. "Robert Stack was right here in this town, and nobody knew it?"

"Somebody knew," I said, and I knew why he'd kept mum about it.

"Newt can run, but he can't hide," Redstone pandered. "I will personally see to it that the State of Georgia and the victim's family receive satisfaction in this matter."

Stack presented a sketch artist's best guess of what Newt would look like now, after a quarter century on the lam, and offered a $25,000 reward in exchange for information leading to his arrest and prosecution. Red eyeballed the camera and wrapped things up in his classic *Dragnet* baritone.

"Like the Bible says: The mills of the Lord's justice grind slow, but *very fine*."

"Well, ain't that a kick in the giblets," said Guy.

He and King stood side by side in the doorway, arms folded, feet set apart, beneath the corbeled arch that separated the bar from the lobby. The partnership that had kept them together all those years was evident in the set of their stance and the same utterly guarded expression on both their faces.

"King, I do believe, you have finally persuaded me to see the error of my ways," said Guy.

King looked startled by this. "I have?"

"I'm leaving tonight," said Guy. "Going to a rehab spot in Nassau. We need to keep it on the down low."

"Nassau?" I said. "No. No, that doesn't work."

"Now, listen." He looped his arm around my shoulders and steered me away from the bar. "We can't let this get out on the street. I need to be somewhere else for a while. That's all anybody needs to know."

"Guy, you can't just leave. You've got court. You've got cases."

"Nothing you can't handle." He grinned and knuckled my jaw the way he always did when I was a kid. "I know I can depend on you to do what needs doing."

– 4 –

If Brinkman Pollard had known the 1963 Convivium was destined to be his last, perhaps he would not have behaved like such an ass. The events of the evening soured several generations of goodwill between his family and mine, which was unfortunate because he had beautiful twin daughters I'd fancied myself dating someday. I didn't know which one I liked better or if it even made a difference, but I'd spent more than a few hours imagining myself kissing one or both of the Pollard twins, and after that night I knew it would never happen.

My parents hosted a Sunday evening after party that took place when all the official Kappa Alpha weekend events were over so lightweights and out-of-towners were on their way home. Extended family, friends, and neighbors remained, along with law students, court colleagues, and various reprobates my father had interacted with in one way or another since his college days. My mother's social circle teemed with old-money movers and shakers, people with political will and the finances to back it up, so the party was a hot ticket for anyone campaigning for state or local office.

That year my father had decided to run for Congress, a rebellious GOP moderate going up against the incumbent Dixiecrat, Big Jim Fabien, a WWII fighter pilot with a solid base of aging veterans, uptight housewives, and Confederate flag fliers who didn't like the way things were headed with JFK and the civil rights movement.

Mother managed a cocktail party like a master chef stirring a well-tempered bouillabaisse, keeping everyone in good spirits with her adroit storytelling and keen eye for an empty glass. Heated but friendly debate over issues of the day—integration, Vietnam, Beatlemania, and Jackie Kennedy's high-handed remodeling of the White House—raged on into the wee hours. The cause of civil rights had always been near and dear to Mother's heart, and that spring, she was freshly inspired by Dr. Martin Luther King's recent "Letter from a Birmingham Jail."

Holding court on the marble-floored patio for a shifting audience of political comers, boozy spouses, and wealthy widows, she said, "I was particularly stricken by his assertion that 'shallow understanding from people of goodwill is more frustrating than absolute misunderstanding from people of ill will.' It pains me to think of myself that way—that my good intentions are more dangerous than the bad intentions of a Klansman."

"Teddi, you know I've always treated my colored people well," said one of the widows. "The separate doorways and water fountains—that's just dog-mean foolishness, and it should end, but right now, we've got more important things to worry about. There's a war on, in case you forgot."

"When is there not a war on?" Mother sighed. "Seems like there hasn't been six minutes of peace since Robert E. Lee sat under this very tree."

"Which is exactly why we don't need people stirring up riots and marching in the streets."

"Critter, honey?" Mother waved me over, deftly avoiding the argument. "Have you seen Tatum?"

"Not for a while."

"See if Bootsy has her," she said, "and help Doc bring up another case of champagne."

"Yes, ma'am."

Doc walked with a pronounced limp after he got wounded in the Marshall Islands in 1942. Back then, as the fraternity houseman, he was still hale and hearty enough to do everything that needed doing.

By 1963, Doc was getting up in years, and he had always been a hard drinker, so Mother hired younger, spryer men to take over the landscaping and maintenance. Doc spent most of his time in the basement, polishing the bar—a massive mahogany relic—and washing glasses that may or may not have been used recently.

I liked hanging out down there with him and Doralee, listening to the great old R&B, soul, and blues records I still love today. Doc taught me to play cards, and Doralee advised me on matters related to the birds and bees. During barbecues and cocktail parties, I was charged with helping Doc haul tubs of ice, cases of champagne, and supplies for making mint juleps and planter's punch, shuttling between the cellar, kitchen, front porch, and backyard. This gave me a good overview of the diverse conversation areas, which interested me to varying degrees.

In the front yard, straddling the low branch of a magnolia tree, seventeen-year-old Bootsy swung her feet over the heads of several goggle-eyed admirers. Perfectly positioned between Marilyn Monroe and Twiggy, she wore cigarette pants and a boxy, sleeveless shirt with big psychedelic daisies and a modest Peter Pan collar. Other girls in the group wore party dresses laden with "if ya got it, flaunt it" enterprise, which I personally appreciated, but Bootsy refused to participate in that caste system. She enjoyed the advantage of a beautiful mother who was savvy enough to teach her beautiful daughter the costs and benefits of flaunting. While the female voices around her flittered up and around all the expected registers, Bootsy held to her own husky alto, and the college boys hung on her words, moths to flame.

"I have grown increasingly tired of those who insist on reading *Gone with the Wind* like it's the Bible instead of satire," she was saying. "It's a modern-day *Gulliver's Travels* is what it is."

Doc elbowed me and said, "Critter. Check it."

He nodded to a stand of tall pines between us and the duck pond. Somebody lurked in the shadows, but I couldn't see who. I wouldn't have seen him at all if not for the glowing ember at the tip of a cigarette that rose and fell, rose and fell.

"Lucky Winfield," said Doc. "He come here about an hour ago to deliver six cases of beer from your daddy's warehouse. Been standing there starin' at Miss Bootsy somewhat longer than necessary. He needs to go."

"What do you expect me to do about it?"

Doc poked the back of my shoulder. "Git on over there. Tell him to take a hike."

"I'm not telling him. You tell him."

"It's your house."

"It's your house, too! You live here same as me."

Doc shot me a cold look that carried a lot of meaning even in the moonlight.

"Go do right by your sister," he said.

I didn't like it, but I headed over there. The thing is, Lucky Winfield was not right in the head. People knew this. He had not been right since the war. There was a vague cruelty that lingered around the corner of his mouth, the twisted product of a cleft palate he'd had fixed as a child and the unimaginable horrors he'd endured during and after the Bataan Death March. Newt Ballerini, my father's partner in the beer distributorship, felt some kind of brothers-in-arms obligation to give Lucky a break, so they hired him to do warehouse work and deliveries.

Lucky was loudly proud of his participation in various Klan activities, which Guy was loudly against. I'd heard apocryphal tales about Lucky hassling and intimidating Othella's father, who owned the Riverside Country Club, a juke joint down by the covered bridge outside of town. I'd seen for myself how he used a slingshot to kill rats, squirrels, and the kittens of the warehouse cats that lived under the loading docks at the warehouse. I was frankly afraid of Lucky and not eager to challenge him on why he was skulking about the place gawking at teenage girls, but Doc made it sound like a point of honor, so I ambled on over there.

"Hey, Lucky."

"Hey," he said without looking away from Bootsy and her friends.

"Thanks for your—your effort there. The delivery and all." I shuffled my feet. "You should probably take off now."

"Why?" He narrowed his eyes in my direction. "I'm not good enough to be at the party with the shit-don't-stink crowd?"

"I just figured you had places to go."

The glowing ember rose and fell. Rose and fell.

"Lucky," I said. "It's not appropriate for you to be hanging around here. You need to shove off."

"Guess ol' Step'n'Fetchit over there told you to give me the bum's rush, huh? Ain't enough for you to run errands for your rich daddy and his faggot partner. You're so candy-ass, you gotta do as that ol' crow tells ya."

"Lucky, I'm not gonna let you bait me into fighting."

"Pussy."

He flicked his cigarette onto the front of my shirt. Startled, I swatted at it like there was a bee on me. He rasped a smoky laugh at that, but he did walk away. When he reached the delivery van, I called out, "Screw you!"

Lucky swiveled his head in my direction. I turned and ran like hell. I wasn't waiting to see if he intended to make some kind of move. As I made tracks around the side yard, I looked over my shoulder and saw the van bump up against the curb at the end of the long driveway. By the time I reached the front porch, the van had disappeared down the street. I fished a stubby bottle of Falstaff beer from a trough of melting ice and brushed the cold glass across my forehead before I opened it.

A cadre of idealistic young lawyers and law students caucused near the porch swing. Some had clerked at Stillwell & Hodges in the past and had moved on to big firms in Atlanta and Savannah. Others were still in law school or flailing away to pass the bar. Their hapless dates in sweet summer dresses perched on the railing like so many bright-colored canaries while the gentlemen held forth about Plato's *Republic* and whether justice is part of the law or merely a moral judgment about the law. Poppy, the sole female voice in the discourse, argued the latter.

"Because justice is a qualitative and quantitative state of the human condition," she said, "and laws are the product of the time and place in which they were made. Hence laws can and must change in accordance with societal norms, while justice remains constant."

"The laws are about right and wrong," said one of her fellows. "The Constitution doesn't change."

"Of course it does!" said Poppy. "It's a living, breathing document. Case in point: Divorce. Slavery. A million things from spitting on the sidewalk to being a witch."

One of the Pollard boys said something with a sharp snicker. I didn't catch his exact words, but I saw Poppy's expression harden to a prim mask as the group of boys laughed long and hearty. Cal Pollard, I think it was, but Mr. Pollard and his wife had eleven children, and all the boys went to law school, and as I mentioned, the rift between our fathers was about to sunder any relationship I had with them, so I'm not sure.

"Hey, Poppy," I said, "don't listen to that asshat. Guy and King both say you're the best law clerk the firm has ever had, and that includes a bunch of these fellas."

She folded her arms and said, "I can hold my own in a conversation, baby boy. I don't need you to step in on my behalf, patronizing me and trying to make like I'm more than I am. I wouldn't have got through law school if I couldn't step over bigger men than these fools, so you just see to your own self."

"Fine. Jeez. Have you seen Tatum? Mother's looking for her."

"Last I saw her, she was with your daddy down by the creek."

I took another beer and loped off into the darkness, heading for the corner of the yard where my father sat at the center of a circle of light from a fire pit. Tatum was curled up on his lap, her head on the flat arm of his Adirondack chair. Guy patted her shoulder, and she smiled like a contented spaniel, pretending to be asleep. Next to Guy was Newt, and to Newt's left was Pollard. So if Guy was high noon, Brinkman Pollard sat at two o'clock with Newt in between. It was a little after midnight. They were all drunk and still drinking.

"Hell of a thing," Guy boomed in his well-watered basso profundo. "This fella was a Green Beret, and he's doing what he has to do. He takes these fellas up in a helicopter over the Mekong Delta. Now, these SOBs are red-handed double agent spies that infiltrated the VC. He gets them up in the air and sweats 'em until he gets a confession of duplicity, and then—" Here he clapped his hands and made a sailing gesture, whistling the high-to-low sound effect of falling. "Up to this point, the war—the *police action*, pardon me—was a function of the CIA, but then Westmoreland comes in, and the army is not on the same page, so they arrest this fella and haul him up on murder charges. That's where I come in and file a writ of habeas corpus. 'Produce the body!' I told the judge, I said, 'The law demands that you demonstrate just cause for detention or let freedom ring!'"

"Such a patriot," Pollard growled. "Wonder how you'd feel if your boy got drafted and killed."

"I'd be proud to have him give his life for his country," said Guy.

It was a bit of a gut punch for me to hear him say that. He had to be circumspect, I understood. He was running for Congress in an overwhelmingly conservative state, a Republican advocating for civil rights in a field of vociferous Dixiecrats, and some of them—Pollard, for example—had a lot of powerful friends. The Green Beret case had brought Guy an infusion of national media attention, and he was hoping to ride that wave of notoriety. But still. I was just a couple of years from the draft, and the war seemed like it was a long way from over.

"Representing colored clientele is one thing," said Pollard, his tongue clumsy with moonshine. "Taking on that nappy-headed gal as a law clerk—that's another."

"First they want to be lawyers," said Red Redstone, "next thing you know, they'll be aspiring to the bench. Women subject to the vagaries of menstruation and menopause, Negroes out for revenge—sitting in a position of judgment? I don't give two cents for a white man's rights if we allow that kind of progressive Republican claptrap. How am I supposed to champion the cause of justice and discharge my duties as D.A. in such a scenario?"

Guy said, "Slow your roll there, Bang Bang. Last time I checked, there was still an election between you and the title."

"You've got my support," said Pollard. "I'm with you, Red. And I like your chances better than I like this fella's," he added, tipping a thumb in Guy's direction.

"We'll see where we are in November," said Guy.

"I guess we will, won't we?"

"Excuse me." I stepped into the circle. "Mother's been looking for Tatum."

Tatum opened one eye toward me and said, "Buzz off."

I tried to gather her in my arms, but she struggled free and scampered up a magnolia tree.

"Tatum," I sighed. "Tate, get down here."

"Leave me alone," she said. "I was just listening to the stories. I wasn't bothering anybody."

"If I have to come up there—"

"Try it and I'll kick your family jewels."

The men in the circle roared with laughter.

"That child's got a mouth on her," said Red.

"It's the pulp fiction," said Guy. "Hammett and Chandler and Cain and so forth. She's a precocious reader like her daddy—with her mother's affinity for kicking a man's family jewels."

The men roared again, and King said, "I do believe we need another bottle of peach brandy over here. Critter, might I impose upon you to fetch that for me? I don't want to fall in the koi pond again."

I couldn't have been gone more than five minutes. Just long enough to go inside and get the bottle from the downstairs bar, plus possibly ninety seconds or so to take a stiff drink of it and gargle with Coke to disguise my breath. By the time I got back to the circle, things had devolved to rancor and fisticuffs. Everybody was standing there unsteadily. One of the Adirondack chairs lay in broken slats on top of the fire.

"I wanna know," Pollard raged. "How is Guy Stillwell in all the papers as the hero of the day? My Jamie's over there in the hospital in Saigon with half his leg shot off while this nigger-lovin' draft dodger stands in court defending rapists and murderers—and then he's got the brass to run for Congress on the premise that what belongs to me and mine should be taken away and given to the Negroes."

King was holding Guy back. Red was holding Pollard. Mother was in between, trying to play the bee charmer. "Now, boys! Now, boys! Stop this. We're all friends here."

"Every time I stand up in court," said Guy, "I'm fighting for *your* goddamn constitutional rights! I fight for the rights of all American citizens, created equal under the law."

"You never fought for shit." Pollard spit on the ground between them.

Newt stepped up and clocked him a good one right in the chops. Pollard stumbled sideways but stayed on his feet. He raised one arm high over his head. Lamplight glinted off something black in his hand, and then there was the earsplitting crack of a gunshot. He fired in the air—didn't point the gun at anybody on purpose—but the birds in the branches of the magnolia tree took flight, and a small object dropped to the ground.

"*Tatum!*" Mother shrieked.

My heart twisted in my chest. But then Tate got up, shaken but unbloodied. She tells me now she doesn't remember exactly what happened, but I figure she got startled and lost her footing. We both remember Mother's wrath.

"Drunken idiots!" Mother wheeled on Guy and his compatriots, clutching Tatum to her hip. "Stupid, drunken fools! Get out, the lot of you. Get on home."

"Come on, Brink." Red eased the .38 from Pollard's grip. "Party's over."

"Ma'am, I-I'm—" Pollard's mouth opened and closed like a goldfish on the sidewalk. He stared at Tatum, blinking away tears. "Jesus . . . Jesus . . . I could've . . . Jesus . . ."

"Mr. Pollard," Mother seethed, "you are no longer welcome in this house."

All in all, it was one of the more eventful cocktail parties I've attended in my time. The Convivium after party would continue to be one of the season's key events for many years to come, and my parents continued to host it side by side, but that particular event left some scars.

When we came down to breakfast the next morning, we discovered that Bootsy had run off to San Francisco in a VW microbus full of chronically disenchanted beatniks. Greatly distressed by this, my parents fought bitterly while Doralee served up a conglomeration she called "Ol' Sober"—sort of an eggs Benedict concoction on beer biscuits with pulled pork—along with bull shots and aspirin. Mother informed Guy that she was going back to school to finish her degree so people would take her seriously, and that meant she wouldn't have time to help him with his congressional campaign anymore. Guy informed her that he'd grown accustomed to the hoarfrost of her indifference and didn't give a good goddamn if she packed off to Paris, France, and took up with Bohemians. I quietly mourned the loss of my already small enough chances with the Pollard twins, and less than a week later, Brinkman Pollard was dead.

– 5 –

The shapely bartender at the Regent polished the brass RORY nametag with a cocktail napkin.

"It looks much better on you than it did on the other Rory," I said.

"Guess that's why you keep studying it like it's the Dead Sea Scrolls," she said. "Johnnie Walker neat?"

I nodded, and she set up a shot. Again with the water back.

"Thank you," I said, "but didn't they teach you in bartender school that *neat* means just the shot?"

"Water helps you be less hungover, but you do whatever makes you feel alive, sugar. C'mon in for a bull shot when you wake up with a supernova behind your left eyeball."

The new Rory was growing on me. King lived in the suite upstairs, so I could credibly tell myself that I wasn't just going in there to ogle the bartender, but I couldn't escape the uncomfortable certainty that she knew I was. It wasn't my usual MO to hang out at the Regent when I had a perfectly good bottle back at the boat. I was loath to pay for the overpriced liquor by the shot. Profligate spending didn't jibe with my plans for early retirement on the open seas.

Twenty years into my career, I'd never purchased a fancy car or big house. I was never tempted by the fancy Italian shoes my father always wore or the engraved Rolex King presented to himself when he retired. I never went fishing in Cabo or skiing at Vail. I lived frugally and sank every available dime into income property. My goal was to retire at fifty, and Tatum's talk about the possibilities of what lay beyond the Arpanet—an internet that would be readily available to most people— got me thinking about how, in the future, a person could live anywhere in the world and conduct business on the computer just as effectively as if they were stuck behind a desk in Athens, Georgia.

Wading through Guy's backlog of neglected cases had me think- ing wistfully about taking a slow boat to the other side of the world. I took a thick stack of files from my briefcase and separated them into three piles: settle out of court, take to trial, and refund the retainer. It galled me to even think about giving back money, but taking on cases for which Guy had cashed the checks months or even years earlier, I was essentially working without getting paid.

At the other end of the bar, Rory was taking notes from a thick textbook.

"I hadn't figured you for a college girl," I said.

"Careful there."

"What are you studying?"

"Getting my masters in social anthropology."

"What do you plan to do with that?"

"Open up a social anthropology store."

The mobile phone buzzed inside my briefcase. Rory gave it a horri- fied glance and said, "Something's buzzing in your luggage."

"Mobile phone," I said. "For important calls."

"Ah. Thank goodness. For a second there I thought it was a sex toy."

"Nah, I leave those at the office."

It was Mary-Louise on the phone. The secretary of state in the Caymans had promptly returned the corporate paperwork, so every- thing was in order with the lien on the yacht. I hung up and went back to the three piles, already thinking about how I could leverage the yacht money to subcontract some of the cases. There were plenty of hungry young lawyers around, and most of these were civil matters—divorces, property disputes, estate issues—amateur stuff I was working on for my father when I was still in high school and college.

When I stowed the phone back in my briefcase, Rory sighed and said, "I hope the whole mobile phone thing doesn't catch on. I don't want to be that easy to get hold of."

I had to smile. "That's exactly what my dad says."

"Hey, Critter." King strolled in and posted up on the barstool next to mine. "How goes it?"

"It goes," I said. "Guy had a lot more outstanding cases than I realized."

"Can you delegate some to your clerk?"

"Not in good conscience. This year's clerk is kind of a knucklehead."

"Let's see whatcha got."

"These are the worst ones." I slid him the pile destined for refund. "I appreciate anything you can do to help me salvage those retainers."

He took reading glasses from his shirt pocket and started flipping through the files.

"Hey, King," said Rory. "Don't you look handsome today."

"Got my hair cut. All three of 'em."

"Club soda with lime?"

"I prefer to call it the sobrietini."

"You got it," she said. "How's your friend doing?"

"Who doesn't enjoy a good stint in rehab?" King said broadly. "The cocaine's so much cheaper there."

The two of them had apparently struck up a jovial rapport, which was not surprising, because King was the jovial sort. He'd been living in a suite at the Regent for over a year, taking his evening meals in the club. I tried to counsel him on the cost-effectiveness of this lifestyle, but he was closing in on eighty and not about to start listening to advice. He liked the daily turndown service, and he was a magnanimous tipper, so the kitchen staff and concierge doted on him.

The bartender went about her business, cutting limes into a little tin container. I enjoyed watching her roll them between her hands before she sliced into them. Vivvy says there's some deep pathology there, but I'd rather believe it's because I appreciate an assiduous craftsperson, whatever their craft may be.

"My sister and I are driving down to Savannah tomorrow," I said. "Care to tag along? I know a great Cajun place. We could have lunch and make a day of it."

"I'll pass," said Rory.

"Maybe another time."

She sliced into another lime, and I didn't press my case.

"Need a menu, King?" she asked.

"Nah, it's Thursday. I'll go with the pork tenderloin."

"You got it."

She went in the back to put in the order, and King set his hand on my shoulder.

"Son, have I taught you nothing? You don't ask a woman to go out on a date with your sister."

I took out my wallet and set a twenty on the bar. King reached in his pocket, set his twenty next to mine, and said, "Go."

"This is a beautiful woman," I said, "understandably cautious, unfailingly professional. I see her dealing gracefully with unwelcome attentions from the less gentlemanly members of the gentlemen's club, and I don't want her to see me as part of that demographic. If I asked her out to dinner, I am, prima facie, just another guy hitting on her. If she turns me down, asking her out again could be misinterpreted, ex post facto, as desperation, harassment, and/or creepiness, hence, the dinner date option is burned. Instead, I invite her on a friendly day-trip with my sister. Old-school. No pressure. Granted, she has declined that offer, but technically, she has not turned me down for a date, insofar as I have not asked her out on a date, per se, therefore the dinner date option is still in the box with Schrödinger's cat, preceding day-trip query notwithstanding."

"Mouthy kid." King pushed both twenties over to me, and I pocketed them. "Next time, be direct. Don't you know confidence is sexy?"

"I'll take it under advisement."

"I think I can do something with these," he said, shuffling the files into alphabetical order. "If not, Mary-Louise can refund the retainers from that 'what if somebody croaks' fund."

"What if somebody actually does croak?"

"Somebody *will* croak. That's the one thing we can count on," said King. "We'll cross that bridge when it needs crossing."

"Yeah, my life is starting to look like a whole lot of damn bridges that need crossing, and I don't see the bridge builders stepping up for any of it."

"I hear ya," he said evenly, "but I think it'll be different this time."

This was a familiar refrain. Guy tended to look at the twelve steps as more of a hopscotch board.

"King, I need you to tell me who's on the yacht."

"Beats me. He never mentioned it."

"A possible criminal matter with a quarter-million-dollar retainer? He never mentioned it? Come on."

"I'm tellin' ya—"

"Is it Newt?"

"Critter, I straight-up don't know. I'm supposed to be retired, remember? And even to the extent I'm still involved in the practice, he's not obligated to tell me every damn thing. You know how it is. Your daddy and I, we always handled our separate cases, each to his own. Information is shared on a need to know basis. That's for the good of all."

"Yes, but *need to know* is a judgment call, and I'm not feeling rock solid about my father's judgment right now."

"Well, I am," said King. "Not once in the past forty years have I doubted the integrity of Guy Stillwell. Don't ask me to start second-guessing him now."

"You remember what it was like, King. You were there—where he is now—with the drinking. He blacks out. He can't eat anymore. Judge Sterling says she's not going to cut him any more slack."

"Judge Sterling . . . she's a tough cookie." King studied the glass between his hands. "If you've got a feeling it's Newt on the yacht, you should probably go with your gut."

"Skipping the bond—that's not a crime in and of itself," I said. "My concern is how he's been getting on in the world since he left Athens.

We may be looking at anything from credit card fraud to actual larceny, not to mention twenty-five years of alimony his wife is owed."

"As I recall," said King, "the wife was all 'stand by your man' until he lit out. Subsequent to that, she was out for blood. I believe a divorce decree was rendered in absentia."

"If so, she must have had a PI on the case. She would have had to prove a diligent effort to find him. I'm curious to know if that investigation turned up anything."

"Let's not get ahead of ourselves. Redstone's on the warpath, but before he can prosecute him, he has to find him."

Rory arrived with King's pork tenderloin and baked potato, and I asked her, "What are the odds of a man being completely surrounded by people who love him so much they'd never turn him over for a $25,000 reward?"

"Two chances of that," she said. "Fat and slim."

"Expert testimony from a social anthropologist. I rest my case." I stood and gathered the remaining files.

"Before you go . . ." King laid a dove gray envelope on the bar. "Your daddy left this for you."

It was the familiar law firm stationary with our navy blue logo in the upper left corner. Front and center, in my father's elegant script, was my name: *August*—not Critter.

"I'll waste no time reading it." I shoved the envelope into my brief-case. "I'll have my clerk dig up Newt's case file. Nothing struck me as wrong at the time, but now, I keep going back to it in my head and . . . I don't know. I was fifteen. There was a lot going on that summer."

"Jeezus, what a goat rodeo." King's eyes were rheumy with memory. "For a while there, it seemed like if the Dixie Mafia didn't kill me, my wife would."

– 6 –

Mimi Hodges—King's third wife, who relapsed and married him again to become his fifth wife—was a svelte, raven-haired equestrienne who'd competed in the 1952 Olympics and subsequently gave lessons in dressage and jumping to local debutantes-in-training. She walked around in tall boots and jodhpurs, and King was utterly in her thrall. He was a polecat and not faithful to his vows, but he loved Mimi and didn't want to lose her again, so a lot of our time was spent dodging her unsparing eye.

Sometimes at a stoplight, I'd glance up at the rearview mirror and find her glaring at me from the vehicle behind us. Mimi drove a bright red Mustang convertible, and she always had the top down, so everyone could see her unmistakable face. She always wore bright red lipstick and Jackie Kennedy sunglasses. A long silk scarf tied over her black hair rippled and shimmered in the sun.

Sometimes I'd deliver King to his front door at the end of the day, and she'd be standing on the porch, riding crop in one hand, vodka tonic in the other. King would whisper, not in dismay, but in awe, "Good God almighty, that is one hell of a woman."

Once a week, I drove King to Miss Jeffie's, a brothel that famously occupied a once-grand mansion on the seedier end of Hill Street. Anyone old enough to know about the facts of life knew what went on at Miss Jeffie's. Red light illuminated the windows at night, and if you cruised by slowly, you'd see a lamplit row of high hairdos that promised a lineup of fancy ladies waiting on a sofa inside the lace curtains. As a red-blooded fifteen-year-old, I was keen to learn about women of sporting morality, so it was a bit of a letdown the first time I drove King over there and discovered that the enticing silhouette was actually a row of plaster mannequin heads with big wigs on them.

This was business and not a social call, understand. The law firm handled a variety of legal issues for Miss Jeffie, who was subject to regular tax audits and occasional police raids. Being a savvy business-woman in a complicated enterprise, Miss Jeffie kept Stillwell & Hodges on a substantial retainer, so King was obligated to meet with her once a week. (I never knew how much of this retainer was bartered with "services in kind.") Mimi did not like it that this meeting took place at the brothel instead of the law office, and one could never know when she might be on the prowl, so I was obligated to drop King off in the carport by the kitchen door, park on a side street three blocks away, and walk back to Miss Jeffie's to wait on the front porch until King and Miss Jeffie had concluded their business. Making sure the latticework hid me from view of the street, I stared at a dime novel, trying not to think about what was going on inside those walls. One of the young ladies usually brought me a glass of sweet tea, and I hardly dared look her in the eye. When King came out, I had to hoof it over to the car and circle back to fetch him from the carport.

This inconvenient protocol chafed on me as the balmy spring turned to a broiling Southern summer, so the first Wednesday morning after the fateful Sunday evening barbecue party, I told King, "Maybe instead of waiting outside, I'll go in today."

"Well, you dog." He grinned at me from the back seat. "Have you got twenty-five dollars to invest? That's what it costs for an hour."

"Yes, sir," I assured him, but when I pulled into the carport, he said, "Keep your money in your shoe. I'll take care of it."

I parked the car on a side street and hoofed it back to Miss Jeffie's, the sidewalk beneath my feet radiating heat through me like a cast-iron griddle. Miss Jeffie met me on the front porch and beckoned for me to follow her up the stairs. We had to pause on the landing so she could catch her breath, fanning herself with a lace handkerchief.

"Enjoy your youth," she said. "Age imparts wisdom, but that's a poor reward for bad knees," she said.

She showed me to a room on the third floor, and it was pretty much what you'd expect to find on the third floor of an Edwardian mansion: antique four-poster with a faded coverlet, a vanity with a beveled mirror and wooden chair, pull-down shades and lace curtains on the window, brocade paper on the walls.

"Wait here," she said. "Twyla will be with you momentarily."

"Yes, ma'am."

I sat on the edge of the wooden chair, feeling like my circulatory system was trading places with my skin. By and by, the door opened, and a young woman entered. She was older than me, but not by much. Five-five, maybe five-seven. Medium build. Bottle blonde. Nondescript hazel eyes. Some acne scarring under a heavy layer of makeup. Her perfume was both floral and citrusy with a vague note of pecan pie.

"Hey, hon," she said. "I'm Twyla."

"Critter." I extended my hand. She smiled and gripped it briefly.

"You got fifty-five minutes," said Twyla.

"I thought it was an hour."

"I get five minutes to freshen up."

"Ah. Right." I felt like I'd swallowed a cinder block. "Well. Nice to meet you."

"Likewise."

"Is your family from Athens originally?"

"No."

"Do you . . . um, do you read much?"

"Yeah, I just finished *Moby Dick*. Are we gonna do this or not?"

"Yes," I said. "Yes, please."

"You sure?"

"Absolutely."

Twyla rolled her eyes and looked at her watch. "Fifty-three minutes."

I bolted from the chair and dragged my shirt off over my head. She set her hands on my chest, drifting her fingers down my torso. When she unzipped my jeans, it was like pulling the tab on a well-shaken can of beer.

"Oops." She laughed, but there was no derision in it. "That one's on the house."

"Sorry," I mumbled. "Sorta nervous."

"How old are you?"

"Eighteen," I said, and when she gave me a skeptical side-eye, I hastened to clarify. "I've got a birthday coming up."

"In a couple of years, maybe. You're big boned, though, aren't you?"

"Um . . ."

"Have you ever done this before?"

"Not with another person in the room."

"Okay. No worries. You'll be ready to go again in twenty minutes. Meanwhile, I'll show you a few good moves. It ain't all about your pecker, y'know. There's all kinds of tools in the toolbox."

It was without question the most instructive twenty minutes of my lifetime, and the half hour that followed was a formative experience in the best possible way. Vivvy has, on numerous occasions, expressed appreciation for Twyla's patient tutelage. My fond memories of our fifty-five minutes together have seen me through some lonely nights.

"You're sweet," Twyla said on her way to freshen up for the next customer. "Maybe I'll see you again."

I had no words.

"Open the window if you're gonna smoke," she said, and then she was gone, and I was alone, a man in full. Things would be different now. I would be different. Stronger. Better. I wouldn't take any more shit from the Lucky Winfields of the world. Or the Poppy Sterlings. And just maybe I would see Twyla again if the spirit moved me. Practice makes perfect.

I was half-dressed when the screaming started somewhere on the second floor. Footsteps scattered up the stairs. The Haitian cook dashed from one end of the hallway to the other, clanging a wooden spoon on a kettle.

"Cops is here! Cops is here! Raid! It's a raid!"

"*Shit*," I whispered. "*Shit, shit, shit . . .*"

I wasn't scared of the police. I was scared of my mother. She'd have King by the short hairs if the cops hauled me out of here in front of everybody. I threw my clothes on, jammed my feet into my loafers, and cracked the door just enough to see down the hall. People were shouting. Cops yanking doors open, dragging folks out of rooms in varying states of dishabille. I closed the door and tried to lock it, but the lock had been disabled—a hole drilled where the skeleton key ought to go—a policy decision that made sense to me, even as a panicked fifteen-year-old. I grabbed the wooden chair from the vanity and wedged the back under the knob.

Think. Think. Think.

The third-floor window opened about ten feet over the columned carport, and it was a ten- or twelve-foot drop from the carport roof to the grass. When I hit the ground, I heard someone yell, "Hey! You there!" I looked over my shoulder and saw a lumbering giant of a deputy everybody called Tiny. He raised a hand to shade the sun in his eyes and started walking toward me, but I was already running, leaping over flowerbeds and lawn ornaments. I dove through a thick hedge of hydrangeas, leaving a blizzard of pink petals in my wake, and I kept going until I reached the side street where the car was parked. I sneaked around the side of someone's potting shed, turned on the spigot, and drank deep gulps of cold hose water. Raking my fingers through my hair, I caught a faint whiff of Twyla's perfume on my hands. I leaned against the cool cinder block wall until my heart slowed to a dull bass thrum.

"Assess the information and control the damage," Guy always said.

Applying that formula, I decided to play it cool, drive the car back to Miss Jeffie's, and make like I'd just gotten there, but the moment I turned onto College Avenue, Mimi Hodges fell in behind me, keeping pace as I made a few false stops and starts. I finally lost her when I circled the public library, and she had to pause at the crosswalk for two black ladies shepherding half a dozen white children from one corner to the other. I whipped around the corner, faked her out with a right turn on Boulevard, and headed back to Miss Jeffie's. When I got there, Mimi Hodges was leaning on a light pole across the street. She smiled and cupped her hand to offer me a little parade queen wave.

"Dang it!" Too late to do anything about it now.

King was out on the front porch with Tiny and Miss Jeffie, who was being quizzed by a rumpled detective—a fella named Hopper who sometimes did PI work on the side for Stillwell & Hodges. King put a protective arm around Miss Jeffie, and I flinched, glancing over my shoulder at his wife. Mimi stood there for a moment with an unreadable expression on her face, then got in her car and drove away.

Under the carport at the brothel, Miss Jeffie was engaged in heated conversation with Sheriff Heck as her ladies were led out in handcuffs. I got out of the car, craning my neck for a better look, and saw Twyla. She crossed the driveway and climbed into the back of the paddy wagon, frilly robe and frothy negligee floating on the breeze behind her.

Uniformed deputies stretched crime scene tape from one newel post to the other, which seemed like a lot of fanfare. I'd seen Miss Jeffie's get raided before with a lot less theater. Then the kitchen door opened, and the coroner's men brought out a gurney with a telltale black shroud zipped shut on top of it. Red Redstone came out and stood there while they loaded the body bag into the back of the coroner's van.

"What the hell . . ."

A heavy hand came down on my shoulder, and I spun to find my father standing there. Before I could offer up a story, he said, "Go back to the office and tell Mary-Louise we need to prepare for all these arraignments. You and Poppy meet me at the courthouse. They'll start processing Miss Jeffie's girls in an hour."

"What happened? Who is that in the body bag?"

"It's Mr. Pollard," said Guy. "Now do as you're told."

"Yes, sir."

I fetched Poppy, and we headed over to the courthouse for the bond hearings. We sat in the front row, right behind the defense table where

Guy and King would take turns if they had to represent the ladies one by one, but they were hoping they wouldn't have to. There wasn't much money in it, because none of these girls had money. Beyond the retainer from Miss Jeffie, Guy and King did this kind of thing for fun. As soon as word got out that the brothel had been raided again, spectators started filling the courtroom. The whole tawdry business was beneath District Attorney Ruckels, so he'd sent his lackey, A.D.A. Redstone, and a couple of clerks to deal with the hearings.

First up was *State of Georgia v. Miss Jeffie Pitcock*, Judge Eustice Talmadge presiding. Before Redstone could get the ball rolling, Guy raised a hand and said, "Your Honor, if it please the court, I was thinking we might be able to dispense with all this unpleasantness in a single proceeding. We all know what's happening here, and it's a waste of everyone's time. I'm sure D.A. Ruckels remembers how he got his nose bloodied in the Sin City—"

"Objection," said Red. "Relevance."

"Sustained. Move on, Mr. Stillwell."

"Judge," Guy said, "do I correctly recall that you played football for Georgia during the 1940s?"

"I did," said Talmadge. "Once a Bulldog, forever a Bulldog."

"Yes, Your Honor, and you are a lifelong resident of our fair city, correct?"

"Bred and buttered," said the judge. "What's your point?"

"Not to be indelicate, Judge Talmadge, but I wonder about the statistical probability of a red-blooded American male playing football and graduating from UGA without ever having visited Miss Jeffie's establishment, which has been regarded as somewhat of an institution around here since 1937."

Laughter rippled through the courtroom, and Talmadge's expression darkened.

"I don't like where this is heading," Redstone piped up. "Clearly, defense is bucking for a canny and sagacious judge to recuse himself, and he's willing to insult the character of a gentleman to get the job done. I am shocked, Your Honor! I am outraged!"

Guy said, "Don't hurt yourself, Little Doo. We're just getting started."

"You're on thin ice, Stillwell," said the judge. "I happen to be a married man."

"As are most of Miss Jeffie's clientele," said Guy, "though we don't see any of them in the courtroom today. Funny how these ladies managed to commit the crime of prostitution all by themselves. Tell me, A.D.A. Redstone, how does one manage that sort of activity all by one's lonesome? I figure if anybody knows how to do it, you do."

The courtroom roared, and Redstone got redder, a rash of crimson creeping above the collar of his crisply ironed shirt.

"Joke all you want," he said. "We'll see how well she does now that the state has seized that house and every stick of furniture inside it."

"Yes, about that," said Guy. "May I bring to the court's attention Georgia statute 117.4 subsection c, and referenced in *State versus Mellon*, when a tax lien was placed against a carpenter—one Percy H. Mellon. The state seized his tools and construction equipment, and in doing so deprived him of his livelihood, which prompted the Georgia legislature to pass the aforementioned statute. To whit: 'In the enforcement of the law, the state is not at liberty to seize the property of any persons within their jurisdiction or deprive them of the tools by which they accomplish their trade.' And I think we can all agree that the tools of Miss Jeffie's trade must and do encompass the house and furnishings, including sofas and beds. Now, it's immaterial whether you approve of her profession or not. The statute makes no such stipulation. Given that and the absence of any injured parties, we are seeking dismissal of the order of seizure and the immediate return of Miss Jeffie's rightful property."

"Your Honor," said Redstone, "Miss Jeffie's place is an active crime scene at this moment. State is fully within its rights to seize the property and conduct a proper murder investigation."

"How is it," Judge Talmadge sighed, "you jokers always end up in my courtroom?"

Guy winked at the gallery crowd. "Just lucky, I guess."

"I'm gonna give you two hours to work it out," said the judge. "I don't care how you do it. Get it done. Time to play *Let's Make a Deal*. If

I see you back in this courtroom two hours from now, expecting me to sort it out, I'll make sure neither one of you goes home happy."

"Your Honor," Redstone started, "if I may—"

"You may not." Talmadge banged his gavel. "Two hours."

He left by the door behind the bench, and Guy crossed the aisle to Red and offered his hand.

"I'm sorry to hear about Pollard," he said. "Let me take you to lunch at Tony's and get this mess cleared up so you can be with the family."

"See you over there." Red nodded curtly and walked away, stiff-lipped, ignoring questions and catcalls from the peanut gallery.

Guy gathered the arraignment midden into his briefcase with hardly a glance at King, who'd fallen asleep in his chair and was snoring softly.

"Critter," said Guy, "get King back to the office and then meet me at Tony's."

"I should be there," said Poppy. "Your clerk should be there, I mean."

"Yes, you should, but today is not a good day to fight that fight."

"There's never a good day to fight. That's why the fight keeps needing to get fought."

"Don't make this about yourself, Poppy," Guy said sharply. "I know my wife has been eggin' you on. She wouldn't let it rest until I took you on as a clerk for the summer, and I don't regret it. You're the sharpest tool that's ever been in this shed. We've never had a clerk as ambitious or as quick a study. You sure as hell work harder than any of those boys we've had. But you're here to learn, not to shake things up. Understand?"

"Yes, sir."

"Take a lesson from what went down here this morning," Guy said. "Talmadge can't recuse himself, because he can't have it appear that he has a reason. But he doesn't want to be on the bad side of Miss Jeffie. She has a lot of friends in high places—many of whom are familiar with her low places. You can bet he's on the phone to Ruckels right now, and Ruckels will give Redstone his marching orders. Two hours from now, the judge goes home happy, Redstone is in the good with Ruckels, Ruckels is off the hook with Miss Jeffie, and we take the rest of the day off with pay. 'God's in his heaven, all's right with the world,' as the poet said."

"Yes, sir. If you say so."

"It'll happen, Poppy. Just not today."

"Trouble is, it's always *today*, isn't it?"

King's head bobbed and he startled himself awake with a loud snort. He looked about the empty courtroom, perplexed. "What did I miss?"

"Business as usual," said Poppy.

We all piled into the land yacht. I dropped Guy at Tony's, then headed to the law office, where Poppy and I helped King up to the sofa in his office. By the time I got back to Tony's, I was profoundly weary and ravenously hungry for lunch. I slid into the booth next to Guy, grateful to see that he'd ordered my usual burger and fries. I wolfed them down while Guy and Red dispensed justice in the matter of the ladies.

"Bottom line here," said Guy. "You need to save face with the conservative voters. I won't begrudge you that. Let's plead no contest across the board, and I'll play the sternly chastised whipping boy for the gallery while you make some bold remarks about law and order and decency. Talmadge can sentence all the girls to thirty days and then suspend the sentences so Miss Jeffie has everybody back to work by this evening. She's agreed to pay the same fine as last time and won't make any noise for Ruckels."

"We need to question every one of those girls," said Red. "Nobody leaves town."

"Understood."

"And the crime scene stays sealed until I release it."

"Inviolate as Grant's tomb," said Guy. "Hand on heart."

"All right, then."

"I truly am sorry, Red. I know Pollard was a good friend."

"None better. It's a goddamn travesty."

"What the hell happened?"

Red glanced briefly in my direction, but he was used to seeing me as an extension of my father, no more out of place than a collar button.

"Between you and me," said Red, "it looks like a professional hit. GBI is already looking into it. I'm not privy to all the information, but they're hypothesizing it has something to do with the Dixie Mafia. It's somehow related to that special agent who got blown up with the car bomb."

"I thought that was bootleggers that did that."

"It's a tangled web," said Red. "I don't know what Pollard had to do with it, but we could help each other out here, Guy. We're gonna find that hit man, and he's gonna need a lawyer. I'll do my best to get you in the room. You get him to roll over on whoever hired him, and I'll make him a sweet deal. We both walk away heroes in our own constituency."

Such was the lunchtime conversation at Tony's, a well-greased crank case for the machinery of law and order.

Back at the office, I sank into an overstuffed easy chair in the corner of the foyer, which was cool and quiet and smelled of old books. Mary-Louise was on the phone, talking a client through his divorce paperwork. Poppy was at the clerk's desk, typing up something in triplicate. Neither one of them looked at me, and I sure as heck wasn't going to look at them. I felt certain my experience with Twyla had transformed me in some graphically apparent way. I was already shaving once a week and wearing a suit with a skinny tie, but this was next-level stuff. I was changed by it and couldn't imagine how anybody would look at me and not know it.

I intended to avoid Mother's curious gaze for as long as possible, but I felt a wave of longing for Bootsy's free-spirited presence. She'd been gone just a few days and had already called Mother twice to get money from Western Union, so I knew she was okay, but I missed her. She would have known my secret the moment she saw me, and that would have been all right, because a secret told is a betrayal and a secret kept is a burden, but a secret fairly discerned is a sigh of relief.

Poppy typed with a firm stride, pecking at the keys with the steady beat of a snare drum. The carbons whispered against each other every time the paper shifted. A little bell pinged every time the carriage reached the end of the line. Lulled by this symphony, I dozed, dreaming of Twyla's tricks and trade. When I woke up, my father's office door was closed, and from the other side I could hear him and King conversing in hushed but urgent tones.

Mary-Louise and Poppy finished their workday and went home. My father's office door remained closed, the voices on the other side rising and falling. Every once in a while, I saw a square button on the telephone light up, which meant they were making a call. It was well after six when they came out. King lurched past me, out the door and down the hall.

"Give him a ride home," said Guy and closed the office door again.

King was hammered, muttering to himself the whole way to his house, mumbling something about Mimi. When I turned down the long driveway, we saw that on the lawn below the big front porch, there was a multicolored mound of dapper linen suits, crisply ironed shirts, tooled leather boots, and silk ties, all in a heap with hundreds of leather-bound books. On the ground next to the cairn was a bright red can of charcoal lighter fluid. A soft summer breeze wafted the smell of accelerant toward the open car windows.

"I can't look." King closed his eyes.

Mimi flicked her cigarette onto the pile, and King's worldly belongings—his suits of armor—ignited with an audible *pfouff*.

I waited a while to make sure Mimi was clear of the conflagration and that the wind wasn't trying to sweep the leaping flames toward the house. When it seemed appropriate to do so, I backed down the long driveway, careful not to go too wide and disturb the flowerbeds. King snored softly, stretched out on the bench seat behind me. I drove home, and Mother helped me put him to bed in a downstairs guest room.

"You must be starving," she said, and I did not deny it. "Doralee's gone home. I'll make you a sandwich."

"I can make it myself."

"I know you can, but I wish you'd let me. Seems like you've had a lot on you lately." She pushed a sweaty lock of hair from my forehead and pressed the back of her hand to my face as if to check if I had a fever.

For reasons I couldn't understand, there was suddenly a hard lump in my throat. The weight of the long day dragged my shoulders down. The inside of my nose burned, threatening tears, but I was rescued from humiliation by the shrill ringing of the phone on the wall. Mother answered it and, after a proper exchange of pleasantries, covered the receiver with the palm of her hand and called down the hallway, "Guy? Red's on the phone for you." He took the call in his office and appeared a moment later in the kitchen doorway.

"Critter, I need you to drive me down to the courthouse. They arrested Lucky Winfield for murder."

Mother insisted on making a ham sandwich wrapped in waxed paper for me to take along. For some reason, I remember that. I remember the smell of iron bars and wet cement floor and the low echo of Guy's voice as he gave Lucky the talk. I sat on a chair in the corner, and they faced each other across a big table with a faded Formica top. Lucky insisted, like most people did, that he hadn't done this thing, and Guy said, "Of course, I'm prepared to take you at your word, Lucky, but I have to ask the questions Mr. Redstone will ask. Why do you suppose he has it in his head that you shot Mr. Pollard?"

"Hell if I know," said Lucky. "He claims these fellas down at the ice-house say I did it, and they all stand to collect a reward when I swing, but I didn't do it. I swear to you, Mr. Stillwell, I did not kill the man. If those SOBs say I did, they lie, and the truth ain't in 'em!"

Guy started to ask Lucky if he knew how much money it cost to have a lawyer defend you for murder, but in the middle of the whole "cold leg iron" bit, the steel door slid open, and D.A. Borley Ruckels came in followed by his toady Redstone and an odd little fella I didn't know.

"Evening, all." Guy stood, unruffled. "Red, I'm surprised to see you. I thought we had an agreement."

"It's not up to him," said Ruckels.

The stranger was small and impeccably dressed with unnaturally fair skin, elfin features, and round wire-rimmed glasses so thick, they made his pale blue eyes look large and irregular. The top of his fedora barely cleared the height of my shoulder as he stepped past me and set his briefcase on the table. The color drained from Lucky's face. Suddenly, there was nothing left of the slingshot bravado with which he usually comported himself.

"What's *he* doing here?" Lucky asked, eyes as big as sweet potatoes.

"Mr. DiLippa sent me," said the stranger. "He's prepared to post bond and cover any additional expenses."

"Go on home, Guy." Ruckels jerked his thumb toward the little fella. "Mr. Tick here will be representing the accused."

"Lucky, is that what you want?" Guy asked. "You want Mr. Tick to represent you?"

Lucky shook his head vehemently.

Guy turned to the stranger and said, "Sorry to have wasted your time, Tick. Seems Mr. Winfield would prefer to retain his own counsel. Best regards to Mr. DiLippa."

"Of course, it makes no never mind to the state if he retains his own counsel," Ruckels said with a pie-eating smile, "so long as it's someone other than you."

"Excuse me?"

"You're his employer," said Ruckels. "I intend to call you as a witness. Seems to me like there's a conflict there."

"Now, hold on a minute," said Guy. "That's not—"

"You . . ." Lucky eyed me with the same narrow squint he'd given me when I confronted him the previous Sunday night. "You framed me up is what."

"My boy's got nothing to do with any of this," said Guy.

"This silver-spoon motherfucker—" Lucky pointed a shaky finger at me. "He's got it in for me 'cause I gave his sister a second glance and refused to kiss his cotton candy ass."

The stranger said, "That's enough, Mr. Winfield."

"Yes, sir." Lucky stared down at the man's cold shadow on the floor.

Ruckels said, "You want Mr. Tick to be your lawyer, don't you, Lucky?"

"Yes, sir," Lucky said, barely above a whisper. I'd never seen a man so nakedly devoid of hope.

"Good evening, Mr. Stillwell," said Tick. "Pleasure seeing you again. You and your boy." He smiled an opaque smile. His teeth were small. Like baby teeth.

"Critter." Guy ticked his chin toward the door. "Wait for me outside."

I vaguely remember raised voices behind me as I left the jailhouse, but truthfully, my attention was focused on that ham sandwich. It was late, and I'd had a long, eventful day. Holy hell. Lunch seemed like a year ago. I sat in the car, ate the sandwich, washed it down with an RC Cola and listened to the radio until Guy came out and got in the passenger seat. He took a flask from the glove compartment and drank in silent contemplation.

"What happened back there?" I asked a mile or two down the road.

"That's not your business," said Guy.

"Who's Mr. DiLippa?"

"Drop it, Critter. You hear me? Some things are outside of what's appropriate for you to be involved in."

"What things?"

"Just drive."

- 7 -

The present day Tatum laughs when she recalls the electronics setup that the 1988 Tatum had rigged in the back of her Toyota Land Cruiser. It involved a state-of-the-art Cambridge Z88 laptop computer that weighed approximately twenty pounds, two small black-and-white TVs, a ham radio receiver, and a police scanner, all powered by an array of tomato can batteries that got so hot they had to be kept in metal lunchboxes. I wanted to call it the Mobile Surveillance Technological Intelligence Tracking System (MS TITS), but Tatum called it Frank, short for Frankenstein.

"I've been doing some freelance fox hunting for the GBI," she said. "Coast Guard has cameras out on the harbor for drug runners, so we should be able to tap into that and poke around a bit."

Drug-running. My heart sank. I hadn't even thought of that as a revenue source for Newt, and it was not something I wanted the firm to get involved in.

It was a four-hour drive to Thunderbolt Marina, and Tatum slept most of the way, slumped in the passenger seat with a black leather jacket over her face. According to Mother, Tate was a nocturnal being now, laboring all night like a mad scientist and sleeping most of the day on a cot in her walk-in closet because Mother wouldn't allow her to cover the bedroom windows with aluminum foil. It would have been easier to lure a wombat out into the sunlight.

Rather than take the freeway, I cut down through the rolling hills of the Oconee National Forest to Madison, a small enclave of antebellum homes that survived the Civil War. As General William Tecumseh Sherman scorched a path across Georgia, burning Atlanta to the ground, he spared about three dozen grand houses in Madison, thanks to the astute politicking of a few locals.

When you see a movie that looks like the authentic Old South, chances are it was shot in Madison. Folks there have kept it pristinely preserved, thanks to an infusion of money from developers in the 1980s, who pegged it as the perfect bedroom community about an hour out of Atlanta. People started retiring there, setting up small horse and hobby farms, living the life of landed gentry, much like the folks who'd built the houses in the first place.

This was the scene of one of the first cases I handled on my own after law school. A cattle rustling case. The defendant was a magazine-handsome fellow, young and athletic. Not terribly bright, but he struck me as guileless. I was as certain as I could be that he was innocent. He enjoyed carnal knowledge of a University of Georgia professor, who put up the bond and paid my fee.

"The prosecution's case is flimsy and circumstantial," I told the jury, and I made my case, but they found him guilty on gut feeling.

"That's how it goes sometimes," said Guy. He tried to comfort me with the fact that my client could get a day off for every day of good behavior and be out in five years, but I could not let this thing go. I told the professor I'd handle the appeal for free, which left Guy and King righteously pissed off.

"Now you're screwing with the billable hours," my father thundered. "That is not gonna fly."

Long story short, I gave that appeal heart and soul, only to discover that the professor had already moved on to another boy toy and my client had been selling the stolen sides of beef out of the local abattoir the whole time. Mary-Louise was the only one in the office who didn't enjoy a belly laugh at my expense.

"This line of work can be hard on your faith in human nature," she said. "You just gotta do what you do to get through the mire so your integrity is still intact when an honest lawyer is needed to defend an innocent client."

"I'm not sure they exist," I said.

"Honest lawyers or innocent clients?"

"Take your pick."

"They do exist," said Mary-Louise, "though not in great numbers. Don't let it make you a cynic, Critter. God knows there's no shortage of those."

I didn't know how to explain to her the creeping rationalization that leads to moral compromise. A lawyer gets used to it, unless one sticks to silk-stocking law. It becomes the customary gait, this walking lie. I'd been introduced to it early, an observer first and then an instrument, and now it seemed like I had only two options: perpetrator or patsy. Something was off about this case, and the one person who might have shed light on it had hightailed it to Nassau.

Traffic picked up as we got closer to Savannah. I nudged Tatum and said, "Rise and shine."

We parked in a commercial fishing lot above the docks, and I scoped the boats with binoculars while she fiddled with Frank. *Rascal* sat comfortably on the blue water between her upscale sisters. She was not the biggest yacht moored at Thunderbolt, but to me, she was the prettiest, pristinely white with proud pinstriped bimini. A slick rainbow on the water near the engines indicated a diesel leak that might be responsible for keeping her here.

Tate tapped one of the TV screens and said, "Check it out."

I peered at the fuzzy video feed, which looked down on Rascal's aft deck. A white-haired man sat, pale legs outstretched, on a rattan chaise.

"Is it Newt?" I asked.

"Beats me," said Tatum. "I was five last time I saw him."

"Whoever he is, he's my client. I guess I'll just go down there and talk to him."

"My GBI guy says they got a lot of tips from *Unsolved Mysteries*, but nothing they could confirm so far. If I hear anything on the scanner, I'll sound the car horn. Two shorts and a long."

"Thanks, Tate. You've been extremely helpful."

"You'll be invoiced."

I strolled down to the docks with my hands in my pockets, trying to look natural. I thought I'd just casually chat the guy up, but as I worked my way around to the port side, I heard a voice call down from the cockpit. "Guy? Guy Stillwell!"

I took off my sunglasses. "Newt Ballerini?"

Newt's expression fell. "Wait . . . *Critter*? Is that you?"

I smiled and waved. "Hey, Newt."

"Jesus H. Christ, you are the spitting image of your daddy. Come aboard, son."

He strode along the rail to a steep collapsible stairway that bridged the narrow gap between the spotless hull and barnacled pier. When I stepped onto the deck, Newt gripped my hand and pumped it with vigor.

"Good to see you, Critter. Good to see you. You don't realize it while you're out in the world, but you miss it. It's great to see somebody from home."

"Good to see you too," I said. "I guess we've got some catching up to do."

He looked past my shoulder. "Is Guy with you?"

"Guy is indisposed."

"Oh. What about King?"

"King has been semiretired for several years."

"I see." He folded his arms, nodding, glancing right and left. "Okay . . ."

"Please, rest assured that I am every bit as qualified to serve your interests. If you're not comfortable with that—"

He huffed a nervous half laugh. "I don't have much choice, do I?"

"I've been studying up on your case, so I have a solid understanding of the charges pending. I'd like to get your perspective on the situation. Is there somewhere we can talk?"

"Sure." Newt gestured toward the stern. "C'mon. I'll give you the nickel tour."

I followed him along the passageway, taking in every linear foot of *Rascal's* streamlined charm.

"This here is the salon level," he said. "Cockpit, aft deck, pilothouse, galley, and dining area. Down below are the staterooms. Up here is the flybridge."

At the top of another short flight of stairs, there was an open-air bar section seating arranged in a relaxed horseshoe. Newt directed me to make myself comfortable, but I stood at the rail, watching a rain squall form on the distant horizon. The evening breeze was full of salt air and sea gulls, and I felt it move through me, pulling toward the mouth of the Wilmington River and the wide open Atlantic.

"The staff's gone," said Newt. "Can I get you a drink?"

"Gone where?"

"Cook didn't speak English, so who the hell knows, but I expect the others are tripping over each other trying to get that reward money."

"I expect so. It's been almost seventy-two hours since the show aired. I'm surprised they haven't already picked you up. My associate is onshore monitoring the police scanner."

Newt opened a cabinet below the bar and brought out a bottle and two highball glasses.

"Forty-year-old Glenfiddich," he said. "No time like the present."

"Hear, hear." I raised my glass. "When you say 'others' . . ."

"First mate, captain, and a very sweet little gal who was effecting some plumbing repairs when the show came on."

"Aren't you the captain?"

"Hell, no, son. You need a professional for that."

"Ah. Of course."

"I paid all three of 'em twice what the reward was, and they were all 'Mum's the word, sir! You can count on us!' Oh, butter wouldn't melt. We were supposed to shove off tonight. My plan was to cruise the *Rascal* over to Trinidad and scuttle her."

"Scuttle her? Why?"

"I need the cash infusion from insurance. I know an outfit over there—Venezuelan pirates—they scuttle the yacht, and then after you get the settlement, they raise her up, do a full refit, and give her a new identity."

"Whoa, whoa, whoa!" I held up my hands. "I did not hear that, understand? As your attorney, I'm advising you, that would be illegal. I cannot be party to any of that."

"Well, I'm strapped for cash, so if you expect a half mil retainer . . ."

"I have a lien on the yacht. If you can't mobilize the cash, I'll sell it."

As the words left my mouth, I could have sworn, I felt an indignant hiccup from somewhere deep in *Rascal*'s substructure.

"Maybe I'll keep her," I said, and again, I swear, she purred, mollified, beneath my feet.

"Okay, well . . . where do we start?" asked Newt.

"At the beginning," I said. "Walk me through it."

"There's nothing to walk through. I never hired Lucky to kill anybody. I was framed."

"Then why did you run?" I asked.

"You wouldn't understand."

"Try me."

"After the war . . . I don't know. They say you can't go home again."

"But you came home a hero."

"All that ticker tape parade shit made me intensely uncomfortable." Newt rubbed his salt-grizzled chin and sighed. "You don't know things we saw over there, Critter. Things we did. And we thought we'd be okay with it all, because the Nazis and Japanese did worse. But after a while, it started weighing on me. I didn't want to be that man anymore—the golden son, the war hero—all that BS. First I thought about how to kill myself. Then I thought, no. I want to live. But I wanted to live a different life. I wanted to be a different man in a different place, with a different name. My parents had passed away. I had no love for my wife. I saw a chance to bolt, and I took it."

"Okay. Please understand, I'm not saying I don't believe you, Newt. It's my duty to ask the challenging questions that D.A. Redstone is bound to ask."

"D.A. Redstone." Newt smiled. "Last time I saw him, he was still brown-nosing Ruckels and begging for crumbs of campaign love."

"Well, he's the D.A. now, and he'll be presenting a whole lot of extremely damning evidence against you."

From a distance I heard the Land Cruiser horn. Two shorts and a long. Two shorts and a long.

"That's the signal," I said.

"When they come for me, Critter, you gotta make sure they keep me in the county jail. If I go to the state prison, I'm a dead man."

"What do you mean?"

"Just see to it," he said firmly.

"It's not likely any judge would allow bail," I said. "Trying to argue that you're not a flight risk—that dog's been walked. My advice is that you turn yourself in. Cooperate with the authorities, but don't answer any questions. Not a word to anyone. I'll head back to Athens so I can be there when they process you."

"And then what?"

The Land Cruiser urged caution. Two shorts and a long. Two shorts and a long.

"There'll be an arraignment," I said. "We'll enter a not guilty plea. Red will probably offer some kind of deal. They don't want to risk a jury trial any more than we do."

"No deal," said Newt. "If you're half the lawyer your daddy was, you'll settle Red's hash."

"Settle it how?"

"You'll know when the time comes," Newt said. His confidence seemed a little shaky, but he was obviously planning to cling to it in hell or high water.

– 8 –

King was in a dark place the first few days after Mimi torched his stuff and threw him out. His drinking scared the girl he had in the apartment, so she left him as well, leaving him there to drink in the dark all by himself.

"I need you to drive him down to Fort Valley," said Guy. "Stay with him while he's trying that bank robbery case. Make sure he gets where he's supposed to be."

"Yes, sir."

"Good boy." My father pushed his knuckles gently against my jaw. "I know I can count on you to do what needs doing."

I picked King up at the Regent first thing in the morning, and by the time we got down to Fort Valley, he was shaking pretty badly. We checked into the motel, and as I carried his briefcase up to the room, I could hear glass clinking inside. King hung his dapper court attire in the closet, propped himself up on the bed, and opened the briefcase to produce two bottles of peach brandy, a small file with a copy of the warrants and arrest report, and a tablet on which he'd scribbled down the names of witnesses and a few other notes.

"I'm gonna stretch out while you do the supply run," said King, and he was snoring before I got out the door.

King could no longer keep food down, so I went to the Piggly Wiggly for supplies to make nog for him. When I got back to the motel, I cracked two eggs into a mason jar and shook them up with milk and sugar. King chugged that down and chased it with half a bottle of peach brandy. We repeated this ritual at breakfast time, which kept the shakes at bay while he was in court.

Steady as Gibraltar, he got up and charmed the jury. He grilled the prosecution witnesses on cross. His opening statement and closing argument were witty and erudite. The small town prosecutor, pope-sober, was no match for King at his inebriated best. I don't recall the specifics of the case, but it was a master class in style and delivery, one of many, from which I learned by osmosis the performance art of practicing law. Two days later, it was all over, and King's client was a free man.

"Home, Jeeves," he said, slumping into the back seat of the car.

He dozed off and on as I drove home, windows cranked down, radio cranked up. We rolled into the driveway outside the law office just before noon, and I was surprised to see Mother on the front porch with Othella. When Mother saw me, she stood up from the porch rocker and waved. Poppy stood off to the side, quaking like an aspen, arms folded tight against her body, but Othella appeared calm and serene. She sat up straight, but not uncomfortably so, on a bentwood rocking chair. Resting on the floor between her feet was a burlap bag, the same type of grain sack her daddy always used to transport bundles of cash and stained leather ledgers when he brought his taxes into the law office every February.

Miss Othella had been running the Riverside Country Club for several years, ever since one night when Klansmen showed up at the juke joint after closing time and beat old Mr. Sterling within an inch of his life, but he insisted on taking care of the taxes himself and would trust no one but Guy to assist him. This went on until he died in 1962. It was a little sad to see Miss Othella bring the burlap sack to the law office without him.

"Why, Teddi! Good morning. And Miss Othella." King nodded to them in turn. "To what do we owe the pleasure?"

"I'm here to speak with Mr. Guy on a matter of some importance," said Othella. "My daughter called ahead and set up a proper appointment with Miss Mary-Louise."

"Poppy?" I said. "You okay?"

"She's fine," Mother said sharply. "You boys go on in now. We'll wait here till your daddy's done with Mr. Redstone."

King and I exchanged a curious glance, and he shrugged as if to say, "*Women.*" I followed him inside, and we paused in the cool foyer. At the top of the grand stairway, Mary-Louise was eavesdropping, flattened against the wall outside Guy's office door, which was slightly ajar. She looked down at us and pressed one finger to her lips, so we stood by the newel post, straining to make out the specifics of the heated exchange happening over our heads.

Redstone strode back and forth by the door, barking and gesticulating. "So don't you sit there stonewalling, trying to tell me you know nothing about it."

"Last time I checked," said Guy, "Lucky was Tick's problem. Your boss saw to that."

"And what about Ballerini?"

"Haven't seen Newt as I can recall."

"Well, next time you *don't see him*, you tell him I got a warrant for his arrest on a charge of murder in the first degree."

"*Murder,*" Guy coughed. "Hold on. Hold on. Red, that's gotta be some misunderstanding."

"Tick came to Ruckels this morning, proposing a deal for your warehouse mutt. As of last night, Lucky Winfield was ready to turn himself in and swear to the fact that your good buddy and business partner, Newt Ballerini, paid him to put a bullet in Brinkman Pollard's head. Now Lucky's conveniently gone missing, and Newt's nowhere to be found."

"That is unpasteurized bullshit—hearsay and conjecture."

"We'll see how Judge Talmadge and twelve angry men feel about it," said Red.

"Show up with some hard evidence, and I might be interested."

"It won't take me an hour to get a warrant to search the beer distributorship. My advice to you: cooperate fully, lest the unsparing eye of the law turns to examine your role in this whole affair."

"I'd take legal advice from a junkyard dog before I'd take it from you."

"I'll have you as accessory after the fact!"

Guy was already up from his desk, escorting the A.D.A. to the door. "You go get your warrant, Little Doo, and I'll meet you at the warehouse."

Redstone stomped down the stairs to the foyer, where I stood gaping. "Close your mouth, boy. You'll catch flies," he said as he brushed by me.

"Mary-Louise," said Guy, "call the warehouse and tell them cops are on the way. See if you can get a bead on Newt. Try Tony's and that place down by the tracks."

"Right away." She scurried down the steps to her desk.

Guy motioned me and King to come up. "How'd it go in Fort Valley?"

King gave him a thumbs-up and headed down the hall to his office.

"Critter," Guy said, "get over to the warehouse and tell the foreman—"

"Guy, darling?" Standing inside the front door, Mother smiled up at us. "Othella needs to see you."

My father glanced at his watch. "Sweetie pie, it's not a good time."

"Yes. Sugar. It is." Her voice was flat, her smile oddly impassive. Something in it made Guy pause and then beckon. She touched my elbow and said, "C'mon up, Critter. He'll need you."

Poppy and I followed her and Othella up to Guy's office. Othella settled herself on the leather sofa, and Poppy closed the door. Guy opened the globe bar, poured himself a stiff drink, and said, "Care for a whiskey, Mrs. Stillwell?"

"Goodness, yes," said Mother.

"Miss Othella?"

"That would be appreciated," said Othella.

He handed her a glass. "What can I help you with today?"

Othella reached into the burlap bag and brought out a bundled stack of cash, which she placed on the coffee table like it was a pineapple upside-down cake.

"This here's five thousand dollars," she said. "My Poppy tells me that's what it cost for a murder case."

"Murder case?"

"On account of I killed Lucky Winfield."

"Fwuh?" I gusted an involuntary croak of surprise, and my father flicked a quick, hard glance in my direction. He pulled a chair close to the sofa and sat, elbows on his knees.

"I'm listening," he said.

"It was self-defense." Othella framed it with her hands, a four-sided figure. "I was attacked. Unprovoked. No provoking was made on my part. And I was under threat of imminent death or egregious injury. And it was a *reasonable* fear I had. And I responded with a *reasonable* degree of force."

"That is the very definition of self-defense," said Guy. "Did Poppy explain that to you?"

"Yes," she said, "and I committed it to memory."

Guy turned to Poppy, who avoided his gaze but never lowered her eyes to the floor. "Did you witness the altercation, Poppy?"

"She was with me," said Mother. "I was helping her study for the upcoming bar exam, and it got so late, I said, 'Poppy, honey, why don't you just stay over in Bootsy's room, seeing as Bootsy is off with the beatniks, don't you know.' So she was there. At our house. You, of course, could not have known that, as you never came home last night. You'll have an airtight alibi, I've no doubt. And Critter was gone to Fort Valley, so he wouldn't know anything about it, either."

"What about Tatum?"

"Sleeping like a baby."

"And Doc?"

"Same."

"I see." Guy pressed his palms together. "Teddi, I think it's best if you go on home now. I'll see you at supper."

"Won't that be nice." Mother stood and smoothed a wrinkle from her skirt. She patted Othella's shoulder and said, "Don't you worry now. We'll get it all worked out."

She went out, closing the door quietly behind her, and Guy poured himself another drink.

"Start at the beginning," he said. "Walk me through it."

"I was all alone, washing down the floor after closing," said Othella, "and Lucky come in with that unprovoked attack and all."

"They can check this for blood and a strand or two of hair." She reached in the bag again and brought forth a cast-iron frying pan. "Check it for evidence, like they do on the *Dragnet* show on TV."

Guy tore the front page off the morning paper and spread it on the coffee table, and Othella set the frying pan down with a weighty metallic *tonk*. The inside was crusted with something that smelled like sausage and eggs. The back was tarred with rust-colored residue.

"Plenty of peoples'll tell ya," said Othella. "He's a no-good SOB to everybody trying to make a living down on the riverfront. He feel free to take whatever he feel like takin'. He got a goat's appetite for humpin' on things he got no business humpin' on. Call the police—they don't do cat shit about it. You ask Miss Jeffie. Ask those little gals down there. They's always been afraid of him. Well!" She regarded the frying pan with a satisfied nod. "They ain't gots to fear him no more, do they? No, they surely don't."

"So the altercation took place at Riverside Country Club," said Guy.

"Yes, sir, it did."

"What time?"

"After closing. About two in the morning. He come in saying I owe him money. He says if I don't give it to him, he'll take it out my hide, and I believed him. Ain't like he never done it before."

"And then what happened?"

"Then old Mr. Skillet happened, that's what."

Poppy covered her face with her hands. "Mama. Please."

"Right upside the head. *Kerbash!*" Othella slapped her hands on her lap. "That's that."

"How do you know he's dead?" asked Guy.

"Oh, he *deeeaaaaad*." Othella drew the word out like dark molasses. "In the river. Caught on a piling under the juke joint."

"How'd that come about?"

"There's a trapdoor in the floor. Boats used to come up under there to do deliveries during Prohibition. When we wash the floor every night, we open up that door and sweep out the peanut shells and dirty water."

"So it was open, and . . ."

"Out he went with the rest of the peanut trash," said Othella. "He slipped and fell in. Nothin' I could do about it."

"Where is his truck parked?"

"On the landing," Poppy said. "Up by the vegetable garden."

"Okay." Guy tented his fingers, thinking for a moment. "I'm glad you came to me, Othella. We've got a lot of talking to do. First, Critter and I need to take a look over at Riverside. When we get back, you'll turn yourself in, and I'll go with you."

"Yes, Poppy explained it all to me."

"Sit right here until we get back. Poppy, you stay with her. Put the money in the safe and give her a receipt."

"Yes, sir." Poppy swallowed, blinking hard. "Thank you."

"Othella, there's some papers you need to sign. Poppy can answer any questions about that. I'll tell Mary-Louise to get you some lunch from Woolworth's."

"Oh, my! I ain't never had lunch from Woolworth's before," Othella said. "Didn't know it would only cost me five thousand dollars."

"Othella," said Guy, "most important: do not repeat a word of this to anybody. Not today, not *ever*."

"I know how to keep a secret when a secret need keepin'. It's the folks I tell who can't seem to keep their mouths shut!" She clapped Guy on the knee and laughed at her own joke.

"If Redstone or Sheriff Heck or anybody else comes poking around here before I get back, you keep mum. Poppy and Mary-Louise will tell them you won't speak a word without your lawyer present. Understand?"

"Oh, yes," said Othella. "I watch the *Dragnet* most every week. Perry Mason, too. Lord! The wrongdoers, they always want to stick their tongue in that mousetrap. Poppy always says, 'Hush, fool! You don't say boo without a lawyer.' They never learn. They surely don't."

"Poppy's a smart girl. Keep doing what she says. We'll work this thing out."

Guy headed for the door, and I followed. Before I went out, I impulsively squeezed Poppy's hand and whispered, "It'll be okay."

She flinched and pulled her hand away. Acted like I'd zapped her with a cattle prod. She didn't drill into me with her usual glare. Her eyes stayed focused on the wall over my shoulder, tears welling up behind the haughty uptilt of her nose.

"Mind your business," she hissed. Arms tight against her shirtwaist, she pushed her hands into the pockets of her dress.

I would remember this moment twenty-five years later. It would come back to haunt me. It haunts me still. At the time, however, it slipped through the chicken wire of my fifteen-year-old attention span—just another instance of typically baffling female behavior—and I was hungry for lunch, so I followed my father down the stairs and out into the sticky afternoon heat, hoping that wherever we were going, we'd stop by Woolworth's on the way.

"Memory is subjective," Vivvy reminds me. "We tend to tell ourselves the story we can most comfortably live with."

My own subjective memory of that summer is creased and faded, folded away in a mental file cabinet with all the subsequent summers piled on top of it. The odd bits that stand out are specific moments related to a particular song or the smell of something cooking. While you're living through a thing, you're focused on what you care about at the time, and that's what you remember, so looking back on it all twenty-five years later, I found vivid images of my fifty-five-minute romance with Twyla while the cases at hand have faded into the backdrop.

I do remember going with my father to Riverside Country Club, heaving the trapdoor open, and stumbling back from the fetid smell. Even now, any time I get a whiff of dead fish under a dock, I get a sickening flash of Lucky's ruined blue face, his neck at a nonsensical angle to his shoulders. Guy used the phone on the wall behind the bar to call Sheriff Heck's office.

"Hey, Josie. Guy Stillwell here. Is Tiny around? No, that's fine. I'll wait on the line. Oh, she's good. Real good. How 'bout yourself. And how are your folks? Good. Good. Bootsy? She is, um—well, it's sweet of you to ask. Bootsy is . . . vacationing with friends. We hope to have her home soon."

It hadn't occurred to me until I saw the tortured look on his face that he might be more concerned about Bootsy than he'd like to let on.

"Tiny, it's Guy. How are you? Yeah, I'm planning to do that whole barbecue thing for the department again real soon. Thing is, I've got a bit of a situation today. Seems like Lucky Winfield ran into some trouble down at Riverside Country Club early this morning. I came over to check on it and found him over here in the water. No, he's in the river under the—correct. No, I'm not gonna try that, Tiny. I don't think that'll do any good. I don't like to step outside my own area of expertise, but I'm pretty sure he's deceased. Best to leave it for the coroner, I was thinking. Yeah. Yes, sir. Critter is here with me, but he knows not to touch anything. Thanks, Tiny. We'll wait here for you and your boys."

I sat on a barstool, wondering if it would be okay for me to help myself to a Coke. On a small black-and-white television over the bar, JFK and Jackie stood before a press gaggle. He waved, buoyant, and she held his arm, smiling in her immaculate pink Chanel suit with matching pillbox hat.

"I thought the TV was black-and-white," says Vivvy, who doesn't miss a trick. "You're superimposing the pink suit from the Zapruder film. That happened just a few months later."

I can't deny that probability, but neither can I unsee the image of the First Lady in her strawberry suit, arms full of roses. It remains in my mind alongside the dryness of my mouth, the smell of death, and the lapping of the sluggish river below the wooden floor.

– 9 –

Redstone strutted into the courtroom for Newt's arraignment, parked two cardboard banker boxes on the defense table, and clapped me on the back.

"Good to see you, Critter."

"Hey, Red."

"I think you'll find some interesting reading here," he said, all sarcasm and swagger. "Weapon, motive, intent, opportunity—the whole enchilada."

"Thanks, Red."

"You'll see on the witness list there, A.D.A. Chastain is working on bringing in Robert Stack to testify as an expert witness—like a celebrity guest star."

"I'm all aflutter."

Redstone raised a bushy eyebrow in Newt's direction and said, "Brinkman Pollard was a friend of mine. Godfather to my oldest boy. We slept side by side in a foxhole on a beach in Normandy."

"Mr. Redstone," I said, "please address your comments to counsel."

He leaned in to hiss a few inches from Newt's ear. "I know what you did, and I will see you rot in jail for it."

"That'll do, Red." I maneuvered to get between them, one hand on Newt's shoulder to keep him in his chair.

Red went to his seat and engaged in a show of hushed conferencing with A.D.A. Chastain, a reed-thin lady who always wore her salt-and-pepper hair in a severe French twist. The two of them whispered back and forth, eyeing me and shuffling their note cards.

Lucky's statement, as it was preserved in Newt's case file, was scrawled in cramped handwriting on a Big Chief tablet. The original was retained by the prosecution, and an eight-by-ten glossy photograph was provided to me, as per the rules of discovery, which call for the prosecution to share in advance any evidence they intend to present during the trial.

The statement was short and sweet: *Newt Ballerini give me this .38 and told me if I kill Brinkman Pollard he give me $10,000 after and I done so June 12, 1963, in the manner of which they say I done.*

"All rise, all rise," the bailiff intoned. "Court is in session. Honorable Judge Olympia Sterling presiding."

"Good morning, everybody." Poppy took her seat at the bench and rapped one sharp knock with the gavel. "In the matter of State of Georgia versus Ballerini, Counsel, please state your appearances for the record."

"Doolittle Redstone for the State of Georgia, and may I say, Judge Sterling, you look exceptionally lovely today. A pleasure to behold."

"Uh-huh," said Judge Sterling. "Defense."

"August Stillwell of Stillwell & Hodges for Mr. Ballerini." I left it at that, knowing there was no use trying to grease the skids with Poppy. She ran a tight ship.

"Mr. Ballerini," she said, "state your full name for the record, please."

"Edward Newton Ballerini," said Newt. "Not guilty."

"Keep your pants on," said the judge. "We've got some protocol to get through."

"Yes, ma'am."

"This is an arraignment for you, Mr. Ballerini. I will read the indictment, which is brief. The grand jury charges count one, murder in the first degree of Mr. Brinkman Pollard on Wednesday, June 5, 1963. Count two, conspiracy to commit murder. In addition, there is a criminal forfeiture allegation. State of Georgia gives notice to the defendant that the state will seek, in accordance with the law, forfeiture of any property, real or personal, constituting or derived from proceeds traceable to said offenses. That's the grand jury indictment from June 1963. Twenty-five years ago. I don't know about y'all, but that is definitely a record for me. Mr. Stillwell, have you discussed the charges set forth in counts one and two with your client?"

"Yes, I have."

"Does your client wish to enter a plea at this time?"

"One hundred percent not guilty," Newt blurted again, and I patted him on the shoulder.

"He will plead not guilty," I said.

"So I hear." She made a note on the paperwork. "Plea of not guilty is entered. Are there any motions?"

"There are," said Redstone, "and I have provided them to defense counsel along with a list of witnesses. It's all pretty cut-and-dried. Once Critter's had a chance to look it over, I expect we'll be engaged in plea discussions."

"Defense has no such expectation," I said. "In fact, I have prepared a motion to dismiss."

I held up the paperwork, and the judge beckoned. "Let's see it."

"Twenty-five years after the indictment," I said, "I think we can all agree that a speedy trial was not forthcoming. Had the prosecution done their due diligence and pursued the defendant rather than leaving him to his own devices until they were shamed into action by one of the secondary players in *Caddyshack II*—"

"Objection," said Red. "Counsel is not familiar with the investigation, hence in no position to impugn the diligence of the state. Furthermore, I will not stand by as the career of Robert Stack is assailed. The man's a golldang American treasure. Am I right?" He turned to the packed courtroom like a conductor to his orchestra, raising a hearty round of applause.

Judge Sterling rapped her gavel. "Mr. Redstone. We're not playing that game. The objection, however, is sustained. Got anything else, Mr. Stillwell?"

"Your Honor, this stone-cold case hinges on a statement made twenty-five years ago under dubious circumstances by a gentleman who is now deceased. The prosecution has no hope short of a Ouija board to produce this witness, leaving no opportunity for cross, therefore it is the worst form of hearsay. I move we toss out that statement, in accordance with the law, dismiss all charges, and enjoy what's left of a beautiful day."

"Your Honor," Red chimed in, "seeing as poor Lucky turned up dead less than twenty-four hours after he swore and signed the statement—an uncanny coincidence that turns out mighty convenient for the accused—"

"Objection," I said. "The state is not in a position to know what is or is not convenient for the defendant. The insinuation there is rank speculation and downright slanderous."

"Sustained," said the judge.

"Nonetheless." Red accepted the ruling with a shrug and moved on. "In light of the witness's untimely demise, I would argue that the statement should be classified as a dying declaration, and as such, it is as admissible as a rooster in a henhouse."

"Dying declaration calls for 'settled, hopeless expectation of death,'" I said. "Red, are you suggesting that Lucky knew he was about to die? Or maybe *you* knew he was about to die?"

"Without dignifying the calumny spewed by the defense . . ." Red puffed his barrel chest. "I would ask Your Honor for some latitude here, considering how the defendant took it on the lam and evaded capture for twenty-five years in a desperate attempt to weasel out of these charges. Now defense is trying to use the very fact of this rapscallion's fleeing the warrant as just cause for throwing out incontrovertible evidence against him. It's an affront to the integrity of this court."

"Your Honor . . ." I stood to head off the impending Cross of Gold speech, but Red was in full campaign plumage, conscious of the press corps behind him, and suddenly there was a cool trickle of apprehension at the back of my neck. I studied the glossy eight-by-ten of the Big Chief tablet on the Formica table in the jailhouse, rummaging my distant memories of that room, the shadow of Tick's fedora on the cement floor, and Lucky's face as the bluster drained out of him.

"I withdraw the motion," I said.

Chastain shot me a curious glance, but Red continued bloviating, holding his courtroom audience on the edge of their seats. I felt a twinge of sorrow for Guy, who would have hammed the hell out of a scene like this.

"Too long, Your Honor—*tooooo looooooong*—the State of Georgia has waited for the smoldering ember of the law to ignite the mighty conflagration of justice."

"What a load of shit," Newt laughed out loud.

Before Red could sputter his disapproval, I placed a firm hand on my client's shoulder and said, "Apologies, Your Honor."

With another sharp knock of the gavel, Judge Sterling ended the playlet.

"Critter, the statement is ruled to be inadmissible. Red, the matter is bound over for trial," she said. "There you go. A little something for everybody."

I raised my hand. "Actually, Your Honor, I withdrew the motion to suppress."

"Mr. Stillwell, are you saying you want the statement back in?"

"Yes, Your Honor. Thank you."

I heard a sharp hitch in A.D.A. Chastain's breath, followed by an urgent whisper. Red whispered back, then cleared his throat. "Your Honor, I withdraw the motion regarding the dying declaration and move that we suppress the statement on the grounds that it is hearsay."

"Two minutes ago, it was gospel," said the judge. "Now you're asking me to suppress your own evidence?"

"Correct."

"Uh-huh. Okay. I see how this is gonna go." Judge Sterling pressed her lips tight together. "The statement is in. The matter is bound over. And in light of the mighty dumpster fire and so forth, I am putting you both on notice: I will brook no further Billy-Bob-BS nor superfluous motions that lead to delays in this trial. For the sake of the victim's family, I am disinclined to drag this out beyond the quarter century it has already gone on. Fast track, understood?"

"Yes, ma'am," I said, and Red huffed a disgruntled syllable of assent.

She made another notation. "Counsel for the defense, please, tell me we're not gonna spend time debating the flight risk of this defendant."

"No, ma'am, but I am duty bound to request bail be set at—"

"Bail is denied." She rapped her gavel and said, "Go on home."

Redstone and Chastain hurried out to meet the press. I stayed with Newt, waiting for the bailiffs to come and shackle him for the trip upstairs to the holding cell.

"That didn't go so great," he said. "I hate to ask, Critter, but are you absolutely certain Guy is unavailable?"

"It went fine," I assured him, "and it's just a formality."

"I thought you were gonna get that statement thrown out."

"I changed my mind," I said.

"Why?"

"If it's thrown out, I can't hang them with it."

"Hang them how?"

"I'm not exactly sure yet, but something about it is off. If the statement is bogus, Lucky didn't kill Pollard, and if he didn't do the murder, you didn't hire him."

Newt grinned a slow-spreading grin.

"Well, all right now. There's Guy Stillwell's boy. He's in there." He rubbed his hands together and hitched his chair closer to the table. "What's the plan, Stan?"

"For starters, I'll have my PI go over the prosecution's discovery submissions and make sure I'm not missing any exculpatory evidence. I'll visit with the witnesses who are still living and see if modern ballistics and CSI methods confirm the conclusions that were drawn back then."

"Okay. Good. Sounds good."

"I'll see you in a few days, and we'll discuss a way forward." I took a few files and stored them in my briefcase to study over a drink or two on the way home. "Got everything you need over there at the jail?"

"I'd be grateful if you could bring me a carton of Swisher Sweets."

"Absolutely."

The bailiffs arrived, and Newt stood, offering his hands behind his back.

"If Lucky didn't kill Pollard," he said, "do you have a good guess who did?"

"Some dude," I said, and I'll admit, I enjoyed saying it.

My father was the master of the Some Dude Defense. I saw a thousand nuanced versions of it played out during my years at Stillwell & Hodges. One example: Guy was defending a fella who'd been caught red-handed with a stolen TV set on the console in his living room. The accused sat there straight-faced and said, "Some dude came up to me on the street and sold it to me for ten dollars."

"What was his name?" Guy asked.

"I don't know. He was just some dude."

"What did he look like?"

"Like any other dude. Black dude, probably."

"And where might I find him now?"

"Beats the hell outa me."

"We can work with that," said Guy, and he did. All the prosecution had was the TV. No physical evidence connected the accused to the crime scene. No witnesses came forward to testify about seeing him break the store window and hightail it with the display model.

Of course, there was no witness to testify about the existence of "some dude" either, but the burden of proof is on the state. The man was innocent until proven guilty, and they failed to prove it. The state's case was largely circumstantial; they deserved a steaming pile of *some dude*—a scenario just as ambiguous and unsupportable as the one they were trying to put forth.

"Create doubt by advancing an alternative scenario," Guy always said. "That's the meat and potatoes of criminal defense."

When I was in college, I had the opportunity to travel to London, and Mother suggested I stop by the Old Bailey and see how things are done at the Central Criminal Court of England and Wales. I sat for an afternoon in the gallery, observing the participants with their powdered wigs, and what do you suppose I heard? The Some Dude Defense was clearly recognizable, even when it was dished up with a PBS Britcom accent.

"If it pleases the court," said the barrister, "my client is the victim of an unfortunate misunderstanding. How could he have known that this television—purchased by him honestly and in good faith—was in fact stolen by some random bloke completely unknown to him?"

The success rate of the Some Dude Defense is far from a hundred percent, but there are moments when that's all you've got left, and it was in that sort of moment that Guy rose to his full potential as a skilled purveyor of reasonable doubt. Most of his clients were people of color, so juries—I'm sad to say—were predisposed to declare them guilty on the basis of purely circumstantial evidence. Guy had to bring the hellfire in those Some Dude closing arguments.

When I explained the finer points of the Some Dude Defense to Rory II, she said, "The dynamics of crime and punishment are fascinating from a sociological perspective. On the one hand, you have the need for public safety. On the other, you have the threat of power-drunk authoritarian assholes. And then you get the jury in there, which introduces group-think behavior and the innate pecking order that develops in that space. Jury dynamics—that's the topic of my master's thesis."

"Seriously?" I was suddenly paying attention to everything above the nametag.

"Voir dire strategy, specifically," she said. "I did my undergrad in psychology just because it fascinates me. Figured I better do something people might pay me for."

"Hell, yes, they'll pay. A skilled jury consultant makes a better than good living."

My father had always decried this sort of thing as "psychobabble and parlor tricks." I refrained from telling her that I would sooner pay a palm reader, but she picked up on something that let her know I was skeptical.

"It's an inexact science," she said.

"I'd be interested to hear your take on it," I said. "What's the substance of your thesis?"

"It's a criterion for sizing up potential jurors based on values rather than predisposition."

"I'm listening."

She set her hands on the bar, framing her thoughts. "Commonly applied methodology uses behavioral markers in an attempt to cherry-pick a certain kind of jury. Speculative, at best, because you have no control over what sort of people show up on any given day. There's only one thing you know for sure going into voir dire."

"They're human."

"Exactly. So no matter who shows up, I double-dog guarantee, they respond to the same basic tribal dynamics that have steered human behavior for thousands of years. I call my system the BELL Curve."

She wrote on a cocktail napkin:

Belief

Education

Laughter

Loyalty

"According to Maslow's hierarchy of human needs, certain universal—"

"Hey. Freud." Some dude at the other end of the bar tapped his martini glass with a fountain pen. "Can I get a drink over here?"

"Sure thing, hon." She crumpled the napkin into her pocket. "Anyway. It's a work in progress."

I sat for a while, sipping whiskey and water, studying the files from Redstone's banker box of discovery files. In addition to Lucky's testimony, they had the .38, which was indeed registered to Newt, and statements from people who'd seen Newt punch Pollard in the face just a few days prior at the party in my parents' backyard. Stories ran the gamut of subjective memory. One witness reported: "Everybody was drinking, and it led to some playful fisticuffs." Another claimed: "Newt goes after Brink with blood in his eye. There was murder in his heart. You could tell it." It was hard to say which ones were still alive or what any of them might recall twenty-five years hence, having aligned and realigned in loyalties the way people do. Whatever it was, I felt certain I could defuse it on cross.

King strolled into the club and posted up on the barstool next to me. "What, is this your satellite office now?"

"Tatum claims there will someday be a complete dismantling of the corporate structure, and everybody will work from coffee shops."

"That kid always had a screw loose." King sighed heavily. "At the risk of sounding like an AA evangelist—"

"King. Don't worry about it. I actually drink less here, because I'm loath to spend the money on overpriced shots. I'm here to see you."

"Here to see somebody," he mumbled.

The bartender returned, and he hailed her with a hearty wolf whistle.

"King, you dog." She set her elbows on the bar close to his. "How's the bum hip?"

"I'm up for a test drive if you are."

"Behave yourself," she said, "or you'll be eating dinner out back with the rest of the alley cats."

He ordered prime rib, and when she went to get it, he said, "I've become fond of Rory the Subsequent."

"She certainly seems fond of you," I said. "I'm jealous."

"She keeps asking about you. In my expert opinion, there's some interest."

"Time will tell," I said. "I don't suppose you've made any headway with Guy's backlog, have you?"

"Settled the two estate cases," said King. "Still working on three others. His departure left some people more than a little pissed off."

"Yeah, I'm one of them."

"How goes it with Newt?"

"Still trying to wrap my head around it," I said. "I don't believe he hired Lucky to kill Pollard. I don't believe Lucky killed Pollard to begin with. The statement doesn't smell right. No emotion. Utterly devoid of details."

"The man had the personality of a doorjamb," King said. "I've heard tales about him giving as good as he got in the Japanese prison camp. He was capable of killing a man. I don't doubt it for a minute."

"That night at the jailhouse, I remember, there was this strange little man who showed up with Ruckels."

"Tick," King said darkly.

"Is he still around?"

"Hard to say."

"I asked Tatum to dig up any information she could find on him."

"Whoa. Belay that," said King. "That's not a good idea."

"Why not?"

"This fella was the go-to attorney for the Dixie Mafia. Back then, they did some bootlegging and ran a protection racket, shaking down riverside business owners, hand in glove with the Klan. Mostly, though, it was chop shops. The underlings would go out and steal cars, take them back to the boneyard, and strip them for parts. Old man DiLippa—you know the DiLippa family that owns the auto body and tire stores—he was the head of the whole operation. He used to bring in Tick any time one of his boys got in trouble. Good ol' Tick, he'd get them out of jail on bond, and you didn't see hide nor hair after that."

"Jesus. How's he gotten away with that all these years?"

"They've got a convenient way of disappearing inconvenient people," said King. "All around the old farmhouses, there's abandoned wells, cisterns twenty to thirty feet deep, five or six feet in diameter. They'd toss a fella in there, throw in a stick of dynamite, and he's gone. Sealed in a tomb. Easy peezy Japaneezy."

"So if Tick came for Lucky, that meant they were planning to kill him?"

"More than likely."

"But why? And why would Ruckels facilitate that?"

King opened his hands and shrugged. "Questions for the dead."

"How much does Guy know about all this?"

"More than he's saying," said King. "I'm not surprised he kept you out of it, and I have to trust he has his reasons for keeping it from me."

– 10 –

Othella's arraignment was the biggest show of the summer of 1963, attended by a diverse crowd that packed the courthouse despite the midsummer heat. Black people who owned businesses on the riverfront had been plagued by Lucky for years, so they showed up to support Othella, who'd always done right by her neighbors. Miss Jeffie and several of her girls sat in the balcony, waving laminated fans printed with ads for Winfrey's Mutual Funeral Home.

Doralee held Tatum on her lap, making room for the help from neighboring households. The gallery on the main floor was filled with white community members, including my mother and her friends from the Progressive Thinkers Book Club, Athens Garden Club, Saint Joseph Catholic Church sewing circle, Junior League, and the gentlemen and ladies of the Jaycees and Jaycettes.

Outside on the lawn, a few fully robed and hooded members of the KKK sat on lawn chairs, handing out mimeographed leaflets that called for the black murderess to get the death penalty and her nigger-loving attorney to get run out of town on a rail. The day was too hot and most of them too fat to march around a lot, but they called out to everyone passing by on their way into the courthouse, "Who among us are safe if we allow some pickaninny to rise up and kill a white man and not swing for it?" and things of this nature. Every once in a while, they raised their hoods to mop their sweating heads, revealing the haggard faces of the rural poor. People of quality kept that sort of sentiment to themselves in the days of JFK, so the Klan dwindled in number, persisting in private like an unseemly itch that continued to tickle the armpit of Athens.

D.A. Ruckels mixed and mingled, slapping cronies on the back and chatting up the Junior League ladies while A.D.A. Redstone organized paperwork on the prosecution table. Guy sat with Othella at the defense table, and Poppy and I sat in the front row behind them. Guy's head was bent over his notes, and I knew not to bother him. Othella looked the way she did that morning on the porch, calm and uncompromising. There was a small book on the table between her hands, which I thought might be a New Testament or pocket hymnal, but when she picked it up and opened it, I saw that it was a book of poems—*Lyrics of Lowly Life* by Paul Laurence Dunbar.

"Look here," she said, turning to show Poppy a verse she'd boxed with an uneven line of blue ink. "*But we all fits into places dat no othah ones could fill, An' we does the things we has to, big er little, good er ill.* That's you, baby girl."

Poppy squeezed her mother's shoulder, Othella placed her hand over Poppy's, and they stayed that way until the bailiff called, "All rise, all rise. Court is now in session, Honorable Judge Eustice Talmadge presiding."

"We'll move things right along," said Judge Talmadge. "It's too damn hot in here to spend a lot of time hashing over frivolous motions and showboating. Counsel, state your names for the record."

Ruckels stood and said, "District Attorney Borley Ruckels the Third for the great state of Georgia," and a patriotic cheer went up from the gallery. My father stood and said, "Guy Stillwell of Stillwell & Hodges, for the defense," and there was a raucous response of mixed cheers, jeers, and calls for gladiatorial whoop ass.

Judge Talmadge banged his gavel and read out the charge of first degree murder and asked, "Miss Sterling, how do you plead?"

In a clear, loud voice, Othella said, "Not guilty," and again there was a rumble of response from both sides of the courtroom.

Housekeeping issues were brusquely taken care of: Guy's pretrial motions for evidence suppression, dismissal, and continuance—all denied. A standard request for renewed bond was also denied, but that was fine with us, because we knew Othella was safer inside the jail-house than out of it. The trial was set to begin on a Monday morning ten days hence, court was adjourned, and people drifted out into the humid afternoon.

Before Mother left the courtroom, she brought forward a basket of fried chicken, hard-boiled eggs, cornbread, and apples she and Doralee had assembled for Othella to take back to jail with her. As the bailiff inspected the contents of the basket, Mother produced a Tupperware container of peanut butter cookies, and said, "These are for you, Melvin, in recognition of the important work you do. It means so much that we can depend on you to keep our Othella safe from harm."

"Yes, ma'am, Mrs. Stillwell. We'll take her up the back way."

"Thank you, Melvin. You're an angel."

"That was sweet of her," Vivvy says now. Vivvy's father was a superior court bailiff for forty years. Her parents divorced when she was small, and she lived with her dad, so like me, Vivvy spent the summer days and after-school hours of her childhood sitting in courtroom galleries. To hear her tell it, we'd be living in some Kafka netherworld if not for bailiffs, the unsung steward heroes of the judicial infrastructure.

Out on the courthouse steps, Ruckels addressed a small gaggle of reporters. "It's well known among y'all that upon the wall in my office there hangs a placard engraved with the words of Isaiah, chapter three, verse eleven: *Woe unto the wicked!* I'll say it again: *Woooooooe unto the wicked*, y'all, for so long as I have breath in my body, the rule of law and the cause of justice will prevail in the great state of Georgia. Rest assured, this heinous crime will not go unpunished."

"D.A. Ruckels," called one of the reporters, "will you be endorsing A.D.A. Redstone in the upcoming election?"

"I will announce an endorsement for my successor—whoever that might be—in August," said Ruckels. "Plenty of time to get out the votes for November. Right now, I'm gonna make sure A.D.A. Redstone and everyone else in the office keeps their eye on the ball. Guy Stillwell is a crafty SOB. He's a goddang snake in the grass. You fellas can adjust the phraseology there in deference to the churchgoers. He's gonna try every lowbrow trick in the defense attorney playbook. The man has a dark past, defending rapists and murderers—the worst kind of malefactors. He dwells in the underbelly of society, working as a minion of the devil. Well, I'm here to tell you, I will not rest until the troublemakers are put down and the good people of Athens sleep safely in their beds at night."

"Mr. Redstone, would you care to comment?" called another stringer.

Redstone puffed his chest and stepped forward, but the moment he opened his mouth, Ruckels draped a heavy arm around his shoulders and said, "That's enough for today, y'all. We got work to do. The cause of justice is a relentless taskmaster, am I right, Red?"

"Yes, sir," said Redstone, though perhaps not with the zeal Ruckels was hoping for. As Ruckels turned him around and steered him back up the courthouse steps, Red's head swiveled for one last, longing glance at the press gathering, and he looked for all the world like one of the hapless marionettes on *Howdy Doody*.

Mother decreed that Poppy should stay with us while Othella was in jail, so the day after the arraignment, Guy and I drove her home to fetch her clothes, shoes, girly appurtenances, and hair paraphernalia from their little apartment above Riverside Country Club. Back in the early 1920s, Othella's daddy had built this place on the river with the enthusiastic support of the black community, who gathered there for a variety of events and activities until the church was built on a hill a mile away, and the preacher declared from the pulpit that, henceforth, Riverside Country Club was for sinners.

Officially, I was never allowed to go to the juke joint, of course, but Doc knew I loved the music played by performers on the Chitlin' Circuit, where Sam Cooke, the Isley Brothers, and James Brown himself came up. Some Friday nights, back when I was in middle school, he dropped broad hints that he and Doralee would be heading down to the river after the Stillwell children—*wink, wink*—were tucked in for the night. I hunkered down on the floor behind the driver's seat so Mother wouldn't see me from the front porch as we drove off.

Above the bar at the juke joint, there was a spectacular thirty-foot mural of a bare-naked lady, painted by the high school art teacher.

Doralee allowed me to sit in on a wooden chair in the corner where I could gaze at this copper-skinned goddess and listen to the band playing up on the makeshift plywood stage. By the time I was old enough to count myself among the sinners, Doc had passed away, Doralee had lost her sense of humor, and in furtherance of my musical and social edification, I was hanging out at hot spots where the college students gathered. But the summer of 1963, when I was fifteen and had seen a total of zero real live naked ladies (Twyla had kept her chemise on), I was still entranced by that mural with breasts the size of pickle barrels and shapely legs that were longer than I was tall.

Mother had sent four empty suitcases for Poppy. Guy directed me to tote those upstairs so Poppy could pack up her things while he checked out the crime scene. I don't believe I ever noticed the rickety stairway on the back side of the juke joint or gave any thought to where Poppy and Othella lived when they weren't at our house or the law office. Following Poppy up to the second floor, I noticed for the first time that there were lace curtains in the windows up there. From this new perspective, looking down from the upstairs porch, I could see a vegetable garden benched into the hillside above the landing where people parked their cars.

Terra-cotta flowerpots blossomed along the porch railing, and two ancient lawn jockeys stood on opposite sides of the Dutch door. The grinning figures were cast from iron with exaggerated black faces, red lips, and white eyeballs. Peeling green and white paint defined their natty vests and caps. They were about four feet tall, including the cut stone pedestals they stood on, and carved into each pedestal was the name *Marblesmith.*

At the time, I figured this meant that the stone must have come from the Marblesmith quarries owned by my mother's family. I didn't know until years later that "Hokey and Pokey" (as Othella called them when she was a child) were actually the property of my mother's family and once stood outside a carriage house belonging to my great-great-grandfather. Poppy's great-great-grandfather, John Taller, a slave who was also the property of my mother's family, had absconded with the lawn jockeys after Sherman's army came through and burned the house and outbuildings to the ground at the end of the Civil War. This still strikes me as an odd thing for John Taller to do, considering the onerous physical and metaphysical weight of Hokey and Pokey, but here they stood, each extending an arm, one proffering a rusted lantern, the other holding up a corroded ring for hitching a horse.

As I made multiple trips, hefting Poppy's jam-packed luggage back to the car, I passed by the juke joint windows and saw Guy walking back and forth with a tape measure and his leather-bound notebook. Poppy and I loaded the last of the bags into the trunk and forced the lid down, and I used the front of my shirt to mop sweat from my temple. The landing was shaded by tall pines, but heat rose up from the river with humid clouds of black gnats and bloodthirsty mosquitoes.

"How much longer do you think he'll be?" Poppy wondered.

"He's got that Perry Mason look. It might be a while. Maybe we should go down and get a cold one," I added hopefully.

"I'll wait up here," she said, but a moment later, Guy stepped out onto the catwalk and called out to her.

"Hey, Poppy?"

"Sir?"

"I need you to come on in."

She swore softly before she called back, "Yes, sir. Coming."

I fell into step behind her. "Hey, maybe we could—"

"Yeah, yeah. You want a cold one. Like beer grows on trees and don't nobody have to pay for it."

Crime scene tape was a newfangled thing in 1963, so the sheriff's men, rather missing the point, had draped it around the place like Christmas garland, carefully tacking it up above the lintels to keep the doorways unobstructed. Poppy went to the cooler and came back with three beers. She handed one to me and one to Guy, who thanked her and drank it at the bar, where he laid out notes and photos in a long row. He'd stood there, watching like a hawk, while they processed the scene, so I couldn't imagine what he might have missed.

"Poppy," he said, "help me pin down the blocking here."

"Mama told you what happened," she said woodenly.

"I need you to walk me through it."

"Mama told you I wasn't there."

"I heard," said Guy. "Now I'm asking my law clerk to help me process our client's account in the context of this crime scene. Ruckels won't go easy. We need to make sure there's no inconsistencies between her story and the evidence."

"Yes, sir."

"According to our client," Guy prompted, "it was about two in the morning . . ."

"She said he came in and started going off on her. Yelling. Hitting her. Beating her with a chair."

"This broken chair here?" He showed her one of the crime scene photos.

"No, this one." Poppy dragged a cane chair from the corner, and Guy knelt to inspect it. "See, these black marks right here—that's from her fending off the blows with the skillet."

"Interesting," said Guy, contemplating the alleged marks that—to me—didn't look any different from the scuffs and scars on the rest of the ramshackle furnishings. "You know what leading the witness means, don't you, Poppy?"

"Suggesting testimony. Injecting narrative that helps your case."

"Are you telling me what Othella told you, or are you telling me what you told her to tell me?"

Poppy didn't answer.

"What happened after the chair?" asked Guy.

"She hit him with the skillet, and he fell down the trapdoor hole."

"Critter, open that trapdoor for me."

I hooked my hand through a hole cut for a handle. The hinges squawked as I hauled the door up and let it down flat on the floor. The thing was heavier than it looked. Or else Othella and Poppy were stronger than they looked. It hadn't crossed my mind prior to this that Othella had always gone back to the juke joint after a full day of work in our kitchen, served beers and busted peanuts all night, and then hauled this heavy door open so she could wash down the floors after closing time. It didn't cross my mind until much later that Poppy had been doing the same thing after a full day at school—or at the law office.

Guy laid out the tape measure about seven feet.

"Your mama said he stumbled?"

"Yes, sir."

"Poppy, they took a lot of pictures of this blood smeared on the floor right here. Even though the floor was mopped, they'll be able to show it. See how it got down in the wood grain?"

"But how would they know it's from last night?" I piped up. "Maybe that's old blood from a fight or something."

Guy raised an eyebrow. "Is it, Poppy?"

"Maybe. Who's to say?"

"Oh, Ruckels will find somebody to say. Rest assured. He'll have somebody who swears up, down, and sideways that this is fresh blood right out of Lucky Winfield's head, and we'd better have something better than *maybe not* and *who's to say* or Othella's goose is well and truly cooked. Look at that and tell me how to answer Ruckels when he says Lucky hit the floor right here and somebody dragged him over to that trapdoor?"

"Maybe the blood was dripping, and he dragged his foot through it when he stumbled," I said. "Or maybe one of the sheriff's men—"

"Critter." Guy's tone was sharp enough to hush me. "I'm asking Poppy. You think that's what happened?"

"Maybe," she said. "Yes, sir. I think it was . . . like Critter said."

"That is one interesting hypothesis," said Guy. "Thing is, I keep wondering if the real story is somewhere between."

"I don't know what you mean." Poppy pushed her hands deep in the pockets of her dress.

"I mean, maybe he was already right here on the floor. Maybe he was on top of somebody. And somebody else walked over and whomped him on the back of the head. And then the two of them dragged him over to that trapdoor, hoping the river would take him. Only it didn't.

Because the water is slower in the summertime, and his belt got caught on a nail sticking out of the piling down there."

Poppy stood, as immovable as cast iron, and said nothing. Guy shook his head in frustration and strode back to the bar. He whisked his notes and photos into a pile and jammed them into his briefcase.

"You've been through law school, Poppy. Clerking for me almost six months—about to take the bar exam and go into practice for yourself. You know goddamn well how important it is for a client to be truthful with her attorney. Whatever happens, it's your job to work it out, but you've got to have the *truth*. If you don't have the facts, you go into that courtroom, bare ass exposed, and you get blindsided."

He came back to Poppy and gripped her shoulders.

"Poppy, think about what's at stake here," he said. "You have a brilliant career ahead of you. Don't do something stupid. You could get disbarred before you even get started. Think about your future."

"Right now, I'm thinking about my mama."

"*So am I*, goddamn it! We all know there's a dozen different ways Othella doesn't make it out of this alive. If there is something I should know, you need to tell me straight up. You need to tell me *now*. You gotta trust me, Poppy. *Please*."

Her chin trembled, but her jaw remained square, and her eyes never wavered from his. After an uncomfortable moment, he turned away, pinching the bridge of his nose as if he had a headache.

"Get on up to the car," he said. "Both of you. Critter, take that cane chair and put it in the back seat. And leave that beer right where it is. I'll let you know how it turns out."

Poppy stomped up to the landing, arms locked tight across the front of her body, and I ambled along behind her. It seemed prudent to give her a wide berth. She kept pushing the backs of her hands against her cheeks, and I knew she wouldn't like it if I saw her crying. She got in the car, slammed the door, and covered her face with her hands, but I could still hear the muffled scream—an elongated primal howl that came from somewhere deep inside her. I went to the far side of the landing and waited for Guy. By the time he came up and the two of us got into the car, Poppy was sitting primly in the back seat, posture erect, nose freshly powdered.

We drove home in silence, and I carried Poppy's bags up to Bootsy's room. She sat on the edge of the bed and smiled a shaky smile. "Thanks, bellhop."

"Are you okay?"

She shook her head. "Huh-uh."

"Tell me what to do. Tell me how I can help."

"No one can help."

"You haven't given us a chance."

"She made me promise, Critter. Made me swear. And now it's too late."

"Too late for what?" I sat on the floor at her feet. "You can tell me, and I'll help you tell Guy. Whatever it is, he can fix it. You know he can."

When she spoke, it was little more than a whisper. "I thought the river would take him. I thought he'd disappear, and we'd never have to say a word. But then the sun came up, and we could see him down there."

"So you were there?"

She nodded tightly.

"The cane chair," I said. "Was she fending him off, or was it the other way around? Or was he . . . was he on top of you?"

"I'm not saying any more about it." Poppy's breath was shallow and fast. Hard trembling had overtaken her, like she was out in the cold.

I did what I'd always seen my father do: I sat there for a minute or two, allowing the kind of silence that begs to be broken. "Nothing sucks truth out of people like a hollow ear," Guy always said, and I seldom saw it fail.

But when Poppy finally spoke, she said, "My aunt Cornelia saw you at Miss Jeffie's."

"Oh. Shit . . ." Itchy flames of embarrassment rose at the back of my neck. "I wasn't—I just—I was there to drop King off. For work purposes."

"Uh-huh." Poppy withered me with a knowing look.

"Don't tell Mother. I'm begging you. Please."

"That's not my circus, and you ain't my monkey," said Poppy. "I have no interest in talking about it."

"Wait. Your aunt works at Miss Jeffie's? You mean . . . like . . . in the kitchen."

"No," she said flatly. "Not in the kitchen."

"Oh."

"Mama says Cornelia was twelve years old the first time Lucky Winfield went after her. Mama made Granddaddy call the police and file a report. Sheriff and his men came out and took down all the information. Took Cornelia's underpants in a paper bag. Photographed her bloody hands and knees and her bruised-up body. Late that night, Klansmen showed up and beat my grandfather almost to death. He had to use a walking stick the rest of his life because the busted eardrum gave him vertigo he never could shake off. He couldn't raise his right arm ninety degrees. Didn't have any front teeth left. But he genuinely considered himself fortunate, seeing as they didn't hang him. Lucky came around next day and nailed a naked picture of Cornelia to a tree up on the landing. That showed everybody he was free to do whatever he wanted—to whomever he wanted—and he did. Year after year. Some people say . . ."

"What?"

"People say he's my father." Poppy stared at the wall, blinking back tears. "Mama says it's not true. But that's what I've been told."

"Jesus."

"It won't matter if you and me and your daddy walk up and down that riverfront till the water turns to stone. There's not a soul who's gonna step out to testify on Mama's behalf, because she won't have it. She made it clear: if anybody steps up to testify, she'll change her plea to guilty. She won't see someone else she loves suffer on her account. She'd rather lay down her own life."

"Okay." I rubbed my fists on my knees, trying to think how this was going to work out as anything other than a total clusterfuck for everyone involved. A jittery doorbell chimed in the hallway between Bootsy's bedroom door and mine.

"That's supper," I said. "Mother'll worry if you don't come down."

"I just need a minute."

"Poppy, I have to tell Guy what you just told me."

"I know."

We ate dinner in a silence quite unfamiliar to our dining room, which was usually filled with banter and debate. Tatum finally piped up, "Why isn't anybody talking?"

"We're simply dumbstruck by Doralee's delicious fennel chicken," Mother said in the lighthearted tone she mostly reserved for dinner parties.

"Poppy, what's wrong?" Tatum asked.

"Nothing's wrong with Poppy," said Mother. "Eat your dinner."

"Poppy's been crying," said Tatum. "You can tell if someone's been crying, because increased blood flow makes your eyes—"

"Tatum. Please." Mother set her fork next to her plate. "Little girls who can't mind their business don't get peach cobbler and ice cream."

"It's science, Mama! I'm just trying to tell you science."

"I need to be excused, please." Poppy dabbed her lips with her linen napkin. Before she left the table, she kissed the top of Tatum's head and whispered, "You can have my cobbler."

After dinner, I went to Guy's study intending to tell him the whole sorry tale, but the door was closed, and I could hear him and Mother going at it on the other side.

"You were one semester from taking the bar," Guy seethed. "It's not like you don't know—"

"What would you have had me do?"

"Not bring the goddamn murder weapon to my office!"

"What—I should have left it here on the kitchen table?" said Mother. "I was trying to make the best of a bad situation."

"And your brilliant idea hinges on me suborning perjury?"

"You don't have any trouble lying to me about your girl uptown."

"A little human comfort doesn't get a man disbarred."

"*Disbarred*," Mother said bitterly. "Yes, that would be terrible. Imagine seeing your lifelong dream of being a lawyer come to nothing due to the callous self-interest of someone who professes to love you."

The door lurched open, and Mother and I both inhaled sharply, startled to find ourselves face-to-face.

"August Stillwell," she said, her cheeks flushed with annoyance. "How dare you skulk about, listening in on private conversations?"

"I was just—I didn't—"

"It's bad manners. You ought to have made your presence known."

"Yes, ma'am."

"We don't have to guess whose side you're on, do we?"

I didn't know how to answer that, and it didn't matter. She brushed past me and stomped up the stairs. Guy waved me in and told me to close the door.

"You and Poppy were having quite a powwow up there before dinner," he said. "Are you about to tell me something I'd prefer not to hear?"

"Maybe," I said uncertainly. "But isn't it better to know?"

"Not always." He sighed and folded his arms. "You can't argue a premise you know for a fact is false. That's another reason to keep your client off the witness stand. Some things you're better off not knowing."

I didn't know how to reconcile that with the whole lecture from the juke joint, so I decided to bite my tongue for the time being.

"Whatever was said up there," said Guy, "bear in mind that Poppy and Othella are as close as mother and daughter can be. Either one of them is capable of lying to protect the other. My client told me her daughter was not on the premises at the time of the incident. Your mother says Poppy was here at the house at the time of the incident. She says she'll swear to it if Redstone calls her to the stand. So that's the story, and unless the prosecution presents me with evidence proving otherwise, there's no reason to jump to any other conclusions or assume any facts not in evidence."

"Like Othella saying Lucky was dead when he went into the river."

"Exactly. She's not a doctor. She wasn't down in the water with him. She made that assumption, and assumptions are based on fear more often than they're based on information. Build your case on assumptions, and you'll end up doing the prosecutor's job for him."

"You can't let Mother get on the witness stand," I said. "She'll perjure herself. She could go to jail."

"Figured that out, did ya?" Guy opened the lower left drawer on his desk and took out a bottle of bourbon.

"What'll you do if Redstone subpoenas her?"

"Same thing I'm fixin' to do right now." He poured three fingers of whiskey and propped his feet up on his desk. "Get good and drunk."

"Isn't there a law about Poppy testifying against her own mother? Like attorney-client privilege or how you can't force one spouse to testify against another?"

"Some states have parent-child privilege, but that's not the law in Georgia. It's been asked and answered all the way up to the Supreme Court."

"There's plenty of people who knew Lucky was bad," I said. "If the neighbors can't testify, then what about cops? Or Klan fellas?"

"If you expect any of those fellas to testify on behalf of a black woman, you're looking under the wrong rock."

"What about Ruckels? He arrested him on a murder charge. He must've had evidence."

"There's a bang-up idea," Guy laughed. "Call Ruckels to the stand. That's the very definition of hostile witness, right there."

"Is it legal?"

"You have to be careful pulling stunts like that. The jury sees you grasping at straws, and they know the prosecution's got your dick in a wringer." But Guy sipped his whiskey, thinking about it. "Lucky was never convicted of murder. The case never went to trial. He could argue that evidence against Lucky doesn't figure as exculpatory, and I don't anticipate Judge Talmadge coming down on my side of any objections. He'll deny it till he's blue in the face, but his Klan sympathies run deep."

"What about Redstone? Mother says Red's a decent man. Maybe he doesn't like how Ruckels operates."

"Oh, I know for a fact he doesn't, but you need to understand, Critter, there's politics involved. Red has put twenty years into playing the game, allowing Ruckels to puppeteer and humiliate him. Now he's on the porch steps where it's all about to pay off. All Redstone has to do is keep Ruckels on his side until the election. Then he'll be the D.A., and he can operate any way he likes. How hard do you think it'll be for him to convince himself this is all for the greater good? Why shouldn't he throw Othella into the volcano? Like the world is gonna suffer that loss? And having Lucky out of the way, everybody's better off. All he did was slither around and prey on people in an effort to make himself feel powerful. The only time anybody treated him like he was worth a damn was . . ." Guy trailed off, and his eyes narrowed.

"What?"

"He'd found a niche for himself—doing things for people who didn't want to dirty their hands. I didn't like it when Newt hired him. Junkyard dogs aren't particular about who gets their fleas."

"But the people with clean hands—they couldn't have him telling stories at the icehouse."

"Correct."

"Did you ever hear tell . . . some folks say Lucky was Poppy's father?"

"*Uff!*" Guy snorted his disdain at the very suggestion. "A lovely, intelligent girl with a fine legal mind like Poppy's—coming outa that microcephalic bootlicker? That's an evil rumor born of jealousy. She's a beautiful black girl with high aspirations. That's all some people need to hate her, and it makes them feel tall to talk that trash about her."

"She's lighter than Othella," I said. "Do you know who her father is?"

"Some amorous young shithead from the university, I imagine."

"She's light-skinned. So it was a white fella, I guess."

"Looks that way."

"It would have been illegal for him to marry her, even if he wanted to."

"Yes," Guy said impatiently. "The best he could do is provide financially and make sure she got through college, which has apparently been done. Moral of the story: *Use a goddamn rubber.* I know you think you're a man of the world now, but you're still a freckle-faced kid, and the last thing you need is some local girl setting the hook in you because you couldn't keep August Stillwell the Fourth in your pants. Understand?"

"Yes, sir."

"Shut the door on your way out." He took his feet off the desk, hitched up his chair, and opened Othella's case file, effectively ending the conversation.

As I pulled the door closed, he said, "Critter?"

"Sir?"

"You'll be a fine lawyer someday. Mind you don't let it chew you up."

Poppy and I spent the next several days following Guy up and down the riverfront, interviewing Othella's neighbors and begging them to testify on her behalf. There was plenty of love for Othella, but even with Lucky in a drawer down at the morgue, people were plain scared. You could see it in their faces and hear it in their nervous throat-clearing and fidgety laughter.

Othella's uncle Cyrus, who ran a lawn mower repair shop, said, "Understand, Mr. Guy, they'll send another fella down here before long, and that won't go well for none of us."

"Another fella?" said Guy.

"To collect the monthly insurance. If you don't pay the premium, they say you'll find your place set on fire and a cross burning out front and you swingin' from an old oak tree right next to it."

"Says who?" said Guy. "The Klan?"

"I ain't saying another word about it, and I sure as hell ain't sittin' up in the witness box, jeopardizing my family. You know how it is," he added with a knowing nudge to my father's forearm. "We ain't forgot what you did for Othella's daddy."

"Thank you for your time, Cyrus." Guy offered his hand, and the old man gripped it.

"I know you won't let her down," he said with great confidence.

"No, sir," my father said with a buoyant smile, but as we drove back to the law office, he stared out the window without speaking. Poppy sat in the back seat, silent, a book in her lap.

"What's that you're studying?" Guy asked her as we turned onto Hancock Avenue.

"School desegregation cases."

"Blaustein and Ferguson?"

"Yes, sir."

"Good girl," said Guy. "Don't forget to review contracts and torts one more time. And don't let this situation distract you, Poppy. It's unfortunate that the trial dates overlap with the bar exam, but that's where your focus needs to be."

"Maybe I should hold off for the next one."

"No." Guy curtly nipped that notion in the bud. "If you miss the bar exam, I won't hear the end of it from Mrs. Stillwell. King is second chair on Othella's trial. Mary-Louise knows more than any of us about the divorce cases that need to be handled. Critter can run errands and cover the clerical issues. You just keep your mind on your studies."

"Yes, sir."

When we pulled into the driveway at the law office, Mary-Louise was out on the front porch with King, who waved and stumbled down the steps.

"Looks like he's ready for a ride home," said Guy.

King was jolly and talkative as I drove him out to his place. He and Mimi had patched things up after he agreed to provide a healthy budget for the remodeling of the house, which had sustained some smoke damage when she torched King's belongings.

"A fresh coat of paint has done wonders," said King. "She's been whistling like a lark every day since the fella started work."

I pulled down the long driveway and observed that scaffolding of a sort—a six-foot plank between two ladders—had been jury-rigged over on the side of the house, and a utility truck was parked out front. On the side of the truck was a cartooned fella in white overalls standing under a colorful typography arch: Casey's Interior and Exterior Painting. Poised above the painter's head was a word balloon saying, "Get the job done right!"

"Thanks for the lift," said King. "Help yourself to a Coke from the fridge on the back porch."

It didn't take me but a minute to get back there, open the bottle with a church key, drink it down halfway, and fill it up with rum from a squat bottle on the potting shelf. Maybe two minutes. King must have gone directly up the stairs, because just as I was taking the first swig of my poor man's cuba libre, Mimi started screaming. I heard King shouting, "*What in the holy hell?*" and then there was the clatter of falling paint cans as a naked man scrambled out of the second-floor window onto the makeshift scaffolding and dropped to the scrubby grass below. He dashed across the yard, yanked a sheet from the clothesline, and draped it around himself like a toga as he hastened toward the utility truck.

"Run, Billy Roy!" Mimi shrieked from overhead. "He's got a gun!"

I stood frozen on the porch steps, the cool bottle neck poised on my bottom lip. A shot rang out, and I flinched so hard the bottle jumped out of my hand and smashed on the floor. The man dropped like a sandbag. A red hibiscus-shaped stain blossomed on the white sheet.

"*Shit!*" Without thinking, I leaped over the porch rail, making a beeline for the fella on the ground, calling over my shoulder, "Jesus, King! What the hell?"

"Git outa th'way, Critter," King slurred, hanging out of the upstairs window, brandishing a snub-nosed pistol. "I don't want to see you get hurt."

"Stop it! Stop it, you crazy idiot!" Mimi pummeled him with her fists. She got him off-balance, snatched the gun away from him, and pitched it into the hedges.

The man in the sheet moaned and swore. He'd managed to get to his feet and was limping toward the truck, repeating over and over again in disbelief, "He shot me. He shot me. Motherfucker shot me in the ass."

"Mister? Hey, are you okay?" I tried to take his arm to assist him, but he shook me off.

"Don't touch me. Don't you come near me."

"Sit down, okay? I'll call for help."

"Lemme alone. I gotta get outa here."

With great difficulty, he eased into the driver's seat of the truck, located the keys above the visor, and started the engine. I ran into the kitchen, grabbed the phone off the wall, and dialed the only number my shaking fingers could manage.

"Stillwell & Hodg—"

"Mary-Louise," I croaked. Suddenly I had no spit for talking. "It's an emergency. Put Guy on."

A moment later, I heard my father's voice, low and calm. "Critter, are you all right?"

"Yes, sir. But King—he shot a man. Shot him in the ass. He's alive, but he's bleeding something awful."

"Okay. Take a deep breath, son. Tell me exactly what's happening right now."

In the time it took for me to inhale, the utility truck lurched over the railroad ties that formed the perimeter of Mimi's vegetable garden and became mired in the loamy soil. The man got out, clutching the bloody sheet around him. He tripped and fell, got up, and limped toward the road. I relayed this information to Guy, my heart pounding louder than King's heavy footsteps on the stairs.

"You're doing fine, August," Guy said evenly. "Where is the gun?"

"I don't know. In the yard. Mimi threw it."

"Did you call for an ambulance?"

"I don't think they'll take him," I said. "He's a colored fella."

"Okay. You need to drive him to Saint Mary's. I'll meet you there."

"Yes, sir."

I craned to look down the hall. King slid to the floor on the landing and retched into a Grecian urn.

"What have you done, you crazy fool?" Mimi wrapped her arms around King, keening and sobbing. "What have you done?"

"Listen to me," said Guy. "Tell Mimi to get King in her car and high-tail it over to the law office. I'm gonna call Sheriff Heck right now, and they need to be gone when he gets there. Understand?"

"Yes, sir."

"Good man. Stay calm. It'll be okay."

Guy hung up, and I relayed his instructions to Mimi. She nodded, wordlessly clutching the front of her silk robe, her face streaked with rivulets of black mascara. I bounded down the porch steps to the car and peeled out of the driveway, spraying gravel on the abandoned utility truck. I reached the road and saw that Billy Roy was still on his feet but had not gotten far. Weaving along the road's thistled shoulder, he didn't even look at me when I coasted up next to him.

"My dad says I should take you over to the hospital," I said.

He stopped and gave this some thought, sweating and shivering in the harsh sunlight. Billy Roy looked only a little older than me, his face smooth and tearstained. I got out and opened the back door so he could lie down on the seat, and he thoughtfully wadded the sheet beneath his backside and haunches, which were caked with dirt and ruby red blood. He was quaking like an aspen, and as I drove toward town, I pretended I didn't hear him crying.

"My daddy's gonna wear me out," he moaned, curling onto his side, covering his manhood with cupped hands.

Glancing in the rearview mirror, I noticed the familiar specter of Mimi's red Mustang burning rubber toward town. When she peeled off toward Hancock Avenue, I could see that the top was up, windows rolled tight despite the heat.

At the hospital, Guy was waiting outside the emergency room with the attending physician, who happened to be an old fraternity brother. The doctor and two nurses whisked Billy Roy through the glass doors. Guy and I waited outside for Billy Roy's father, William Royal Casey Senior.

"I've settled a few nonpayment disputes for him over the years," said Guy. "He's a hard-nosed negotiator. This is going to cost King a pretty penny, but at the end of the day, we all know it would be bad for everybody involved if this gets out on the street. King goes to jail. Mimi's ruined in this town for all time. Billy Roy gets run off—or worse—and Casey might as well close the doors on his business. That don't sound like any kind of justice to me."

Mr. Casey listened stoically to my father's assertions that boys will be boys, men have their pride, and the girly bullet removed from Billy Roy's butt was obviously intended for target range purposes, on account of King had been teaching Mimi to shoot, and the snub-nosed .25 itself lacked the stopping prowess of a weapon that aspired to kill a man at any sort of distance. Guy didn't have to point out to Mr. Casey that, should he decide to press charges, Billy Roy—whose baby face camouflaged a draft-age man of nineteen—would probably be doing so in front of a jury of white men whose blood ran cold at the idea of their wives flirting with the old "once you go black, you never go back" precept.

"King is prepared to cover the medical bills, of course," said Guy, "and he'd like to pay college tuition for Billy Roy, plus a thousand dollars each—to Billy Roy for his pain and suffering, and to you, Mr. Casey, for your inconvenience."

Mr. Casey inspected his perfectly tended cuticles and said, "I notice the law office building looks a little tatty these days. Seems like you might want to get that painted this summer. Outbuildings too, of course."

"Agreed," said Guy.

By the time Sheriff Heck arrived with Tiny, Guy and Mr. Casey had established that this was an unfortunate mishap Billy Roy would undoubtedly laugh about someday, telling this story about how he dropped that gun and accidentally shot himself in the ass.

"Moral of the story," Guy said as we drove back to the office. "If you're gonna get shot in the ass, get shot in the ass by a lawyer."

I expected to find King drunker than twelve sailors, but he was quite the opposite—cold sober and trembling with DTs—and when Guy offered him a drink from the globe bar, he declined.

"I've hit rock bottom," he said, choking back tears. "Rock bottom, I tell ya. I won't take another drink. I promised Mimi I'd take the cure and start fresh, and this time, I mean it. And I do mean it . . . just not with her. I feel like I've wakened from a fever dream. I'm seeing clearly."

"I'm glad for you, King," Guy said, but he didn't sound especially glad. He sounded a bit forlorn.

"Thank God for Critter." King turned to me and said, "I could've lost it all today, little brother. Everything I ever cared about. I was sure I was about to be divorced, disbarred, trying to dry out in a jail cell without morphine . . ." He pressed his palms together, rocking on the leather sofa. "Jesus. Guy, I don't know what to say. I put you in a terrible position. Witness tampering. Suborning perjury. Accessory after the fact. I owe you my life, partner."

"To our partnership." Guy raised his glass. "And God damn a man who won't commit a felony for a friend."

– *11* –

Guy's suite at the law office was actually a little smaller than mine, because I'd moved into King's spacious office suite when King retired in the early 1980s. Guy's office had bigger windows that faced the street, however, and I was beginning to understand why he spent so much time standing there, looking down on the comings and goings of Athens. The rush hour traffic didn't amount to much. The commuters were mostly busy squirrels and baby carriages. Gnarled roots and tree knees jutted up through the broken sidewalks here and there as the street mellowed and aged like the town around it. There was a bad moment in the late 1970s when a few old houses were torn down and replaced with strip malls, but for the most part, Athens protected its Greek Revival architecture and cherished its gentle character. For more than forty years, my father stood at these windows, surveying the growing city—not as a would-be potentate surveying his turf, more like a goatherd observing an unruly flock.

Since Guy's departure, I'd found myself standing at those same windows at the end of the day, pacing between the old globe bar and the tastefully shabby seating area. I sat in his worn leather chair, propped my feet on the desk, and opened the bottom left-hand drawer. There was a glass in there, but it didn't look particularly clean, so I drank from the bottle.

Tatum arrived as Mary-Louise was heading home for the evening, and their voices echoed softly in the foyer at the bottom of the stairs.

"Why, Tater Tot!" Mary-Louise enthused. "What a treat."

"Hey, Miss Mary-Louise."

"We missed your mama at the Bush-Quayle brunch last Saturday. And you know what happens when you don't show up for a Junior League brunch. You get put on a committee."

"I'll let her know."

"What brings you in this afternoon?"

"Critter asked me to cast an assiduous eye over some evidence."

"He's up in your daddy's office." Then Mary-Louise lowered her voice to say something I didn't catch. I heard the brisk click of her less-than-sensible high heels going out the door as Tatum clomped up the marble stairs in her motorcycle boots.

She joined me at the window and said, "You're not gonna like this."

"Tick?"

"He was a Dixie Mafia fixer who turned GBI informant twelve years ago, and about six months after that, they found pieces of him under a dock at Thunderbolt Marina."

"Did you find any connection between him and Newt—Newt and DiLippa, DiLippa and Pollard—anything that puts Tick in the room that night?"

"Not yet."

"I've got nine days to figure this out and make some kind of case. Newt swears he was framed, which is possible, but he maintains he has no idea who did it, which is bullshit."

"You'll get it out of him, brother. You're good at that," said Tatum.

I laid out the crime scene photos on Guy's desk, Pollard murder photos on one side, Lucky Winfield photos on the other.

"Exactly what am I looking for?" she asked.

"Anomalies," I said. "Incongruities."

"So you have no idea."

"Correct."

She picked up one of the Pollard photos and said, "Well, cause of death seems obvious."

"The hole between his eyes kinda gives it away."

"The deceased appears to be wearing a lady's corset," Tatum observed.

"That's one of the crime scene details they kept out of the press," I said. "They figured whoever did it wouldn't be able to keep that to himself."

"They figured right, apparently."

"Maybe." I couldn't deny the possibility that it was that simple. Like Vivvy says: "Sometimes a cigar is just a cigar."

"Walk me through it," said Tatum. "According to the D.A. . . . . "

"Sunday, June 2, 1963: Newt and Pollard get into an argument over politics, during which Newt makes some crack about Pollard going to Miss Jeffie's every Wednesday. The following Wednesday morning, June 5, Pollard is found dead at Miss Jeffie's."

I handed her the photo of Pollard, tightly corseted, a small hole dotting his head.

"Wednesday afternoon: A couple of fellas down at the icehouse report to the police that Lucky is down at the juke joint, drinking and talking about the kinky circumstances of the Pollard murder and insinuating that he had a hand in it. The detective on the case, Burl Hopper, goes to an icehouse where Lucky is known to hang out, and sure enough, he's sitting there drunk and talking about indelicate details, which—according to them—could only be known to the killer."

I handed Tatum that paperwork and a copy of Hopper's subsequent report.

"Lucky's arrested, supposedly cracks under interrogation, and his lawyer makes a deal with Ruckels. In exchange for a ten-year sentence, Lucky will confess to the murder and testify that Newt paid him ten thousand dollars to do it."

I passed her the photo of the statement and photographs of the physical evidence.

"Lucky supplies the gun, which is indeed registered to Newt and has two sets of fingerprints on it: Newt's and Lucky's. They hook up bank records verifying that the ten grand was withdrawn from Newt's account on the same day ten grand was deposited into Lucky's account. Tuesday, June 11: They go to arrest Newt, but he's lit out for points unknown. Wednesday, June 12: Lucky turns up dead. Fast-forward twenty-five years, and here we are."

Tatum whistled softly. "That's one damning pattern of facts right there."

"It is."

"But at the start, all they had on Lucky was hearsay from the icehouse."

"Crime scene details corroborated by Detective Hopper."

"Even so, the kinky stuff—whatever they withheld—they can't sell that as 'the killer is the only one who could have possibly known' because what about . . ." She ticked the cast of characters off on her fingers. "Killer, investigators, anybody the killer told, anybody the investigators told, anybody told by the people who were told, plus anybody who might have been at the crime scene before the investigators even got there—like Miss Jeffie and literally any hooker who worked in the brothel."

When Tatum sat in Guy's big leather chair, her feet didn't touch the floor. She pushed against the edge of the desk with her foot, swiveling in a slow, thoughtful circle.

"So before the gun and everything came into it, isn't that plea deal kinda lame?"

"It was enough to bring him in for questioning," I said, "but if he'd stuck with Guy and kept his mouth shut . . ."

A fleeting memory brushed by the back of my brain. Ruckels's certitude. Tick's smile. *Pleasure seeing you again. You and your boy.*

"Then he makes the deal, and suddenly, it's airtight," said Tatum. "If there was ever a prosecution wish list—statement, gun, bank records—all that's missing is a side of fries."

"Newt swears he was framed, and the argument could be made. There are no wrong turns. No loose ends. When you look at the paperwork, it doesn't even feel like an investigation. It feels like insurance."

She laid the statement photo next to the photo of the gun.

"I wonder what this is, right here." She pointed with her pinkie finger. "This crescent-shaped shadow. I don't see it on this photo with the gun, even though you can tell from the chips and scratches, it's the same table."

"That's in the jailhouse interview room."

"I'd like to take a closer look at these." Tatum gathered the two lots of crime scene photos into separate manila envelopes. "An acquaintance of mine is planning to unveil something called a 'digital camera' at a German trade show in September. It allows you to capture an image as data and store it in metal-oxide-semiconductor memory cells."

"Let's imagine I know what that means," I said. "How does it help?"

"You look at the image on a computer screen, so you can blow it up like a billboard. We'll be able to see a flea on your vic's johnson. They're not for sale yet, but I know where I can borrow one. Fuji's behind it. Come September, Fuji stock is gonna go apeshit."

"Good to know." I wrote that down. "I don't have much time, though, so don't go too far down the rabbit hole."

"I don't have a lot of time either," she said. "I have other clients."

"Anybody I know?"

"If I told you, I'd have to kill you," she said. "But I've been thinking it's time for me to get serious about the business. Form an LLC. Set up a proper computer lab. I need a real office."

"Good for you." I smiled my patient big brother smile. "Mary-Louise can put together the LLC paperwork. If you like, I'll help you clear out that big storage room down behind the kitchen."

"Actually . . ." She ran her hands along the edge of Guy's desk. "I was thinking I could move into Daddy's office."

"You mean . . . until he comes back?"

Tatum regarded me with an unreadable expression.

"He's coming back, Tatum. And if he did decide to retire, I think it's pretty obvious I'd be moving into his office."

"You have King's old office—a perfectly grand office—right down the hall. Why shouldn't I have Daddy's office?"

"You know why."

"Yeah, because you're determined to relive his life instead of coming up with a life of your own."

"That's a load of crap."

She pulled open the lower left drawer and took out the bourbon bottle, which was about empty. "What happened here?"

"Must've had a hole in it."

"Hm." Again with that inscrutable expression.

I folded my arms and said, "Look, if I need a sobriety monitor, I'll call the Temperance League. Meanwhile, what I need is a PI, and you might want to tread lightly, little sister, because if it was up to Guy, that PI would be someone other than you."

This time, the look on her face was clear—stunned, then wounded, then flat pissed off.

"You think I don't know that?" she said, blinking back furious tears. "I've known it since I was five. Bootsy's the beautiful one who's got him wrapped around her finger. You're the golden son who can do no wrong. And then I come tagging along like a lovingly tolerated household pet."

"Tate. C'mon."

"Good luck with your case, brother."

She tossed the manila envelopes on the desk and flipped me off with both barrels on her way out the door. The heavy footfall of her motorcycle boots echoed on the marble stairs, and a moment later, I heard the front door swing open and bang shut.

This was a problem. Guy's short list of go-to PIs consisted of a few octogenarians who winked and said *gumshoe* and couldn't stop talking about the bygone decades leading up to their retirements, most of which had been forced by case-toppling errors and egregious violations of political correctness. None of them had ever heard of the geeky gadgetry Tatum had been playing with since she was a child.

"Well, shit . . ."

I polished off the remaining dribble of bourbon and decided that, given the time constraints, I was better off on my own.

– *12* –

There was some study of voir dire in law school, of course, but I mostly spent that class time doing paperwork for a law firm in Atlanta, where I clerked until I could check all the boxes and sit for the bar exam. My checkered academic past prevented me from going to an Ivy League law school, so I clerked all day, went to law school in the evening, and partied till the wee hours.

I learned two things in law school: case study—such and such precedent set by Hungadinga v. Hungadinga—and how to be an egotistical SOB. Solid SOB training is essential to the profession, because it takes a kernel of arrogance to get up and brawl, bare-knuckled, day after day for causes you may or may not believe in. You believe in the cause of fighting, not the cause you're fighting for, and in that fray, a defense attorney wins no points for civility.

Everything practical I know today about lawyering, I learned on my feet at Stillwell & Hodges. This includes the delicate art of voir dire.

Twenty-four jurors were called for Othella's trial, and in keeping with 1963 norms, seventeen of them were white men. Ruckels and Guy took turns questioning them, romancing them, winning them over, and winnowing them down to twelve. I wasn't thinking about it much at the time, but when I look back on the way Guy navigated the process of jury selection, God help me, I can see it in practice as clearly as I saw it written on a cocktail napkin:

Belief—not in the sense of religion, but a system of values.

Education—not in the sense of academics, but in an apparent willingness to learn.

Laughter—that openness that allows a person to breathe differently, even for a moment.

Loyalty—the strength to stand firm once one has been won over.

"I guess you've heard about the trouble being stirred up this summer," Ruckels said to Juror 1, a sunburned workingman. "What do you know about this fella Martin Luther King?"

"He's a preacher," said Juror 1, "and he wrote that letter from jail."

"A preacher. What religion is he ordained in, I wonder?"

"I wouldn't know, but he seems like a strong Christian. Talks about poor folks same way Jesus did."

"State exercises its first strike," said Ruckels.

Prosecution and defense were allowed six strikes each. Ruckels used strikes two and three to eliminate the only two black men who'd made it past the voter suppression and other obstacles that prevented most black people from being called up for jury duty. Guy used his first strike to eliminate a man he recognized as a Klansman whom King had defended for malicious mischief a year prior. He used his second to eliminate a young woman who cried when he asked her if she'd feel comfortable looking at photos of a dead man and his third strike to remove a lady who refused to serve certain people in her candy shop. Ruckels asked a few questions about domestic violence and eliminated the three women who remained.

"Did you happen to serve in the armed forces?" Ruckels asked an old man with readily evident tattoos. Because you don't ask a question unless you know the answer.

"Surely did. I got the bad leg and Purple Heart to prove it," said Juror 16. "I was in the Pacific Theater during the Second World War."

"World War II." Ruckels turned to Guy and clarified, "That was the conflict going on overseas while you were dancing at the fraternity cotillion."

Such baiting and barbing was allowed by the court and encouraged by the enthusiastic gallery. I thought Guy would exercise his fourth strike, but he didn't, and I understand now that doing so would have alienated anyone who'd been in the military or was family to a serviceman. The tactic might have worked for Ruckels back in the 1950s, but in 1963, potential jurors were just as likely to know and love someone who lived in fear of being sent to Vietnam. So, Guy laughed a good-natured laugh and watched for an opportunity to skewer the old man in return. He was already planting seeds. Guy saw almost everyone as a potential ally, so his voir dire was more about sympathy and seduction than it was about carving away potential hostility. At the end of the day, a jury of twelve white men was impaneled.

When trial commenced the next morning, the courthouse was packed with spectators, funeral home fans wafting. Below the bench and witness box, the stage was set, props and all. In front of the defense table, Guy had parked the cane chair. The prosecution table was covered with a red-and-white checked tablecloth on which Redstone placed the frying pan, a watermelon, a carton of eggs, and a slab of bacon.

"Planning a picnic after the dismissal?" Guy said affably. "Because we all know damn well demonstration is not allowed during opening statements."

Ruckels glowered at his notes, not even bothering to look up. As Guy took his place behind the defense table, Poppy whispered, "What's he up to?"

"No good," said Guy. "He's going to pull something and then apologize, for what it's worth. But you can't unring the bell. Once the jury's seen him pull his dirty trick, they've seen it."

She darted a glance toward the cane chair. "What were you planning to do with that?"

"Same thing."

"All rise," said the bailiff.

Everyone rose up and sat down as instructed, and Judge Talmadge went through the housekeeping details, getting everyone's names for the record, and issuing a repeated warning about the tactical hijinks and melodrama everyone in the gallery was counting on.

"Mr. Ruckels," said Talmadge. "Make your opening statement."

Ruckels stood and nodded his thanks.

"The facts of this case are plain," he said, "as the evidence will show. The victim, Mr. Lucky Winfield, walks into the Riverside Country Club, that old juke joint down by the covered bridge, on the night of Wednesday, June 12, 1963. He's a thirsty man at the end of a hardworkin' day."

Redstone scurried from behind the prosecution table and cast a sheet of clear plastic on the floor in front of the prosecution table.

"Objection," said Guy. "Demonstration is not appropriate during opening statements."

"Your Honor," said Ruckels, "in order to lay out the facts of the case as accurately as possible, leaving nothing to interpretation—or mis-interpretation—it's necessary for me to employ a minimal display of visual aids. Within your discretion."

"I'll allow it," said the judge.

"Outrageous!" Guy made a great display of stunned indignation and then settled back to watch the show.

"The defendant, by her own admission, offers to make him some-thing to eat," said Ruckels. "She turns on the stove, invites him to come over and sit down. *Come into my web, said the spider to the fly.* She takes out a frying pan identical to this here cast-iron skillet . . ."

He raised the frying pan up—using both hands to make much of its weight—displayed it to the jury, and then set it down with a heavy *clank*.

"She cracks a couple of eggs . . . put some bacon in there . . ."

There was an undeniably sinister sound to the crunch of the egg-shells and the soft plop of dead meat in the pan, and Ruckels smiled a lascivious smile as he rattled it back and forth the way you would on a hot stovetop.

"Poor old Lucky. He thinks he's about to tuck into some breakfast. He's sitting there, sippin' a cold one. And then for reasons known only to whatever devil makes a person do a thing like this, the defendant, that woman sitting right there, with malice and fury and the unfemi-nine musculature typical of her African heritage, *bashed—his—head*."

Ruckels brought the frying pan down hard on the watermelon—once, and again—leaving it shattered, dripping red innards like brain matter and seeds that suggested broken teeth and bone fragments. Even now, I shiver at the image. It was a masterful exercise that would be spoken of with awe in the halls of law schools for decades to come—on a par with a Texas prosecutor who brought a queen-size bed into the courtroom, tied her paralegal to the headboard, and straddled him to reenact two hundred stab wounds that had been inflicted on the victim.

"She bludgeoned him until he was dead as a wedge." Ruckels handed the skillet to Redstone, who carefully set it aside. "Now, I'm gonna give you a chance to examine the real murder weapon. Hold it in your hands. Feel the substantial weight of it. You'll hear the coroner's testimony regarding the damage an implement such as this might wreck on the skull of an unsuspecting victim. But right now, I want to tell you what you won't see.

"You'll not see the slightest bump nor bruise on the body of this woman who's gonna try to claim she was being so savagely beaten that she felt justified in taking this man's life. You'll see no weapon *proven* to have been wielded against her. You'll see no *proof* that Lucky Winfield ever turned a harsh word on her. You'll see only her devious plot to hang a murder on this man, who was never tried or convicted of any crime, and when she could not get the state of Georgia to carry out her evil intent, she struck him down with her own hand. *Struck—him—dead!*"

He clanged the skillet on the prosecution table—once, and again—and let that resonate for a moment before he strolled over to the jury box.

"Gentlemen of the jury. Keep your eyes open. This fella over here—Guy Stillwell—you all know how he operates. He is slicker than the whiskers on a harbor cat. He will try to lead you down his *yella* brick road. Don't you pay him any mind. You have a duty here. Duty to the truth. To justice. Pay attention to the evidence, and when it's all laid out before you, you ask yourself if you want to live in a world where a known troublemaker can dispatch a regular workingman and then waltz off scot-free. I ask that you rule on the evidence, disregard the dog and pony show, and return a just verdict: guilty of murder in the first degree."

"Defense," said Judge Talmadge. "Opening statement."

"I'm happy to wait while they tidy up over there." Guy gestured to the dripping gore and shattered green brainpan.

"Get on with your statement," said Talmadge.

"Your Honor, it's prejudicial." Guy sprang to his feet. "Now, I sat here patiently while the D.A. put on a show like Cecil B. DeMille with utter disregard to your instruction expressly forbidding such a display. If you allow that mess to remain, undermining my sincere and respectful—"

"Would you prefer to forego your opening statement, Mr. Stillwell?"

Guy stood silent for a moment, during which there was not a breath taken between the bench and the back of the room.

"No, Your Honor, I will not forego my opening," he said quietly. "I would never allow my personal indignation to impede the most vigorous defense to which my client, as an American citizen, is entitled by law. And I'll tell you something . . ."

He strolled over to the prosecution table, scooped up a hunk of watermelon and ate it on his leisurely way back to the defense table.

"I'm willing to bet that the gentlemen of this jury are smart enough to know the difference between *The Greatest Show on Earth* and the God's honest truth."

Guy turned and spat a watermelon seed onto the floor in front of Ruckels and then pulled the cane chair over to face the jury. He sat down and crossed his legs, as if he was chatting up guests on his own front porch.

"Let's cut to the chase," he said. "The evidence will show that this man needed killing. He shows up at the juke joint, three o'clock in the morning. What do you think he intended to do there? She tried to cook something for him, hoping that would distract him from forcing himself on her as he had time and time before. He got impatient and went to beating her with this here chair I'm sitting on, and damn right, she gave him a taste of old Mr. Skillet there, and in his drunken stupor, he stumbled off the edge of the access port in the floor. Does that mean she killed him? I don't know. Not so as anybody has proven it to me *beyond a reasonable doubt.* Maybe he cracked his skull on the piling down there. Maybe there was a rock under the water. But I'll tell you this, if she did kill him, she killed him to save her own life, for sure, as the evidence will show, and in doing so, she most likely saved a number of other lives as well. Because here's what the D.A. knows very well but neglected to mention: the deceased was a stone-cold murderer."

"Objection."

"Sustained."

"Not long before Lucky Winfield accosted my client—"

Ruckels bolted from his chair, talking over Guy, but Guy kept right on going while the judge banged his gavel and the court reporter got saucer-eyed and frantic trying to type it all down.

"He showed up at the local whorehouse—"

"Objection."

"Sustained."

"—placed the barrel of a gun between a man's eyes—"

"Objection! I object!"

"—and blew that man's brains out the back of his head."

"I object!" Ruckels bellowed. "Facts not in evidence!"

"You brought it up." Guy opened his hands with an air of innocence. "You said the man was never tried or convicted. Let's discuss that."

"Your Honor, he's yapping on facts not in evidence in this case or any matter pending. Defense pulled that straight out of his—out of—"

"Sustained."

"And that," said Guy, "is what passes for the D.A.'s *duty to the truth*, ladies and gentlemen."

The two lawyers faced each other below the bench like a couple of banty roosters hackled for battle.

"This is an outrage," Ruckels sputtered. "Grounds for mistrial. I object, goddamn it!"

"Enough," Talmadge said. "The objection is sustained."

"Imagine my surprise," Guy said to the gallery and got a good laugh.

"Defense will direct comments to the court," said the judge. "Stay within the scope of this case, Mr. Stillwell, and mind your p's and q's, or I will hold you in contempt. Prosecution, keep your skivvies on. If we declared a mistrial every time somebody went over the line, we'd still be grinding our teeth over Cain versus Abel."

"May I continue?" Guy asked.

"Are you encouraging me to state a preference?" said Talmadge.

"No, sir." Guy returned to the jury, hands in his pockets. "It must be mighty convenient to live in a world where things are so clear-cut— good or evil, thumbs-up or thumbs-down—based on the most super- ficial interpretation of the evidence and of the applicable laws. A world where *facts in evidence* can be adjusted to suit the narrative of the strong and silence the stories of those at a disadvantage. Like you and me."

He set his hands on the rail in front of the jury box, taking his time to look each member in the eye.

"I see good men sitting here. I see honest men who want to do the right thing. The D.A.—he sees a ship of fools, easily swayed by theatrics, vulnerable to the prejudices and biases designed to keep every one of us in our place. Somebody said to me the other day, 'There's never a good day to fight. That's why the fight keeps needing to get fought.' Well, gentlemen, I guess this day right here is as good as it gets. I'm gonna fight like a pit bull for this defendant over here—Miss Othella—and every time the D.A. tries to tell you she's anything less than *innocent until proven guilty*, every time he plays to anything less than your better angels, I will call him out. I will call *you* out. Because I believe in your integrity, in your honest desire to see justice done."

I watched Ruckels, waiting for him to object, but he just sat there simmering, and Redstone looked like a whipped dog sitting next to him. I'd not seen before—and never seen since—two opening state- ments that went so far out of bounds.

"The evidence will show that Miss Othella Sterling decided it was a good day to fight." Guy moved back to the defense table and stood behind Othella, his hands resting lightly on her shoulders. "In fear for her life, she rose up before a monster and struck him down. The evi- dence will show that Lucky Winfield cast a long, dark shadow over the riverfront community for decades, a shadow made longer, deeper, and more terrifying as it was facilitated by the very authorities employed by *you*—law-abiding taxpayers—to protect and serve the citizens of this county. I'm gonna lay out for you a history of violence and complicity that will leave no question in your mind. And then I'll ask you to do the decent thing. Return a just verdict. Not guilty."

There was little conversation over dinner that night. The next day, court reconvened for the second day of Othella's trial, and the prosecution promised "a series of damning witnesses, relentless as a freight train," starting with the county coroner.

"Dr. Cowell," said Ruckels, "how long have you been the coroner in Athens-Clarke County?"

"Long enough to know better," Cowell chortled, and Ruckels chortled along, but the jury and spectators were silent. Sensing that the joke hadn't landed, Ruckels quickly moved on.

"Seven years?" he nudged.

"Correct," said Cowell, "but I've been a board-certified forensic pathologist for nine years total."

"You personally performed the autopsy on the savagely murdered victim—"

"Objection," said Guy.

Talmadge waved it off. "Overruled. Let's not get tangled up in semantics."

"I'll rephrase," said Ruckels. "As a courtesy. Dr. Cowell, you performed an autopsy on, uh, the deceased fella with the inexplicably flattened head."

Cowell chortled again, and this time the rest of the room snickered with him.

"I did," said Cowell. "Cause of death was blunt force trauma to the skull."

"And in your opinion, this here cast-iron skillet was the cause of said trauma?"

"Yes, sir. That is entirely consistent with my autopsy, yes."

Ruckels held up a copy of the autopsy report. "And does your report here jibe with the defendant's story about the deceased coming after her with a chair? Like this part right here. Would you please read that out loud for the jury?"

Cowell put on a pair of diopters and read stiffly: "The skull was crushed in the posterior right occipital region just beneath the lambdoid suture, causing massive trauma and sending bone fragments downward into the occipital lobe and cerebellum."

"Doc, I'm just a Southern lawyer, and those are some mighty big words. In simple English—"

"Mr. Winfield was struck with a downward motion toward the back of the head."

"He was hit from behind."

"Correct."

"Like he was sitting on a chair, minding his own business, and somebody came up behind him, quiet as little cat's feet—not like he was going at somebody and she was defending herself."

"Objection," said Guy. "Leading the witness."

"Overruled."

"That self-defense scenario would not fit the injuries," said Cowell. "Looks to me like a blow to the back of the head propelled the victim forward so his face came in contact with the wooden table, breaking his nose and loosening a couple of front teeth."

"You think he was rendered unconscious at that point?"

"Objection," said Guy. "Calls for speculation."

"Calls for common sense, as far as I can tell," said Talmadge. "Overruled."

"I suspect he was unconscious or dead," said Cowell.

"How do you suppose he ended up in the river?"

"I object," said Guy, on his feet this time. "*I suspect* this. *How do you suppose* that. It's speculation, plain and simple."

"Overruled," Talmadge grunted. "Take it up on cross."

Emboldened, Ruckels said, "In your expert opinion, Dr. Cowell, how did the victim end up down there in the water?"

"I'd say he was dragged," said Cowell. "There were wood slivers in his face and one arm, indicating that the other arm was lifted up as she dragged him over there."

"Holy cats," said Ruckels. "That sounds like an unpleasant way to go."

"I'm sure it was quite unpleasant," said Cowell.

Ruckels shot a meaningful look at the jury and said, "Your witness."

Guy sat for a contemplative moment before he said, "Unpleasant, you say?"

"Without a doubt," said Cowell.

"But just a minute ago, you said he was unconscious or dead."

"Yes. Correct."

"So which wild speculation are we supposed to go with? Perhaps you and the D.A. could pick one story and stick with it."

"Objection," said Ruckels.

"Sustained."

"Was he dead, unconscious, or none of the above?" said Guy. "Was he suffering some sort of unpleasant excursion after smacking his face on the wooden table, or did he perhaps stumble away from a violent altercation and smack his face on the wooden floor? Did he get dragged across the floorboards, or did he step in the hole and get those splinters attempting to grasp at the edge as he fell in?"

"There's no way to say exactly."

"So your testimony is that you don't know."

"I didn't say that."

"Are you saying you *do* know?"

"Not for certain, but I can make an educated guess."

"No, sir!" Guy spun to point his finger at him. "No, you may not. Not in a court of law. Not when a woman's very life hangs in the balance. A trial does not convene for the purpose of your guesswork."

"Objection." Ruckels slapped his palm on the prosecution table. "I object."

"State your grounds," said Guy. "I have a feeling it'll go well for you."

"Badgering, testifying, and being a horse's ass."

The courtroom rewarded Ruckels with hoots and spattered applause.

"Objection is sustained," said Talmadge. "Defense, I don't like what you're implying."

"Apologies, Your Honor."

"Ask a question, Mr. Stillwell, or I'll excuse the witness."

"Not so fast," said Guy. "We still need to discuss the matter of that injury to the back of the head."

Cowell folded his arms, guarded now. Tight-lipped.

"Dr. Cowell, according to the defendant's statement to the sheriff's deputy, she was accosted by the deceased, and during that altercation, she managed to whomp him upside the head with the frying pan."

"I don't see how that's possible."

Guy produced a small round can and held it up for everyone to see.

"Dr. Cowell, having known you for several years, I've observed you have a habit of dipping snuff. Rooster brand, correct?"

"Yes . . ."

Guy opened the can and inhaled a deep snort as he covered the last three paces between the defense table and the witness box. Right in front of Cowell, he reared back and let rip a prodigious sneeze. Cowell ducked, tucking his face into his raised arm. The courtroom roared with laughter.

"Oh, my stars. I am so sorry. Here." Guy produced a clean handkerchief and swiped at Cowell's lapel. "Begging pardon. Here you go, Doc. Let's see the back of your shoulder. Ah. Yeah. There it is. On account of the way you flinched when you saw it coming."

"Objection," said Ruckels. "For the love of—"

"Sustained."

Cowell took the handkerchief and swiped at the back of his shoulder, chin tucked with distaste.

"I do apologize, Doc," said Guy. "But maybe you'd like to rethink that whole thing about how someone standing in front of you can't possibly hit you in the back of the head?"

"I didn't say *possible*. I said *probable*, didn't I? There is a difference."

"Yes, there surely is," said Guy. "The scenario described by the defendant, is that possible or probable?"

"It's . . . possible."

"If someone lunged at you, swinging a heavy object, such as a cast-iron skillet, isn't the most natural human reflex to turn away, as you did just now?"

"Yes."

"So now, we've gone from possible to probable, haven't we?"

Cowell looked at Ruckels, but Guy stepped into his line of sight.

"Don't look at the D.A., sir. We already know what he wants you to say. Doc, does the autopsy report disprove the defendant's claim that she was being accosted and swung that skillet to defend herself?"

"*Disprove* it? No," said Cowell. "But it doesn't *prove* it, either. And neither does that stunt you just pulled."

"Again, we agree. But the burden of proof is on the prosecution. The defendant is innocent until proven guilty beyond a reasonable doubt, isn't she?"

"Yes."

"Dr. Cowell, does this autopsy *prove*—beyond a reasonable doubt—the scenario concocted by the prosecution? 'Little cat's feet'? That whole confabulation?"

"No."

"Thank you for your honest testimony," said Guy. "No further questions."

Talmadge cocked an eyebrow toward Ruckels. "Redirect?"

"Nah," said Ruckels, "let's move on."

After the coroner, who detailed Lucky's violent demise, and then Sheriff Heck, who talked about the questionable circumstances of Othella's arrest, Ruckels called Lucky's sister, Ladine, who told the moving tale of a scrappy little boy who grew up to fight the axis of evil in World War II and got maimed by Japs for his trouble.

"But still, *still and always*," she tearfully testified, "he arrived on time every Sunday morning to take our aging mama to church—until that fateful morning when he did not arrive, and we had to tell her, 'Mama, something terrible has happened to your baby,' though we truly didn't know if her failing heart would withstand the blow."

Guy wasn't about to cross-examine this witness with members of the jury still dabbing their welling eyes in sympathy.

"Miss Ladine, I'm sorry for your loss," he said. "No questions."

"Prosecution calls Detective Burl Hopper," said Ruckels.

Guy didn't flinch, but I knew Hopper would be a tough nut to crack.

– *13* –

Burl Hopper ("Barley Hops" in Guy's lexicon of nicknames) was a grizzled but meticulous detective who retired from the sheriff's department not long after Othella's trial and freelanced, often for my father, in the decades that followed. If you'd asked me when I was fifteen, I would have said he was old, but when he sat down across from me at a picnic table outside his RV in 1988, a large bottle of inexpensive rye whiskey between us, he looked to be about eighty, so he must have been in his midfifties during the summer in question.

"I retired early," he said, and without being asked, he added, "Came into a bit of an inheritance."

"Looks like it worked out well," I said. "Beautiful spot you got here."

He surveyed his kingdom, a few acres on the water adjacent to the land the developers had gotten me to invest in. When they tried to buy Hopper out, he threatened to shoot them, but he was old and without family and hadn't paid his taxes for several years, so we knew we'd acquire the land from the state erelong, and we didn't mind biding our time.

Hopper knew I wasn't here about that.

"To be honest," he said, "I didn't think it would take this long to unravel. People go, but they don't stay gone. They lie, but sooner or later, 'the truth will out.' So sayeth the bard."

He poured whiskey in a glass for me and refilled a silver flask for himself.

"I brought these to refresh your memory." I took the manila envelopes from my briefcase and nudged them across the table, but I had a feeling he didn't need to look at them. "Let's start with Pollard."

"It was a clean hit," he said. "No sign of struggle before or tidying up after. Somebody opened that door, did the deed, and . . ." He illustrated the hit man's smooth departure with a whistle and a flick of two fingers. "Wham bam, thank you ma'am."

"Dixie Mafia?"

"Maybe. Pollard was backing a fella in the congressional race. DiLippa was backing somebody else. The two families had a history of conflicting business interests."

"Do you think Lucky did the hit?"

"I interviewed all the ladies, and not one of them mentioned seeing him. They all knew him. Despised him. I figured, if he'd been there, he'd have come up in the conversation."

"Did they mention anyone else? Anyone who seemed out of place?"

"Only you."

I coughed, whiskey burning my sinuses. It had never even crossed my mind that my name might have come up in the investigation. But of course, it had.

"Jesus. Hopper, surely, you know I had nothing to do with it. I was just—that day was—"

"I know, I know." He laughed a long, rolling belly laugh. "She told me all about it—the young lady. I forget her name."

"Twyla." I winced. Oh, Twyla. The betrayal.

"Ah. Yeah. It was the source of some merriment in a rather dark day. They told the story for years—how the virgin Critter Stillwell jumped off the roof without his pants."

"I had my pants."

He shrugged. "Not the way I heard it."

"Stories tend to shift with the storyteller."

"That they do."

We sipped our whiskey in silence for a long moment, listening to the songbirds and a summer breeze in the pines. Hopper held the silver flask between his hands, as if tipping it no longer gave him the absolution he was looking for.

"Had this thing gone to trial," he said, "I don't know what I would have done. I was a good cop. Never once in my career did I knuckle under to pressure from the D.A. to see things a certain way or fudge on evidence I'd rather not see."

"But Ruckels was pressing hard on this one. Why?"

"I won't pretend to know the answers, but I had questions," he said, "and I got paid well not to ask them."

"Your convenient inheritance—that was actually a payoff from Ruckels."

He nodded, unable to look me in the eye. "The shame ate at me. That's not who I am. But they'd already hung it on Lucky, and Lucky was dead, so I figured . . . maybe that was beneficial to all parties involved."

"Except Othella."

"That's a whole different situation."

"Is it?" I wondered. "Because I keep thinking the two cases must be related somehow."

"She saw an opportunity, that's all."

"An opportunity?"

"The lady who found Pollard's body was her sister."

"Cornelia . . ."

"She was set up to join him for his usual appointment. Walked in and found him dead," said Hopper. "Those crime scene details that got withheld—the corset and such—she got herself an eyeful."

I hated the scenario that immediately unfolded in my head. I thought of Othella chuckling at her own joke. *I can keep a secret. It's the people I tell who can't keep their mouth shut.*

"So Cornelia told Othella," I said, "and Othella fed the details to Lucky, knowing he'd go shoot his mouth off about it."

"That's how I figured it." Hopper looked out over the water, and I watched the weight of memory lift from his shoulders as he unburdened himself. "For years, he was trouble to her and her folks. He skated on one thing after another. I looked into more than a few incidents where he was the bad actor. Ugly incidents. Violent. I did the legwork, every time—did the paperwork down to the jot and tittle. I wanted that SOB to go to jail. No charges ever came of it. Reports somehow got misfiled. Evidence mysteriously went missing. I didn't know why Ruckels was protecting him, but it was plain as the bulbous nose on his face, and it got to be more than I could have on my conscience."

"So it was you that tipped off my father."

There was the slightest tic of a smile at the side of Hopper's mouth.

"Funny thing about those misfiled reports," he said. "Turns out, some of 'em were filed in a plastic bin under my front porch."

"But during the trial . . ." I pulled the trial transcript from my briefcase, revisiting Hopper's damning testimony about the particulars of the crime scene. There was nothing, not a whiff of subtext. "Why didn't he ask you about all this when he had you on the stand?"

"Because we were friends," said Hopper, "and Guy Stillwell would never throw a friend under the bus."

But he'd thought about it. Hopper must have sensed that. I could see it now, when I set aside the dry pages of the old transcript and searched the faces in my living memory: Hopper on the witness stand and Ruckels rising to hammer that final nail in the coffin, taking it all back to the scene of the crime.

- *14* -

I sat in the front row behind Guy and Othella as Hopper described the details of the crime scene without embroidery, and Ruckels filled in between the lines.

"Detective," said Ruckels, "am I correct in my understanding that the man was killed, his body was dumped in the river, the floor was washed, and then finally, ten hours later—*ten hours later*—the sheriff was called, not by the defendant, mind you. By her lawyer. That's who she called. Her lawyer. Because that's who you call when you did something bad and know you're in trouble deep."

"Objection," said Guy. "Prosecution is leading by testifying."

"Overruled."

"Okay, then he's bloviating."

"Knock it off, Stillwell. Ruckels, get on with it."

"Yes, sir, Your Honor," the D.A. said. "Detective Hopper, every police report filed in this county crosses my desk. I pay great attention, and it's seldom one gives me a chill of the spine like this one did. With regards to the previous relationship that existed between the deceased and the killer—"

"Objection," said Guy. "Prejudicial, and I can already smell the hearsay."

"I'll allow it," said Talmadge.

"I was told the relationship was of a personal nature," said Hopper.

Sitting directly behind Othella, I saw her backbone go rigid. Guy whispered to her, quietly urging calm.

"In fact," said Ruckels, "according to some neighbors, the victim was the father of Miss Sterling's daughter, wasn't he?"

"Objection!" said Guy.

Ruckels winked at the jury. "Hell hath no fury like a woman scorned, am I right?"

"Objection! This is vile hearsay and lurid speculation." Guy stood with a sweeping gesture. "I want all that stricken from the record."

"Sustained," Talmadge said, and Guy looked momentarily flummoxed.

He looked over his shoulder and mugged. "Oh. You're talking to me?"

"One more crack like that and I'll be talking to you about contempt."

"Apologies, Your Honor. I trust you'll instruct the jury to disregard Mr. Ruckels's statements."

"So ruled," said the judge. It was easy for him to throw Guy that bone in order to make himself appear less biased. The jury could be instructed to disregard, but you can't unring the bell.

Guy sat and patted Othella's hand, but her backbone was still as rigid as a railroad spike. I was glad this was the day Poppy was away taking the bar. A pulse of brotherly love, protective and outraged on her behalf, surged through my heart.

"That SOB," I whispered.

Without turning, Guy raised his index finger. That was enough.

"Your witness," Ruckels said with an affable grin.

Guy stood, his face drawn tight with indecision. Now I understand why, but at the time, I expected him to wheel around and shred Hopper's testimony down to bare rebar, like he always did. I was focused on my father, so I never noticed Hopper's inability to draw a breath. The silence lasted long enough to arouse whispers and foot-shuffling in the gallery.

Judge Talmadge drummed his fingers on the bench in front of him and said, "Defense? Your witness. Move it along."

As Guy flipped through several scrawled pages of a yellow legal pad, I detected an unfamiliar tremor in his hand. Things weren't going well for Othella, and he knew it. Ruckels had crafted a story that played to all the stereotypes and fears that swoop into deliberation when a jury's better angels fly out the window.

Guy leaned forward, palms flat on the table. Othella looked up at him, her face full of uncertainty.

"No questions," he said.

The whispers came together in a collective gasp.

"Witness is excused," said Talmadge.

Hopper left the stand and didn't stop walking. He made a beeline for those double doors at the back of the courtroom, and he was gone for good. We heard later, he went back to his office at the precinct, cleaned out his desk, and scrawled his resignation on the back of a take-out menu from a Chinese restaurant. Twenty-five years later, it all made sense to me, but at the time, I was wondering—along with everyone else in the room—what the hell just happened.

A.D.A. Redstone looked deeply suspicious, whispering urgently to Ruckels until Talmadge pointedly cleared his throat and said, "Prosecution, what's next here?"

"Prosecution rests," Ruckels said.

"Well, all right, then." Talmadge pushed out his lower lip and shrugged. "Defense, call your first witness."

Guy stood and said, "Defense calls District Attorney Borley Ruckels."

And then there was chaos.

– 15 –

I left old man Hopper contemplating his life on the riverbank. Driving along the winding road toward Athens, I cracked out the car phone and called Bootsy.

"Are you calling me on that goddang car phone?" she said. "You sound like you're talking to me from the bottom of a garbage can."

"Do you know if Othella's sister Cornelia is still around?" I asked.

"As I recall, she passed a few years back," said Bootsy. "Breast cancer. I'm afraid Othella's going the same way. Last time Mama and I saw her, she was as thin as onion paper, and I don't know if it was moonshine or pain drugs or both, but she was baked like a powder-milk biscuit."

"Dang. I'm sad to hear that."

"What are you and Tatum up to, asking questions about all that? Mama's very uncomfortable with it."

I felt a rush of relief; Tatum hadn't completely written me off. But Mother had good reason to be uncomfortable, and that worried me. Bootsy went off on something about the paperwork for our parents' impending divorce, and I started looking for a graceful way out of the conversation, but the car phone took care of it for me, cutting Bootsy off midsentence with a blast of static and ending the connection with a bright death-chirp.

Miss Othella's elderly caregiver answered the door, looking harried and happy to see someone from the outside world.

"Well, my stars! Critter Stillwell. What a treat."

"Oh, hello . . ."

"It's Lizzie Mae," she said, sensing that I was having trouble coming up with her name.

"Miss Lizzie Mae. Yes, of course. Nice to see you again."

It took me a moment to recognize her as a lady who used to make the ham biscuits for the law firm's annual holiday brunch. Every year, the Saturday before Christmas, Guy and King hosted an open house, serving Lizzie Mae's renowned ham biscuits with Bloody Marys and bull shots—a potent blend of beef bouillon, vodka, and Worcestershire sauce with celery salt and lime. Everyone did their shopping downtown back then, so they'd park their cars at the law office, stop by the foyer to load up on good cheer, and then weave on down the street with a renewed spirit of giving.

"Come on in, honey. She's here in the sitting room. Othella? *Othella*," Lizzie Mae enunciated, "Critter's here to see you. Lawyer Stillwell's boy, remember?"

Othella didn't look away from the window. Out in the side yard, a pair of mockingbirds chased each other and dive-bombed a portly tabby cat.

"Would you be a pet and sit with her for a few minutes?" said Lizzie Mae. "I just need to run to the post office."

"Of course. No problem."

"Bless your heart." Lizzie Mae dragged a chair over and parked it next to the window. "More than likely, she won't move a muscle till I get back. Poor old thing is pretty much in a state of hypnagogia these days. Can't really tell if she's sleeping or awake."

The moment the door closed behind Lizzie Mae, Othella's shoulders started shaking with laughter that bubbled from her belly and lit up her eyes. I couldn't help but laugh with her until we were both dabbing at our eyes. Just when things started to settle down, she fanned her hands at me and said, "*Hypnogotcha!*" and we sailed off laughing again.

"Don't you look fine today." She slapped my knee, rocking in her wheelchair. "I've missed you."

"I've missed you too, Miss Othella."

"Your sisters come around to see me, but I don't see you."

"I'm sorry." I thought about making excuses, but I wasn't sure how much time we had, and I didn't want to devote any of it to flimsy rationale she'd see through in a second anyway. "Do you know why I'm here?"

"Poppy told me Newt showed up out of the blue, and you're his lawyer."

"That's right."

"She said your daddy run off."

"No, he's just . . . indisposed."

"I know what he is," said Othella, "and I know what you are, so don't try to get around me with your lawyer crap."

"I'm just trying to figure out what happened, Miss Othella. Not just for Newt. I need to know for myself."

"Need to know what?"

"Did Lucky Winfield see that crime scene for himself, or did you feed him the information?"

"I'll tell you the best way to poison a rat," she said. "Mix up a little cornmeal with Ovaltine and baking soda. Rat can't resist that sweet chocolate. He eats it right up. And then he goes off and dies on account of the baking soda in his belly."

"Walk me through it."

"My sister Cornelia—God rest her soul—she was one of the girls at Miss Jeffie's. Mr. Pollard went there every week. All the girls liked him real well. She walked in, ready to do the usual business with him, and there he was. She called me, all in a panic. She was afraid she'd get blamed. Like a flash—like that—" Othella clapped her gnarled hands. "Inspiration come to me, and I told Cornelia, I said, 'Girl, you stay put. Stay quiet. I'll be right over.' By the time I got there, I was thinking about some sweet chocolate powder old Lucky would eat right up."

"The corset."

"Took me and Cornelia some effort to get him out of his pants and into that thing."

"*You* put the corset on him? After he was dead?"

"That was the special sauce." She chuckled softly. "Ol' Lucky, he came into the juke joint Sunday night, like always. Came in to get the protection money and take a few bottles of whatever he wanted, but this time, I had a little something extra for him, and he was all ears for it. Oh, that was a story he enjoyed hearing. I knew he'd get excited and want to hump on me, and that made me sick on my insides, but I knew it would be worth it, so I told him. I told him real good. All the details."

"Details only the killer would know."

"Ol' Lucky, he couldn't wait to get up in the icehouse with the white mens and tell 'em all about it—impress 'em with all the down and dirty information. He had the inside skinny on the big murder story." Othella clapped her hands and crowed. "I figured they'd turn him in faster than you can peel a Vidalia onion, and they surely did."

"After he got arrested and then bailed out, he came back."

"He did." Her smile faded. "He was crazy. Scared. Thrashing like a wounded animal. Said he had to git gone and needed money. Said it was my fault, and he was gonna leave me dead or wishing I was."

"Poppy was there, wasn't she?"

"I was there," Othella whispered, rocking, rocking. "I was there."

"Othella, did he hurt Poppy? Did he rape her? Is that why you killed him?"

I glanced up at the sound of fleet footsteps on the front porch. The door flew open, and Poppy stood there, eyes blazing, as if speaking her name had pulled her in from the heavy, humid air. She pushed a wild curl from her forehead and straightened her skirt.

"Critter," she said. "What a pleasant surprise."

"Hello, Poppy."

"Where's Miss Lizzie Mae?"

"Post office," I said.

I couldn't decide if Othella was playing possum again. She seemed to have retreated into herself, her eyes riveted on the dogwood tree in the yard, the angry mockingbirds, the tabby strutting unimpugned.

"May I speak to you in the kitchen?" said Poppy.

"Sure."

I followed her to the back of the house, where she immediately set to tidying up, shifting spices on the spice rack, banging butter knives and tablespoons from a basket in the sink to a drawer full of flatware.

"I don't want you pestering my mother," she said. "She's an elderly lady. Terminally ill. There's no good reason for you to be poking around here."

"She was happy to see me."

"Oh, really! She was happy to see you. Was she happy to have you grilling her with questions?"

"What makes you think I was *grilling* anybody?"

"Oh, no." She waved her finger. "Don't even waste my time with that."

"What do you expect me to do here? I have a duty to my client. I have a duty to the court. It's my responsibility to make sure the man gets a fair trial."

"Oh, now, I coulda sworn that was *my* job, me being the judge and all."

"Poppy, before this goes any further—Jesus. Help me out here. You know that whole story about Lucky killing Pollard is bullshit. He was framed, which means Newt was framed, and I don't know how to keep you out of it."

"Are you accusing me of something, Lawyer Stillwell?"

"No, I'm just asking—Poppy, please. I'm begging you. Recuse yourself."

"On what grounds?" She folded her arms, jaw set hard. "By law, either I recuse myself on the grounds of financial gain or on the grounds of undue bias. Which one have you decided I'm guilty of?"

"Poppy, if I can't—"

"Counselor," she cut in, "when we are engaged in professional discourse, you'll address me with the deference I have earned."

"I apologize. Your Honor." I took a breath, trying to step back. "Judge Sterling, I must ask you again—"

"It's been asked and answered. I don't intend to recuse myself in this matter. Is there anything else?"

I shook my head.

"Then you should be on your way," she said. "There's an important matter before the court, and you've got a job to do. Lay off the sauce, get your shit together, and prepare your client for trial."

"I will do my job, Your Honor. It's my obligation to provide a vigorous defense, and if that means turning over a few old rocks, so be it."

Her gaze never wavered from mine. "You do what you gotta do. I'll do what I gotta do."

"Okay. Fine. I just hope you know what's at stake."

"What's at *stake*?" she flared. "In the history of this town, I am the first and only black woman to sit on the superior court bench. In the history of my mother's family, I am the first and only woman to go to college. In the history of my father's family, I am among the first generation of people not *owned*—in one way or another—by your family. Do not presume to lecture me about what's at stake, because *frankly, my dear*—"

The old-fashioned phone jangled on the wall, and Poppy answered it brusquely.

"Judge Sterling." She glanced up at me with an odd expression. "Miss Teddi. Hello."

For Christ's sake. I pinched the bridge of my nose.

"Have I seen Critter . . . today, you mean?"

No, I mouthed, shaking my head emphatically.

"As a matter of fact, he's standing right here." Poppy thrust the phone in my face.

"Hey, Mother. What can I do for you?"

"August . . . Critter, honey . . ."

My mother's voice had a frayed edge that told me this was the call I'd been dreading since I was old enough to understand the very idea of dread.

"You need to come to the hospital right away," she said. "It's your daddy."

Before I left by Poppy's kitchen door, I said, "We're not done."

"Go see your daddy," she said. "I'll arrange for a continuance."

When I got to Guy's hospital room, he was intubated but awake. His eyes were yellow and full of fear, but when I took his jaundiced hand, I felt a firm grip returned. Pretty nurses came and went, adjusting the flywheel on his IV, straightening the sheets, and making notes on a clipboard that dangled from a hook on the end of the hospital bed. I looked at the chart and found a few recognizable words among the incomprehensible jottings and figures.

I knew what was happening. I was ten years old the first time I went to the library and looked up *cirrhosis* in a heavy medical tome, and from the moment King went on the wagon, he couldn't stop talking about it. King's situation that summer was straight out of the textbook, same as Guy's condition now.

Circumstances notwithstanding, Mother sat beside him, engaging him in lively conversation. "You know how Bootsy says every time she files for divorce, she gets three proposals of marriage. Well, not to be outdone—"

A truculent grunt emanated from behind the ventilator.

"Oh, no, not Red. Don't worry. No, the first was Peatus Vastapole." Mother laughed and slapped Guy's arm. "Oh, stop! You're always calling names. 'Penis Asshole'—yes, very mature. Well, dear old Penis—*Peatus!* Peatus, I mean to say. See, now you got me doing it. Well, *Peatus*, you recall, owns that chain of convenience stores, which he's now expanded to add video rental places with the adult video rental area in the back. He's in his nineties now and has come to realize that his previous three wives—and I believe you handled all three of those divorces—these little gals were all in their early thirties, and surprise, surprise, they were not eager to dedicate themselves to the sort of eldercare he hopes to receive."

"Mr. Stillwell?" A young doctor beckoned me over to the doorway. "Your mother tells me you have medical power of attorney."

"That's correct."

Mother chattered away like a debutante, distracting Guy as the doctor and I conversed about his case just outside the door.

"Proposal number two," said Mother, "was from Wade Epps, a comparatively spry octogenarian. He's a confirmed bachelor, lifelong, and his mama, Mrs. Minnie Epps—bane of the Athens Centenarians Circle—she would like to see him settled before she shuffles from this mortal coil."

With clinical coolness, succinct without being unkind, the doctor laid out the particulars. Advancing cirrhosis had morphed to primary liver cancer. Alcoholic cardiomyopathy dragged at the rhythm of his stuttering heart. A cascade of strokes and transient ischemic attacks had altered his brain function to an extent that was unknowable, because the ventilator tube down his windpipe made it impossible for him to speak, and the dt's made it impossible for him to hold a pen in his hand.

"What's the treatment plan?" I asked.

"We're looking at palliative care now, Mr. Stillwell. This level of decompensation is irreversible."

"He was in court a few weeks ago," I said. "He was fine."

"Fine?" The doctor looked at me with a sort of bemused sympathy. "It's remarkable how we adapt to these things. His condition probably seemed normal to you. That's what you knew all your life. But, no, he was not fine. He has not been fine for a very long time. I don't offer this as consolation, but statistically, he is at the upper end of life expectancy for an alcoholic."

"He's sixty-three."

Guy groaned.

"My third offer," Mother nattered on to distract him, "was from Lindy Calvin. Bootsy's orthodontist, remember? Lindy took me to lunch and tearfully confessed she's been in love with me ever since we were both involved in the effort to desegregate the municipal swimming pool back in 1964. Well! This was quite a surprise. Miss Lindy invited me to run off with her to some unpronounceable island country where Sapphic marriage has been de rigueur since the days of Queen Isabella. She was as serious as a skull fracture. Had it all worked out."

Guy's shoulders lurched, and his eyes crinkled the way they did when he laughed.

"I gently declined," said Mother, "but that was, without question, the most attractive offer of the three."

I asked the doctor, "What happens now?"

"His liver has failed. His body is trying to shut down. If you sign a DNR directive—do not resuscitate—the next cardiac episode will likely be fatal."

I stood still for a moment, paralyzed in the unsettling focus of Guy's watery gaze. I think I saw him nod. Vivvy says I saw what I needed to see. The doctor proffered a clipboard with a pen tethered to it, and I signed the directive allowing my father to die.

"How long?" I asked.

"A few days," she said. "Maybe a week. We'll keep him as comfortable as possible."

"You should call King," said Mother. "And Mary-Louise."

I agreed, grateful for a reason to leave the room.

"Call Poppy," said Mother.

"Why?"

"For a postponement." Mother hesitated for less than a second before she said it, but I felt a cold breeze down my spine.

I went down the hall and made the calls. Mary-Louise cried quietly and said she would order spiral-cut ham for the funeral and a dozen tenderloins for the after-gathering. King said he'd be over directly and asked me how Mother was holding up.

"She told me to call Poppy," I said. "Can you think of any reason why I should do that?"

"Because your mama said so."

"I need a drink," I said.

"I'll meet you downstairs at the Regent." King tacked on a gruff goodbye and hung up.

From the hallway outside Guy's room, I watched Mother turn off the harsh overhead light and adjust the blinds to allow for the golden light of late afternoon. She lay on the bed next to him, her legs stretched out alongside his, and for a moment, I flashed on an early childhood memory of the two of them in a hammock that was slung between two trees outside a summer cabin in the piney woods of North Georgia.

It came back to me in a rush—the rustic log structure surrounded by dark, fragrant forest—and at the center of this remembrance was the sound of her alto laughter underscored by his teasing growl. The quality of the moment was textured with a sensuality I didn't understand at the time, and now that I did, it made me profoundly uncomfortable.

I stepped away from the door to afford them some privacy.

Leaving my number at the nurses' station, I went out to get some air, knowing I'd end up at the Regent. King was in his usual spot at the end of the bar, finishing up his daily special. When the shapely bartender came to take his plate away, he said, "Hey, Rory, did you hear about the two ladies who got thrown out of Junior League?"

"One had an orgasm, and the other got a job." She bounced an olive off his forehead. "Male chauvinist pig."

King laughed. "Careful, Critter, she's in rare form today."

"Usual?" she said to me.

"Nah, I'm gonna be frugal and get the bottle."

She and King exchanged a glance.

"Sorry to hear about your daddy," she said, without meeting my eye, and then disappeared into the back.

"King, please," I sighed wearily, "don't share my personal business with the bartender."

"I was sharing my own personal business," said King. "I'm about to lose the greatest friend I've had in my life. Because I failed him. Failed to haul him back from the precipice. That's the kind of thing a man can only confide in his bartender."

"Of course," I mumbled. "Sorry."

"Besides, she always asks about you. I told you there's interest."

"Really?"

"Yup. And you could do worse. Gal's smart as a bullwhip, and take a look at those legs."

"Admiring my getaway sticks, are ya?" She set a bottle of Blanton's on the bar, poured the first shot for me, and said, "Proceed with caution."

"Don't worry about it," I said, and it came out sharper than I intended.

King sighed and raised his club soda with lime. "Guy Stillwell. One of a kind. A goddamn rascal, and I love him."

"Hear, hear." I raised a glass to that and added, "You didn't fail him."

I don't know if this toothless assertion was supposed to comfort King or reassure myself, but it didn't do much either way.

"I was sneaking nips out of my daddy's stash by the time I was twelve," said King. "It was something I took to. Your daddy didn't really start drinking till he was most of the way through law school. Trying to fit in, I think."

"What difference does it make now?" I said curtly.

"You tell me."

"I don't want to talk about it."

"I hear ya," said King. "How'd you do on the continuance?"

"Two weeks."

"Got a strategy worked out?"

"No, but I've got it narrowed down to a rock or a hard place."

Proving my client's innocence would require the absolution of Lucky Winfield, a thoroughly execrable human being, which could in turn implicate Othella, Poppy, Mother, and possibly Guy in crimes for which any or all of them could still be prosecuted. I could think of no better strategy than a slow boat to the Bahamas.

"You'll figure it out." King set his hand on my shoulder. "Your daddy always said we could count on you to do the right thing."

As he got up to leave, Rory the Subsequent called from the other end of the bar, "Hey, King, know what they call a lawyer who doesn't lie?"

"Deceased." He grinned and went on his way with his deep belly laugh trailing after him.

I sat at the bar, sipping my whiskey and outlining my opening statement on a yellow legal pad. By closing time, the bottle was two-thirds down, and next to it, there was a growing pile of crumpled pages. I'd been purposely ignoring the object of my affection as she went about her barback duties, preparing to shut the place down.

"Drink up, gentlemen," she called to the room. "Time to call yourself a cab."

She came over to me and lifted a trash can so I could throw away the little heap of drafts and redrafts.

"Productive evening, Lawyer Stillwell?"

"Not terribly," I said. "I'm preparing to try this case in a few days, and I was hoping to talk to you about your master's thesis. The BELL Curve thing."

"Wait. Not the guy on *Unsolved Mysteries*."

"The very one."

"Oh, that takes the whole thing to another level, doesn't it?"

"It does."

"I'm surprised the trial is taking place here in Athens."

"Me too," I said, "but the D.A. didn't ask for a change of venue, and I think it actually works for us. He's got kind of a D. B. Cooper folk hero following."

"It's good for the jurors to see that," she said, "but you don't want any groupies on your jury. They'll trigger the opposing mindset—conservatives who see nonconformity as sin. Paint him as a well-funded Jimmy Buffet. He's a rule-breaker, but he could never really hurt anybody. He slipped the surly bonds of societal expectation and sailed off into the sunset, just like we all secretly wish we could, in the pursuit of Frank Sinatra 'did it my way' self-determination."

"Point of clarification," I said. "How does one actually implement the whole BELL concept?"

"You assign one, two, or three in each category." She wrote the list on a napkin again:

Belief

Education

Laughter

Loyalty

"Go for the twos," she said. "No zealots, no sleepers. You want those open minds in the middle."

"Do it to me so I know how it works. Ask me a question."

"Okay." She tapped her pen on the bar, contemplating. "Have you ever been in love?"

"Yes."

"And . . . how'd that work out for you?"

"Not great, so far, but I figured if I feign interest in this BELL thing—"

"*Oh!* Up yours." She laughed and bounced the wadded napkin off my forehead. "You're worse than King."

The last of the late-stayers drifted out the door while Rory wiped down the taps and the barback bussed the tables.

"Can I call you a cab, Lawyer Stillwell?" Rory asked.

"No, I'm fine."

"Critter, I don't want to overstep, but—"

"Oh. Right. You're right. I'll take the cab. Of course. Thank you."

While she made the call, I took a deep breath or two, girding my loins. She was concerned about me driving. She cared. I found that encouraging, and bottom line, I needed someone that night. *Human comfort*, to put it quaintly.

"Hey, Rory-ish." I tried to make it sound like a term of endearment. "If you don't have other plans tonight, I was hoping we could—"

"Critter." She bit her lip. "Let's keep it casual."

"Is that what we've been doing?" Exasperation got the better of me. I abandoned my circumspect plan in favor of a boneheaded candor dump. "Look, I don't want to overstep either, but I like you. Very much. And I find you very attractive. I thought the feeling was mutual. Please, tell me if I got that wrong."

"You're not wrong."

"Okay. Great. So . . . help me out here." I searched my game brain and found it sadly rusted. "Maybe start by telling me your name."

"Look," she sighed, "you're having a difficult day. I lost my dad. I know what that's like, and I feel for you. I do. So please, don't make me spell it out."

"Spell what out? You won't date a lawyer?"

"I'll date a lawyer," she said. "I won't date a drunk."

"Excuse me?" My face felt hot, as if she'd slapped me.

"I already spent two years of my life with a drunk, and that was too long by about 730 days. I won't say I don't want you, but I'm interested in the authentic Critter, not the liquored-up version. If this version is all that's available, I'll pass."

Those violet eyes drilled into me, and for the first time, I saw how much sadness lay beneath the surface.

"See, Critter, the hard part is . . . when a woman closes in on forty, the talent pool for quality hookup gets pretty shallow. It's more like a talent puddle. When she meets a man who's pleasant to look at, intelligent, good soul—a fella who gives every indication of being great in the sack—oh, Lord! It is tempting to overlook this one little character flaw. She can almost talk herself into the idea that he's a garrulous social drinker and not an asshole who keeps himself just sober enough to conceal a mean streak. She can almost believe he'll be worth it. *Almost*. But not quite."

I took this in, slack-jawed and offended, surprise rapidly hardening to irritation. I tried to sound sober when I assured her, "I am not a drunk."

"You're half in the bag right now, Critter. You come in here drinking almost every day."

"I come in here to see *you*. Okay? Jesus. I didn't know you were sizing me up on your BELL Curve."

"Cry me a river," she scoffed. "We both know what curves you been sizing me up on."

"Wow. I don't even—that's—*wow*."

I stood and chucked the yellow legal pad into my briefcase. I waited for her to look me in the eye again, and when that didn't happen, I felt a sinkhole open up somewhere inside my rib cage.

"Your cab's here," she said.

Outside on the deserted street, the night air was muggy and ripe, and I felt utterly played out. This day was an official cluster all the way around: my client was quite clearly a guilty liar, I was still as baffled by the minds of women as I was when I was fifteen, and for all her academic patois, the bartender didn't know shit about jury selection.

– 16 –

Othella sat at the defense table, calm as the eye of a tropical depression, and Guy stood beside her, one hand on her shoulder. The courtroom was in full disorder with people asking each other, "Can he do that? He can't do that, can he?" But my eyes were fixed on the jury. Uncomfortable glances were exchanged. Postures shifted. Legs crossed and uncrossed.

The jury sees you grasping at straws, Guy had said, *and they know the prosecution's got your dick in a wringer,* but they wouldn't think it from the look on his face. He appeared patient, as if there was nothing out of the ordinary.

Judge Talmadge rapped his gavel, calling for order.

"Mr. Stillwell," he said, "I advise you to proceed with caution."

"Defense calls District Attorney Borley Ruckels," Guy said again.

"I heard you the first time, and I am in no mood for this tomfoolery."

"Your Honor, I know it's somewhat unorthodox, but some new evidence has presented itself, and I believe it has great bearing on this case."

"I move to have this so-called evidence excluded from trial," said Ruckels. "No disclosure. My office has had no time to review and verify these documents."

"The D.A. is, in fact, quite familiar with the documents." Guy held up a file folder in each hand. "I'm prepared to provide copies to yourself and opposing counsel, and I would like this series of documents entered into evidence."

Ruckels seized the offered file and flipped through it, commenting on each of the first few pages. "No. No. *Hell* no. Judge, presentation of these documents would compromise ongoing investigations."

"Ongoing till hell freezes over," said Guy.

"Now you're crossing a line!" Ruckels puffed up, his neck going crimson. "Now you're assailing the integrity of my office, and I will not have it. Your Honor, I demand an apology. I demand a formal—"

"Hang on, hang on," said Talmadge, fumbling with his reading glasses. "Give me a dang minute here."

"Your Honor," said Guy, "as a courtesy, I'd like to give the D.A. the opportunity to testify. No one's better qualified to speak to the nature of these documents while navigating the minefield of sensitive information." He turned to Ruckels. "Unless you'd prefer to have A.D.A. Redstone testify."

"Well, now—now, hold on—" Red stammered. "I'm not—I got no clue what this is about."

"Have a look." Guy tossed the file on the table in front of Redstone, who looked at it like it was dipped in napalm.

"No one from my office will be participating in this high-diving horse trick," declared Ruckels. "No one."

"Your Honor, I believe my opponent has knowledge that is vital to the outcome of this case," said Guy. "He can cooperate with my request or we can have him declared a hostile witness and brought to the stand in handcuffs. I'm more than happy to get a subpoena—if folks don't mind waiting around for an hour or two."

A groan went up from the gallery, and Ruckels turned to the jury box with a conspiratorial wink. "You see that? You see what he's trying to pull here, friends?"

"Hold up there, Ruckelnuts. These are not your friends," said Guy. "This is an impartial jury, impaneled before an unbiased judge. Theoretically."

"Defense, you'll refrain from name-calling and innuendo or I will hold you in contempt," said Talmadge. "Mr. D.A., kindly direct your comments to the bench. Or unkindly. I don't give a damn. I've had it."

Guy and Ruckels both started talking at once, and Talmadge banged the gavel.

"Goddang it! Both of y'all—in my chambers. Right now. Gentlemen of the jury, my apologies. There's a matter we need to take up outside the presence of the jury. You may retire to the jury room for a fifteen-minute recess."

This was a great disappointment to the crowd for whom things were finally getting interesting. As the jury filed out, escorted by the bailiff, folks in the gallery fanned themselves, grumbling and hooting, searching pockets and purses for snacks. Guy patted Othella's shoulder and said, "Hang tight. Tell Critter if you need anything."

As he followed Talmadge and Ruckels to the judge's chambers, she turned to me and smiled. "I don't know what he's up to, but I knew he'd get up to something."

"Do you want me to get you a Coke?"

"No," she said. "I don't want to have to pee."

In the coming and going traffic at the back of the courtroom, we saw Mother and Poppy working their way through the crowd, hurrying to join us, dragging Tatum by both hands between them. When law clerks talked about taking the bar, they always made it sound more arduous than Dante's climb from the ninth circle of Hell, but Poppy looked fresh and undaunted.

"How was it?" I asked. "Was it hard? Did they ask about—"

"Never mind that now." She leaned over the rail to put her arms around Othella. "Mama, how are you holding up?"

"No, *you* never mind!" Othella said, stroking Poppy's face. "Baby girl! Baby girl, you did it!"

"I did it, Mama."

"I'm sorry I wasn't there, baby. We should be having a big party tonight."

"We'll celebrate when you get out of here," said Poppy. "Besides, I don't even know if I passed."

"Oh, you did. I know you did. I know it like I know my middle name."

"You got mail," said Tatum. She handed me a postcard. It was from Bootsy, postmarked Oswego, New York. On the front was an old-timey photograph of Niagara Falls; on the back, Bootsy had written: *Hey, Baby Bruddah.* *"Our plans never turn out as tasty as reality."* ~ *Ram Dass*

"Tell us what's happening," said Mother.

While I brought them up to speed, Mother slipped Othella a Baby Ruth bar, some fresh lipstick, and a compact mirror. I hadn't noticed before that Othella was wearing a yellow-and-pink houndstooth suit I'd seen Mother wear for a bridal luncheon a few weeks earlier. She must have had it tailored to fit Othella, who was smaller by a third.

As the jury filed back into the box, Tatum tugged on my sleeve.

"Can I sit on your lap, Critter? Otherwise I can't see."

"Sure."

I lifted her onto my lap and rested my chin on the crown of her head. Guy and Ruckels returned to their respective seats, and the bailiff announced that court was back in session.

"Gentlemen of the jury," said Talmadge, "I've had a chance to review the evidence, and I am ordering District Attorney Ruckels to take the stand. I have warned defense counsel that he is on an extremely short leash." He arched one bushy eyebrow in Guy's direction. "You hear me, Stillwell? I won't have you turn this thing into a vaudeville show."

"This is ridiculous," Ruckels groused on his way to the witness stand. "A lot of showboating BS, that's all it is."

"We appreciate your cooperation, Mr. District Attorney," said Talmadge. "Now haul your ass up here."

The bailiff proffered a black leather-bound Bible. "Do you solemnly swear to tell the truth, the whole truth, and nothing but the truth, so help you God?"

"I do."

Ruckels took the hot seat, and Guy let him sit there sweating for half a minute before he quietly said, "District Attorney Ruckels, are you familiar with the documents I've just shown you?"

"I wouldn't say I'm *familiar*, no."

"But you've seen them."

"Well, now, I can't rightly recall. I peruse a lot of documentation in the course of my relentless pursuit of justice for the citizens of Athens and the surrounding county."

"Sir, you said earlier in this trial that there was not a police report filed that didn't cross your desk. Are you saying now, under oath, that was an exaggeration?"

"I saw them."

"Yeah, you saw them . . . and saw them and saw them and saw them, didn't you? These reports go back four and a half years. Do you want to explain the nature of the reports to the jury, or shall I?"

"The nature?"

"This area where it says 'Offense Classification'. Would you say these are nuisance complaints? Misdemeanors? Shoplifting? No, these reports pertain to violent, felonious assaults, don't they?" Guy held them up one by one. "Assault battery. Assault with a deadly weapon. Assault. Sexual molestation. Rape. Aggravated assault. Battery and sexual assault. Rape. Sexual assault."

"Objection," said Redstone. "I'm not hearing a question here."

"Sustained. Ask your question, Stillwell."

"Fine! Here's a question for you: *What the hell?*"

"A serious question," said Talmadge.

"I notice every single one of the complaining parties has one thing in common," said Guy. "They're all Negro women. Or Negro girls. And do you notice one thing in common about this box right here? The one where it says 'Assailant'?"

Ruckels locked his arms across his chest, his lower lip pushed forward.

"Mr. District Attorney, would you please read the name in the box where it says 'Assailant'?"

"James A. Winfield."

"The *A* stands for Aloysius, doesn't it? Is that why they call him 'Lucky'? Or did he start to be *Lucky* when he climbed into your hip pocket?"

"Objection," said Redstone.

"Sustained."

"I'll rephrase," said Guy. "District Attorney Ruckels, wasn't Lucky Winfield an informant for your office and for the GBI? Isn't that why you allowed him to skate on a series of sadistic assaults? Because he was useful to you, and the victims were just a bunch of colored folks?"

"Sir, you mischaracterize—"

"It's a yes or no question, sir, and you are under oath."

"I know what I am!"

"So do I," Guy snarled, "and I'm about to make sure the jury knows it, too."

"Objection," said Redstone. "Badgering."

"Sustained," said Talmadge.

"I'll ask again," said Guy. "District Attorney Ruckels, did you knowingly bury a long string of felonious assault reports in order to keep Lucky Winfield out of jail?"

"There were other concerns to be—"

"Is it true—yes or no—that what you call a 'personal relationship' with the defendant was actually a well-documented series of sexual assaults?"

"If we ran a man in every time some woman claims an offense to her honor—"

"YES. OR. NO," Guy bellowed.

Redstone leaped to his feet. "Objection! Badgering!"

"Overruled," said Talmadge. "Witness will answer."

Ruckels looked up at him, startled, betrayed, but he muttered, "Yes."

"No more questions," said Guy.

The courtroom seemed to take a collective breath and then fell strangely silent. Tatum tugged my sleeve again and whispered, "Why is Mama crying?"

I looked over at Mother. Her eyes were shining with tears and focused on Guy's face, full of pride and love and a mix of emotions I wouldn't understand for a good many years. Or maybe ever.

Talmadge asked Redstone if he wanted to cross, but Red wasn't about to touch that with a vaccinated cattle prod. The judge told Guy to call his next witness.

"Defense rests," said Guy.

"All right, then. Closing arguments tomorrow," said Talmadge. "We're adjourned."

Late into the night, I lay listening to the floorboards creak below my bedroom window as Guy paced the front porch, practicing his closing argument. He always worked it out on a yellow legal pad and practiced it like a Shakespearean monologue so he could tread the boards and deliver it on cue without notes. He was out on the porch again first thing in the morning, pacing and muttering quietly.

Getting coffee in the kitchen, I watched Doralee shake up two eggs in a mason jar with milk and sugar. The sound of it sloshing made me feel sick inside. She poured it into a glass tumbler with a stout shot of rye and handed it to me.

"Take this out to your daddy."

"Yes, ma'am." I did as I was told.

"You did a lot of that," Vivvy points out now. "Doing as you were told, I mean." She says she wishes I was still that easy to boss around, but I know she's just playing.

That summer morning was spectacular as most Georgia mornings are—summer, winter, spring, or fall—so I wasn't surprised to see that Mother had let Tatum sleep out on the porch swing. That's how Athens was back then. A five-year-old could sleep out on the porch, and no one blinked twice about it. Guy was out there most of the night anyway. When I handed him the nog, I could see the thready capillaries in the whites of his eyes. He probably hadn't slept more than an hour.

"Mama?" Tatum sat up and rubbed her eyes and called into the open living room window. "Mama, Bootsy's home."

"What?" Mother hurried to the doorway.

"I can hear that funny car," said Tatum. "Like the night she ran off."

Mother gasped and seized Guy's arm. A multicolored VW microbus rolled around the corner and up the driveway, desperately in need of a car wash and muffler repair. The side door opened up, and Bootsy tumbled out, wearing a long, gauzy dress and sandals. She had a greasy headband over her long, stringy hair and a psychedelic sunburst painted on one cheek. The microbus sprouted a dozen arms, all waving out the windows as the vehicle rattled away.

"Hey, baby brother!" Bootsy called as she twirled across the lawn. "Tater Noggins! Come give Sissy a hug."

Tatum scrambled over the porch rail like a squirrel and met Bootsy in the yard. Bootsy swung her around by her skinny little arms and left her giggling, flat on the grass.

"Hey, Mama!" Bootsy danced up the porch steps, into Mother's arms.

"Baby girl, baby girl," Mother said over and over, petting Bootsy's arms and kissing her face.

"Hey, Daddy. Good to see you." Bootsy broke away from Mother's embrace and tried to take his hand, but Guy stood there looking like he was made of stone. Bootsy took the mason jar from him and set it on the side table.

"You don't need this, Daddy. Let me make you a proper breakfast. You know what we've been eating for breakfast in California? Toasted brown bread with avocado slices and an egg over easy right on top of it like a crown. And I've been working all day in the garden and reading Mahatma Gandhi by candlelight at night. And I'm thinking about going to law school. Or maybe getting a master's in poetry. Or going out to this subsistence farm in Vermont."

"If you're coming to court with us," said Mother, "you need to take a bath and wash this hair."

"Oh, yes, a hot bath, please," said Bootsy. "I've been washing up in an ice-cold creek all summer at the commune."

With a deep, hiccuppy breath, Guy pulled Bootsy into his arms. He gripped her against his chest, pressing kisses to her unkempt hair and painted face.

"Okay. Okay." She laughed uncomfortably.

"Don't you ever scare me like this again." He set his hands on her shoulders and shook her gently. "Not ever. Hear me?"

"Yes, sir."

Bootsy linked her arm through Mother's, and they went inside. We could hear their animated chatter as they went up the stairs. Guy cleared his throat and went back to his task, pacing and muttering, but there was a sea change in the way he held himself now—erect and ready, hands clasped behind his back—instead of hunched and weighed down the way he'd been lately.

Bootsy had that effect on him, back then and always.

Right down to the last day of his life.

- 17 -

Every time I entered my father's hospital room, the heart monitor pipped and chittered like a cicada; whenever Bootsy took his hand, the rhythm slowed to a stoic march. Through that last afternoon, I sat in a chair by the window, standing watch like a hollow bronze general on his hollow bronze horse, as family and a few close friends made brief visits. Mary-Louise came and tidied things that couldn't have been tidied any harder. King came and said a gruffly formal farewell, blinking rapidly and blowing his red nose. Poppy came as evening shadows fell. She sat next to the bed and whispered for a long while, her hand cupped against his cheek. A tear rolled back from the side of his eye, and she caught it with a Kleenex before it got to his ear. She squeezed my shoulder briefly as she was leaving, but neither of us said a word.

Mother returned and sat beside me.

"Hungry?" she asked, and I shook my head. "You need dinner. When Bootsy comes back, you should go."

"I'm fine."

"I still haven't been able to reach Tatum. I really should get one of those mobile phones. You just never know when you'll need one. Tatum says someday, a mobile phone will be as small as a deck of cards, and everyone will have one in their pocket. Patently ridiculous, if you ask me. I can't imagine anything more bothersome."

She drifted her fingers across my forehead.

"My beautiful boy. You need a haircut. It's genetic, you know. You got the hair-growth gene from my nana. And you've got my mother's earlobes. Attached, not free. Everything else, though—you are the image of your daddy."

She took a deep breath, and it caught in her throat.

"I'm just gonna run down the hall and try Tatum again," she said and hurried away.

I sat alone with my father in the gathering gloom. You'd like to think a man goes peacefully in his bed, but that's not usually how it is. More than likely, there's clattering and wheezing, as he clutches after every last breath, and that death rattle seems to go on and on. Every raked inhalation feels like death itself.

Bootsy was better with this than I was, so I was relieved when she came back from dinner. As shallow sips of air jangled in and out of him, she sat next to the lowered rail of the hospital bed, holding the back of his hand to her cheek, stroking his wrist, and speaking softly. "It's all right, Daddy. It's all good. Let it go, now. All that's left is love, Daddy. Just love. Just go with it. Nothing else matters."

I didn't realize I was dozing until my head bobbed with a jerk. Bootsy stood beside my chair, her hand on my shoulder. Two nurses bent over Guy, checking and rechecking for vital signs. One said, "Time of death 2:25 a.m.," and the other made the notation on the chart. An orderly arrived, and they cranked the bed flat and straightened the twisted sheet. When they extubated the body, drawing out the long tube, a low groan rose from Guy's throat.

"That's normal," said the nurse. "Just the lungs releasing air."

Bootsy uttered a broken giggle and said, "You just had to have the last word, didn't you, Daddy?"

The nurse and orderly resituated the equipment, draping the tubes and wires on the IV tree before they wheeled the whole works away.

Bootsy said, "I'll call Mama." Before she left, she kissed Guy's cheek, and then she kissed mine. "You okay, baby brother?"

"I'm fine."

I sat there in the void of my father's fresh silence, feeling everything and nothing at the same time. Lightness and leadenness. Bottomless depth and reeling height. Whelming gratitude and bleak, free-falling grief. The ability to breathe—to imagine breathing—left me. I gripped the arms of the chair, my whole body clenched against a sensation that genuinely scared me. I rocked forward and pushed my fist against my mouth in an effort to stifle it, but it was no use. Weeping overtook me like a tide.

I became aware of the metallic shuffle of motorcycle boots on the floor behind me and felt Tatum's wiry arms around my neck. She didn't try to hush or comfort me, just rested her chin on the crown of my head until the passing anguish dissolved, replaced by funereal aplomb and a useful detachment I'd come to depend on.

– *18* –

Guy stood to give his closing argument.

"Gentlemen of the jury," he said, "this has been a difficult week. I thank you for your fortitude and vigilance. That is what troubled times require. Vigilance. Fortitude. You've been confronted with some unpleasant images—crime scene photos, graphic descriptions—and I know you're tired of being here. I've hardly slept a wink this week myself. I'm ready to go home, and I assure you, none of us is as desperate to leave here as the defendant. We have a duty here. A duty to do what's right. Sometimes it's not immediately clear what that means."

Midday sun radiated a sleepy warmth through the courtroom. The wafting of funeral home fans sounded like a low tide lapping at a quiet shore.

"I was moved by the testimony of Lucky's sister," said Guy. "I don't doubt she loved him. And I don't doubt that he loved his mother, but is it really so laudable that he took her to church every Sunday? I don't know a Southern boy who doesn't love his mama, and I know a whole lotta people who use church the way a drunk uses a lamppost—more for support than illumination."

He got a good laugh from the jury and admitted borrowing from Mark Twain before he went on.

"That family has heard some ugly things about their boy. Must be heartbreaking. They'll now face a reckoning about their role in his wrongdoings, even if all they ever did was stay silent and let it continue. Unless they simply choose not to believe it. When it comes to the people we love, we tend to create the reality we need. We choose to see things in whatever way makes us most comfortable. A way we can live with. But you don't have that luxury when you go back to that jury room. You don't get to turn away from the ugliness, the violence, the depravity of this man's choices, just because you find it disturbing. You don't get to ignore the callous indifference of our own district attorney, who prioritized the power and the glory of his office over the well-being of the citizens who pay his salary. That's what these women are, lest we forget. They are tax-paying, law-abiding citizens of this county. They deserved better.

"The Lord might chide me for lack of charity, but I'll say it again. The man needed killing, as surely as the mad dog that gets put down by Atticus Finch in *To Kill a Mockingbird*, and given no other option—with her survival depending on it—Othella Sterling killed him. That is not murder, gentlemen of the jury; that is *self-defense*, and this woman has the legal right to defend herself same as you or me. She had the right to defend herself that night from a man attempting to cause her grievous bodily harm, and she has the right to defend herself now from the complicit law enforcement agency that seeks to use you as a murder weapon. They won't dirty their hands on the rope. No, they leave it to you to put her in the chair and throw the switch."

Guy paused and sat on the edge of the defense table. I could tell he was trying to get a read on the jury. They seemed a bit sleepy. Before Guy ever got on his feet, the court had agonized through the prosecutor's closing argument, which was long and pedantic. Guy had whispered to me that Ruckels was running the clock, making it so that Guy's closing would be late in the day and deliberations would be rushed because people wouldn't want to come back again tomorrow.

"*To Kill a Mockingbird*—that's the big movie this summer," said Guy. "Everybody loves that movie. Hard to go wrong with Gregory Peck. Now, I don't want to ruin it for anybody. Who all's seen it?"

Everyone on the jury and most of the folks in the courtroom raised a hand.

"Ah! Good. If you haven't seen it, stick your thumbs in your ears. I'm gonna be the contrarian. I didn't like it on several levels. At the end of *To Kill a Mockingbird,* having been served up a preponderance of compelling evidence proving the innocence of Tom Robinson and not one jot of physical evidence to the contrary, the jurors proceed to find the man guilty, simply because he is a black man and the woman accusing him is white. And then they go on to make sure that the movie ends with Tom Robinson gunned down by law enforcement for no damn reason. That's a pretty cynical view of Southern justice. It's painful to think about ourselves in that light, but then a case like this comes along, and it's impossible to deny—things happened that should not have happened, and people got away with it because the people being harmed are not white. Somehow justice for these folks came a distant second to justice in the matter of a car theft operation—what they call a chop shop—about which Lucky was providing information.

"Lucky Winfield was a sadistic rapist, enabled by morally corrupt law enforcement. Great harm was done, and you can't undo it, but you don't have to make it worse. There's a thirteenth juror with you back in that jury room where you'll deliberate and arrive at a verdict. That thirteenth juror is *zeitgeist*—the sum total of who we are as a society in this moment. You can't help but carry it with you. Sometimes it argues for vengeance. Sometimes it speaks for compassion. Sometimes it is shackled to old ideas of prejudice and bigotry, and right now—at this moment in history—it's urging us to evolve, to become a better, more just society, appealing to the enlightened conscience of us all.

"I do believe that is the goal of Miss Harper Lee in writing her book, *To Kill a Mockingbird.* I just wish she'd given old Atticus a better closing argument. He comes out mewling and pleading, 'Gentlemen of the jury, in the name of God, do your duty!' Well, of course, they return the outrageously unjust verdict—guilty as charged—because that is the Hollywood notion of who we are as Southerners. We are Southerners and therefore small of mind. We say *y'all* and *meemaw* and *fixin'* to go to *church*—therefore we must be ignorant and ignoble of spirit. The gospel according to Gregory Peck. That's what New Yorkers choose to believe so they can sleep at night. The plight of the Negro in modern society—oh, that's all on the crackers and Dixiecrats south of the Mason-Dixon Line. That's not on the sophisticated Northerners. Heavens, no. But the fact is, someday, somehow, there will be a reckoning for wrongs that have been done from sea to shining sea, and every one of us will be forced to examine our role in the history of it all.

"I want to tell you something about the criminal trial in *To Kill a Mockingbird*—the case Miss Harper Lee wrote about in her book—that's not fiction. She based it on a case that happened in true life, down in Alabama, and in the true-life chain of events, the real-life jury returned a just and wise verdict: *not guilty*. They ruled with the hearts and minds of true Southerners—not some ignorant Hollywood caricature—genuine Southern people with authentic Southern values: decency, intelligence, literacy.

"Do not tell me, Mr. Hollywood Movie Man and Miss New York Book Editor, that a Southern jury is incapable of such qualities, for I have seen it in this very courtroom, time and time again. I've seen the good people of Georgia set aside their personal bias and simply *do the right thing*. Jurors impaneled to execute a sacred duty—people of moral courage—these are the Southern juries I know. True Southern jurors sit before me today. I know you. I believe in you. I trust you to do the right thing—not deliver the cynical cracker verdict Hollywood wants to put in your mouth. I trust you to come back with a just and fair verdict: *not guilty.*"

– 19 –

Guy Stillwell's send-off was one for the history books, the social event of the year, attended by anybody who was anybody and anybody who was nobody and everybody in between. Winfrey's Mutual Funeral Home outdid themselves in Southern style. Guy had repped them on several occasions for free, as they were an excellent source of client referrals—plenty of lawyering needed in the milieu of the dead and dying—so they stepped up now, pulling out all the stops and refusing to accept a penny from the family. It was somehow fitting that a black funeral home provided this service, which was a social taboo for a white decedent—then and now. Down South, white funerals tend to be rather constipated affairs with organ music piped from the balcony and muted sobs muffled in lace hankies. Black funerals are earthy and loud, filled with visceral mourning and boisterous memory.

"Black funerals are more fun," Guy always said. "More about life than death." So this suited him.

The church service took place at St. Gregory the Great Episcopal Church, where Guy regularly scandalized the old ladies by loudly describing himself as a "devout Whiskeypalian" and showing up Sunday mornings with Saturday night still on his breath. The church as a community accepted him as he was and pressed him into service as a Sunday school teacher for two decades. It was a nice place for a funeral. We walked the last half mile to the gravesite at Oconee Hills Cemetery, following a brass quintet that played a mournful dirge on the way there and joyful cakewalk music for us to walk away with after he was laid in earth.

Back at the house, Mother exercised an Elizabethan authority over the reception, commanding a battalion of caterers, bartenders, dishwashers, and waitstaff serving Doralee's fried chicken and tenderloin beef tips with funeral squash and all the fixings to about three hundred people. I made the rounds, visiting knots of conversation huddled here and there in the house and scattered across the yard, people sharing tales of Guy's exploits, talking politics, and asking after Doralee's old family recipes. I moved among them as if I was passing through the disparate eras of my own life and the lives of my loved ones.

Mother and Red Redstone talked politics with their contemporaries in the dining room. There was little talk about Red's current campaign, which had taken up most of the oxygen at the table lately. Instead, they overviewed the wins and losses and watershed events of Guy's lifelong involvement in the GOP.

"He was born early," said Red. "Republicans are on the rise now. You watch. Bush'll get in there on Reagan's coattails this fall. If we can get past the Democrat gerrymandering, we'll dominate the House and start stacking the federal benches the way they ought to be."

"Trouble is," said Mother, "you can't tell who's who anymore. They say the northern Democrats are progressive, but you wouldn't know it by the way they all rolled over for Strom Thurmond and his lot down here. Back in the 1960s, when Guy ran for Congress, all the rednecks and Holy Rollers were dead set against the Republicans—the progressives in favor of integration and social justice. Democrats were the segregationist party of the Old South, putting up Confederate monuments and colored water fountains, fussing about miscegenation of the races. Now it seems like Jerry Falwell and the Southern Baptist Convention are running the GOP, and I don't like the words out of their mouths. They're taking the party backward, and those of us with the sense to see it are getting pushed aside."

"Theodora," said Red, "you can't be thinking about voting for Dukakis."

"Good Lord, no," said Mother. "But Poppy's talking about running for legislature as a Democrat next term, and I've decided to be independent so I can vote for her and a few other Democrats down ticket."

"Woman!" Red clutched his chest. "You're killin' me."

"We all want the same thing," she said. "Normalized acceptance of black and white. Some want to go too fast. Others want to go too slow. Politics is the art of compromise."

"I miss the friendlier days of backdoor dealing," said Red. "How the hell are we supposed to get anything done when it's all out there on cable TV?"

Mother laughed and consoled him with a hand on his knee. She would marry him, I was certain. It was inevitable. Bootsy would organize some small, impeccable event, and I'd have to sit on a daintily slip-covered chair in some charming venue, pondering the warped reality of Red Redstone as my stepfather. Propriety demanded that they wait some period of months, but in truth, Mother was widowed a long time ago; I just refused to see it.

There was a good crowd downstairs in the rec room where Doc and Doralee used to dance to James Brown, Sam Cooke, and Otis Redding records and tell off-color jokes. As I made my way through the throng and received condolences from the owner of Gresham Body Shop—another great source of client referrals springing from the twisted business of people crashing into one another—I was surprised to see Rory of the Regent behind the bar.

She nodded. "Lawyer Stillwell."

"Hello," I said. "What are you doing here?"

"Doing what I do." She made an expansive gesture toward the teeming bar. "I moonlight special events for the catering company. Our signature cocktail in honor of this occasion is the Tequila Mockingbird. Can I get you one?"

"Club soda with lime."

"Critter," she said, "I apologize for speaking out of turn. Please, don't feel like you can't have a drink on my account."

"I don't. I'm just trying to lose a few pounds."

I didn't want her to think I was kowtowing to score points with her. I wanted her to know that I march to the beat of my own drummer and don't take that kind of shit off anybody, if I think it's not right, and I wasn't saying she was right, but I was man enough to acknowledge the possibility that she wasn't completely wrong, while reserving the right to set her straight without hesitation.

She set up the club soda. "I'm truly sorry for your loss."

"Thank you," I said, drowning in the violet ocean of her eyes.

"Critter, you asshole! There you are." A hand clapped onto my shoulder, and an old law school buddy steered me away from the bar, toward the pandemonium outside the wide-open patio doors. "Get out here and settle a bet between me and Mchlman. I'm arguing Pierson versus Post as a matter of precedent in a case between the estates of two cranky old fart neighbors who shot each other in the stomach . . ."

On a plywood stage, the band cranked up a lively rendition of Cab Calloway's "Jumpin' Jive," and from there, it was a good old Southern throwdown, just like Guy would have wanted. I followed the music to a mosh pit of lawyers and judges and court reporters congregating around a pyramid of beer kegs down by the creek. The old folks drifted off with the dusk, leaving sturdier legs to dance and drink under the stars. Sometime after midnight, somebody called the cops. The responding officer, a young fella who clearly didn't know Guy, made his way through the crowd to find me.

"Mr. Stillwell?"

"He's dead," I said, "but his spirit lives on. Am I right?"

A cheer went up. Everybody drank to that.

"Your mom said I should talk to you."

"Start talkin."

"Your neighbor called about the noise."

"We're paying our respects to my father. The night is young, and I don't think it's all that loud, so . . ." I shrugged. "That's how it is. The neighbors are welcome to join us."

"I'm sorry for your loss, Mr. Stillwell, but we need you to unplug the band. Noise ordinance violation."

"What's that? Can't hear ya over the music."

"Very funny, but it's too loud, sir."

"Says who?"

"Says me."

"And you are . . ."

"Deputy DuVernay."

He hooked his thumbs on his belt, sensing what was coming. He looked so fresh-faced and innocent, I couldn't resist.

"Okay, well, 'too loud'—that's a subjective term, Deputy DuVernay. Exactly what qualifies you to judge the ratio of existent volume relative to legal ordinance? Under what criteria? Decibels per square acre? What sort of instrumentation are you using to quantify this alleged loudness, and how recently has the relevant instrumentation been calibrated?"

"It's within my discretion," said the young officer. "I've determined that you are in violation of the law, and now you're compounding the problem with obstruction, resisting an officer, and displaying a generally shitty attitude."

"Whooooooah!" The assembly roared like they were watching Sunday night wrestling.

"Fine," I said. "Write out a citation, and I'll see you in court. If you're right, I'll pay the fine. If I'm right, I'll walk out with my head held high. Either way, you can pound sand up your ass."

"Dude, I'm sorry your dad died, but that doesn't give you the right to disturb the peace. Now, we can do this the easy way or the hard way—"

"Again—easy, hard—totally subjective. What does that even mean?"

"It means turn off the golldang music or I'll take you downtown and book you into the county jail with your murderer pal."

"What?"

"You heard me."

"You got some kinda beef with my client, Officer?"

"Turn around, Mr. Stillwell. Hands behind your back."

"Booooo!" the crowd around us hooted and jeered, but I assumed the position.

"That's okay, folks. That's all right," I said. "Deputy DuVernay is gonna do what he has to do, and I'm gonna do what I have to do. Somebody follow me over to the jail and post bond, if you would, please."

"Right behind you," King assured me. "Nobody else is sober enough to drive."

DuVernay slapped the cuffs on me, and the band struck up "Jailhouse Rock" as he led me away. I bonded out and was back at the party in less than an hour, and less than an hour after that, DuVernay showed up to arrest me a second time, but by then, it was almost three in the morning. DuVernay decided to be punitive about it and said he was going to tell the jailer to hold me overnight.

"Fine with me." I opened my arms to the assembled family and friends and said, "Y'all stay here and drink up. Meet me at the hearing tomorrow, and we'll keep this soiree rockin' all weekend. How 'bout it?"

"Yeah!" The enthusiastic response rang up through the trees.

As the deputy led me across the yard, Bootsy followed, scolding, "Critter, is this truly necessary? Poor Mama is emotionally and physically spent."

"See you at the arraignment, Boots. Tell Mother I'll write her every day from the chain gang."

"August," she said gently, "I miss him, too."

"Then let me do this my own way."

She ruffled my hair. In the flash of the red-and-blue lights, I saw tears in her eyes.

"Hold up," Tatum called, charging across the yard. "Officer, may I please give my big brother a hug before you take him to the big house?"

DuVernay rolled his eyes and stepped aside. Hands cuffed behind my back, I leaned down to nuzzle Tatum's cheek, and she whispered in my ear, "Tell Newt you know about Bari."

"What?"

"Just tell him." She glanced over her shoulder at DuVernay. "Be careful."

He reinstalled me in the back of the patrol car. Before he shut the door between us, Tatum said, "I'll send Mary-Louise with the Contempt Kit."

"You're a good man, sister."

When we reached the holding cells on the fourth floor of the court-house, DuVernay rolled the iron door open and shut with a decisive clang, startling Newt from a sound sleep in the neighboring cell, where he was being held for his impending court appearance. I'd met with Newt several times since he was apprehended, and he was in surpris-ingly good spirits, even after a few weeks in captivity. He sat up on his cot, looking as tan and relaxed as he did the day I first saw him aboard the *Rascal*.

"Five minutes," said DuVernay. "Then it's lights out."

"Thanks, Officer. See you at the arraignment."

"Arraignment?" said Newt. "What in hell? I thought you were at your daddy's funeral."

"I was."

He laughed, long and hearty. "Like Guy always said, it ain't a party till somebody gets arrested."

I shucked out of my funeral clothes and folded them as neatly as possible on the end of the cot, just in case Tatum couldn't get past the gatekeepers with the Contempt Kit, which Mary-Louise always kept handy just in case Guy got thrown in jail for contempt. The kit con-tained fresh underwear and socks, a crisply pressed shirt and pants with a coordinating necktie, plus a shaving kit—everything he needed so he could show up for court looking like a lawyer instead of a reprobate—packed neatly into his spare briefcase.

I stretched out on the cot in my boxers. The lights winked out, leaving only the ambient glow of streetlights outside the wire-meshed windows.

"Sure wish I could have been there today," Newt said.

"A lot of folks asked about you."

"I'll bet." There was a cynical edge, but it softened, and he said, "I've been hearing from a lot of old friends. Didn't even know how much I'd missed the old stomping grounds. I even got a kick out of seeing Red Redstone at the arraignment, inflated like a hot air balloon."

"Some things never change."

"Truth." Newt sighed in the echoing gloom of the cellblock. "When you called to tell me your daddy had passed, I got thinking about all those departed. Ones who died in Italy during the war. And then Korea took their sons. And I'll go ahead and say it—Pollard, too. It's a damn shame he had to go like that. The man pissed me off sometimes, but he was a proud son of the South and good to his family."

"I haven't been able to put it together," I said. "Why would somebody want Pollard dead?"

"Beats me. Politics get rough, but not like that. He was a successful businessman. War veteran. Church deacon. Klan member. Just a regular fella."

"Why do you suppose Lucky pointed the finger at you?"

"You know. To get out from under it. To—to cut the plea deal."

"But why *you*, in particular?"

"Why is the moon made of green cheese?" Newt said. "It was bullshit. That's all. Maybe he resented me for coming from money. Maybe he didn't like the way he was treated down at the warehouse."

"And yet, his first call was to Guy, who was also wealthy and also his boss at the warehouse."

"Yeah, go figure. Fella like Lucky gets arrested for murder, and his first call is to the only lawyer in town lowbrow enough to slum with the white trash and coloreds. There's a shocker." Newt shifted on his cot. "No offense."

"None taken."

"Jesus, I wish your daddy was here," said Newt.

"Me, too."

"I didn't mean to speak ill of the dead. I just don't care for the implication you're driving at."

"What implication is that?"

I lay in the dark, hands locked behind my head, allowing the kind of silence that sits there like the black keys between the white.

Newt said, "I could do with another box of the Swisher Sweets."

"I'll bring you some."

"I appreciate your efforts," he said. "The, um . . . the situation may be a bit more complicated than I said."

"Did someone tell Lucky to implicate you? Did someone have some sort of ax to grind?"

"There were a few people."

"The DiLippas?"

"Yes," said Newt, "but not for the reasons you might think."

"Did it have anything to do with the beer distributorship?"

"No! No. Hell, no. Guy wouldn't stand for that."

"Newt, don't make me be an archaeologist here. Whatever it is, we'll work with it, but I need the *truth*. If I don't have the facts, I go into that courtroom, bare ass exposed, and get blindsided."

Don't ask a question, Guy used to say, *unless you already know the answer—or you're sure you want to know it*. I wasn't sure, but I trusted Tatum.

"I know about Bari," I said.

Newt took in a sharp breath. "You been talking to the FBI."

"I'd like to hear your side of the story."

"Understand, Critter, I didn't know what I was getting into."

"Of course not."

"Old man DiLippa—he's a family man to the bone," said Newt. "He heard through the grapevine that I was stationed over in Italy, and he saw an opportunity. He reached out to my mama and arranged for me to meet Fernanda. She was introduced to me as his niece. I didn't know until later, she's his daughter—on the outside. Illegitimate. But he loved her and felt an obligation. He wanted her to marry a wealthy American and get out of Italy, because anybody who'd been pro-Mussolini, of course, they were well and truly fucked the minute that mob strung him up."

"Sure."

"Anyhoo. I went up to Bari to meet her, and I tell you what—this girl was eighteen years old with piston hips and Cadillac headlights. I was like a fly in a spider web. Before I knew what hit me, her uncles had me up in front of a priest, swearing to love, honor, and suck it up till death do us part."

"So you married a fascist mafia princess," I said. "What could possibly go wrong?"

"I'll tell you, brother, the minute we walked into the family manse, she changed. It was like pulling the rip cord on an inflatable raft. This woman has a fiendish temper. She can drink twelve men under the table. Arm-wrestles like a longshoreman. And she is a bona fide nymphomaniac. I'd have got more sleep in a crate full of weasels. I tried to divorce her, but she's Catholic and wouldn't go along with it. I finally told her, 'It's over. I'm leaving.' Before I got twelve miles down the road, DiLippa's goons roll up on either side of my car and force me into a drainage ditch. He made it very clear that if his daughter was not a happily married wife, she was gonna be a financially comfortable widow. He advised me to make the best of it, so that's what I did. For eighteen long years. Always watching and waiting for an opportunity to get out."

"Are we closing in on the part where Lucky frames you for murder?"

Newt chuckled softly. "Here's where the strategy comes in."

"Lay it on me."

"Lucky didn't frame me for murder," Newt said. "I did."

"You framed . . . *yourself*." I sat up on my cot, the whole caper falling into place in my head.

"I started thinking like DiLippa," said Newt. "When they picked up Lucky for the hit on Pollard, I saw a unique opportunity all around: Lucky confesses to the murder, swears I paid him to do it, I throw in a little supporting evidence, and it's case closed. DiLippa's off the hook for ordering the hit. And in return . . ."

"You're off the hook with his daughter."

"Free at last, free at last." Newt raised his grateful voice toward Heaven.

"But what was in it for Lucky?" I said. "Why confess to a murder he didn't do?"

"Who says he didn't do it?"

"Did he?"

"What difference does it make?" said Newt. "He was a no-good, swamp-crawling shit-heel of a human being who shoulda been in jail for any number of reasons. Plus he'd revealed himself as someone who couldn't keep his mouth shut. This was his one chance to sit on a prison cot, jerking off for ten years, instead of disappearing down a dry well on some Dixie Mafia horse farm. You better believe he jumped at it."

"The plea deal," I said. "Ruckels was in on it?"

"He'd been running interference for DiLippa since Prohibition days, but he wouldn't have been able to let this one go. Pollard was a goddamn pillar of the community, not some piece of trash you could sweep under the rug."

"Like Lucky."

"Hey, that's not on me," Newt protested. "All I did was leverage the situation. Somebody else set him up for the murder."

"I know."

I lay there for a while, trying to build out the timeline in my head. I searched my memory and realized that I was not in Athens the day after Lucky's arraignment. Guy had sent me to Fort Valley with King.

"Walk me through it," I said. "They pick Lucky up for the murder. You and DiLippa come up with the plan. Ruckels and Tick post bond."

"You got the idea," said Newt. "Guy drew up the divorce papers, and I put two million dollars in an offshore account. Only way Fernanda could get the money was to sign on the dotted line. They were supposed to sit on him for forty-eight hours. Long enough for me to get to Costa Rica."

"And then what?"

"That dumbass ran off and got himself killed. I didn't even know he was dead when I left. I read about it in the *Atlanta Constitution* three weeks later, sitting in a bar on the beach in Tamarindo."

"They just happened to have the Atlanta paper? At a bar in Tamarindo?"

Newt said nothing.

"Guy knew where you were the whole time."

"Not the *whole* time."

"What then? Most of the time? Some of the time?"

"Part of the time," Newt conceded. "Look, he's been a good friend to me. You can't condemn a man for being a good friend."

"So I've heard."

"Look, if things don't go our way next week, I'll help you find a buyer for *Rascal*. I won't let you get screwed on this whole deal."

"I appreciate that," I said, "but I was actually thinking about keeping her. Is she fit to cruise? Mechanically, I mean."

"She's been having some engine trouble, but once you get her started, you're good," said Newt. "I'd avoid Trinidad, if I were you. Those Venezuelan pirates seem to think they're owed some money."

In the morning, Tatum arrived with the Contempt Kit. When she handed it to me, I read the question in her eyes, and I nodded with a furtive glance toward Newt.

"See you down there," she said.

"Thanks, Tate."

Since every judge in Athens had been at Guy's funeral wake and had to recuse him- or herself, an elderly part-time municipal judge agreed to come over from a neighboring town.

"His name is Bogus," said Mary-Louise when I took my place at the defense table. "I know you'll have a hard time staying off that, but for your mama's sake, would you please try?"

"Yes, ma'am."

The courtroom was packed to the rafters with partygoers, some who looked like death warmed over, having woke up with their regrets, and others who were still rolling with it from the night before. Half the folks in the gallery wore Free Critter! T-shirts. Others waved signs: Amicus Critter or Run Critter Run! Members of the offending band were at the back of the room, still drunk and egging everyone on.

When the bailiff called *State of Georgia v. August Stillwell III*, Redstone's greenhorn A.D.A. spoke up for the prosecution, because Red was also at the party, and I said, "August Stillwell III here, and I'll be defending myself."

"Well, your client sounds like an ass," said Bogus. "Somebody explain to me how this isn't a waste of my time."

I piped up, "I'm in complete agreement with you on that, Your Honor—the second part, that is. It's a shameful waste of the court's time and resources. The noise ordinance cited in the complaint is unconstitutionally vague and utterly unenforceable. I move for immediate dismissal. If I learned anything from my father, it's that you have to challenge authority now and then. You can't just accept things as they're presented to you. If a city ordinance is instituted improperly and does not fulfill the requirements of the law, it's our duty as citizens to stand and challenge it, lest we deliver ourselves and posterity to a Kafkaesque nightmare of sloppy legislation and kangaroo authoritarianism."

"Oh, for Christ's sake." Bogus rubbed his forehead. "Somebody help me out here."

"Your Honor," said the A.D.A., "District Attorney Redstone would like to speak as a friend of the court."

I started to object, but Red said, "Shut your yap, boy. I'm trying to help you."

"Proceed," said Bogus.

"Your Honor, the state takes no pleasure in prosecuting Mr. Stillwell, as his grieving mother needs him at home and would like to settle this unpleasantness without further ado. Now, I've spoken with the complainants, and they've agreed to retreat to a spa in Buckhead for the rest of the weekend—at Mr. Stillwell's expense—so the festivities might continue."

"At my expense?" I piped up. "Why should I pay for—"

"Don't be such a goddang skinflint," said Red. "Boy, you'll squeeze a nickel flatter than a dime. Meanwhile, your mama is the sweetest, most generous lady I ever knew, and Guy Stillwell—he never begrudged a helping hand to friend or foe. The man vexed the fool out of me on many an occasion, but he was a gentleman and a lawyer of the old school. His passing marks the end of an era."

Red seemed genuinely choked up. It wasn't just histrionics.

"I know the Young Turks around here scoff at the way we used to do things," he said. "Just the other day, my new A.D.A. here took me to task over the old custom of awarding the murder weapon as a trophy to the defense attorney when he got an acquittal. I know, I know—it wouldn't be right these days, what with DNA and all the technological claptrap that's coming in, but back then, it was a sign of respect for the most dearly held principle of law and order—that every defendant is entitled to a vigorous, well-orchestrated defense.

"Guy Stillwell was hard to beat, and that's as it should be. It was an honor to go up against him. He held our feet to the fire and demanded that we rise to the highest standards of justice. But he knew when to hold 'em and knew when to fold 'em. He was always willing to make a deal in the interest of the greater good, Critter, so you know it is in the spirit of justice, as a salute to Guy Stillwell, that I propose this compromise, and if it is agreeable to all parties, I'll move that charges be dismissed."

I swallowed the lump in my throat and said, "Defense agrees to settle as stipulated."

A cheer went up from the courtroom, and folks were cakewalking out the double doors before Bogus brought the gavel down. I crossed the aisle to shake Red's hand, and then I leaned over the rail to hug Mother and my sisters.

"It was a fitting send-off for him," said Mary-Louise. She threw her arms around me, tearful and still tipsy, and over her shoulder, I happened to see Poppy still sitting at the end of the front row. Something about the expression on her face—or maybe Red's mention of the trophy case—suddenly dovetailed with a distant memory. I thought of that moment when I squeezed her hand, and she flinched away. Back then, as a kid, I assumed it was her stubborn pride. But now I knew it wasn't.

It was pain.

– 20 –

The jury deliberating Othella's fate remained cloistered until late into the evening, and then we got word that they were being sequestered at a local motel. The next day, we waited all morning at the law office, making perfunctory efforts at paperwork. At noon, Mother and Doralee brought her the usual offering of chicken, biscuits, and coleslaw.

"Y'all three should go over and have lunch with Othella," said Mother. "She must be climbing the walls right now."

On the way over there, Poppy fiddled with her watch and said, "Almost nine hours."

"That's fine," said Guy. "If the jury comes back quickly, it's usually with a guilty verdict. That's the easy call. We know we got them thinking about it."

Poppy took a deep breath before she told Guy, "I know you did your best, and I thank you. But if they come back with a guilty verdict, I'm going to go to Mr. Ruckels and tell him I did it."

"None of that foolishness," said Guy. "You know how it works. If they come back with a guilty verdict, we'll appeal. Keep your lawyer hat on. I need you to be on deck and thinking straight until King gets back. After that—who knows? He might not be worth a damn when he's sober. As soon as you get word that you've passed the bar, you'll be ready to roll on cases, and King and I would be proud to have you, if you'll have us."

"I appreciate the offer," said Poppy.

"But you've had others?"

"Houston, Baton Rouge, Atlanta—but nobody else in Athens."

"Well, I don't see a piano tied to your ass," Guy said gruffly. "No reason you can't move on to the big city if you so choose."

Mother was right about Othella. When they brought her to the inmate visiting room on the fourth floor of the courthouse, she looked gaunt and exhausted. Poppy fixed her a plate, and opened a bottle of Coke for her, but both sat untouched on the table.

"Take heart, Othella," said Guy. "I think they'll come back before the end of the day with the verdict we're hoping for."

"And then what?" said Othella.

"Then it's over. Critter drives you home. You're free."

"Is that what you call it?"

"Othella . . ."

"I'm black. I'm a female. If I step out of line on somebody, I get slapped down. If somebody steps out of line on me, the law don't give a shit. I wonder where Lucky Winfield would be right now if he'd killed me. They'd've sent him to prison for offing a white man, but if he'd killed me—" She shrugged and snapped her fingers. "Nuthin' to see here. Move along, folks."

"Let's wait and see what the jury has to say about it," said Guy.

"Either way, I'm grateful for everything you've done."

"It ain't over till it's over." He sounded hopeful, but there was a slight tremor in his hand when he tipped his silver flask to drink.

"I don't mean to talk out of turn," said Othella, "but I've made a living running booze most of my life. This puts me in the company of those that imbibe on the regular. There's those that enjoy it. And those that need it. And those that use it as a crutch. I wonder lately which crowd you're running with."

"That's not your worry."

"No," she said, "but you made an effort to save my life. I'd feel wrong if I didn't return the favor."

There was a quick knock on the door, and the jailer poked his head in to say, "Jury's back."

Guy thanked him and said, "Poppy, help your mama get her things. Hopefully, she won't be coming back. Critter, go call your mother. She'll want to be here. Call Mary-Louise and tell her I might be spending the night in jail."

Poppy put her arms around her mother and said, "It'll be okay, Mama. I'll make it be okay."

Downstairs in the courtroom half an hour later, Talmadge took his seat at the bench, and the bailiff called, "Order in the court."

"Has the jury reached a verdict?" said Judge Talmadge.

The foreman produced a folded sheet of paper. "We have."

"Let's have a look." The judge beckoned to the bailiff, who brought him the paper. The judge looked at it, stone-faced, handed it back to the bailiff, and said, "Principals and jury members, please stand."

Guy stood and offered his arm to Othella, who stood beside him, trembling. Sitting beside me in the front row, Poppy folded her hands in her lap, collected and resolute. The gallery was as silent as that airless moment between lightning and thunder.

The judge nodded to the foreman. "Go on and read it."

"In the case of the State of Georgia versus Othella Sterling, on a charge of murder in the second degree, we, the jury, find the defendant not guilty."

Poppy uttered a small, involuntary cry. She leaned forward, clutching her skirt in her fists, and hid her face. I saw Othella's grip tighten on Guy's arm, but neither of them moved as reaction rushed forward from the courtroom. Angry shouts from the good ol' boys at the back. Murmurs of shock and dismay from some of the white people on the main floor. Jubilant cries and tearful celebration from Othella's friends and neighbors in the upper gallery.

"All right, now. Settle down." Talmadge banged the gavel and spoke above the din. "Gentlemen of the jury, we thank you for your service. You are hereby dismissed. Court is adjourned, and the defendant is free to go."

Poppy scrambled over the railing—starchy dress be damned—to get her arms around her mama. Othella crumpled into her chair, covering her face with her hands, rocking forward and back, saying over and over, "Thank you, Jesus, thank you, Jesus, thank you, Jesus . . ."

"I'd like to know where this Jesus fella went to law school," Guy said wryly. "He seems to win all the hard cases without me."

Othella and Poppy laughed, but they both sounded deeply, truly, badly shaken.

"Guy Stillwell, I don't have words to thank you," said Othella. "I don't have words."

"That's plenty," said Guy.

Mother pushed through the madding crowd and put her arms around Guy, planting kisses on his neck, leaving lipstick on his collar.

"Well done, my love, well done," she said.

"That's what I like," said Guy. "The direct approach."

"Everyone come on home," said Mother. "Doralee's fixing a celebration supper. We should go out the back way. It's madness out front."

"Othella," said Guy, "did you want to say anything to the press?"

"Hell no."

"All right, then. I need Poppy and Critter at the office for a bit. We'll see you all at supper."

Shortly after we got there, a file box arrived at the law office on Hancock Avenue, and Mary-Louise poked at it like it was full of snakes. In it was the cast-iron frying pan that had opened eternity's portal for a luckless Lucky Winfield. Guy opened the glass front of the trophy case and placed the skillet in his trove of lethal weapons, between a heavy glass snow globe featuring the Cincinnati skyline and a thickly coiled E string off a Spanish guitar.

After dinner that night, Guy pushed his chair back and said, "It's been a long day. I do believe I'll retire to the front porch for a cigar. Join me in a shot of cognac, Teddi?"

"Sure," said Mother, "if you think there's room for both of us."

Bootsy and I exchanged hopeful glances, and Tatum perked up with hopeful notice. Every once in a while, off and on throughout our growing-up years, there were moments when we could almost believe things would be okay.

Guy took Mother's hand and said, "Critter, would you please drive the ladies home?"

I lugged Poppy's suitcases down the stairs and piled them in the trunk of the car. Othella had nothing but her purse and a brown paper bag with the Paul Laurence Dunbar book and the suit Mother had given her. She'd left everything else for her cellmate.

"She's not as fortunate as me," said Othella. "I had good friends on my side."

We drove without any chatter. I put some music on the radio, but not too loud. Poppy and Othella huddled close together in the back seat, gripping each other's hands as if they'd never let go of each other again.

Well before we reached the landing above the Riverside Country Club, we could see the ominous orange glow. It intensified as we came closer, tall pines standing in stark black silhouette against the smoky red sky. We did not speak. There was no gasp of surprise. Perhaps Othella knew all along that, if she made it home at all, she would find the juke joint engulfed in flames.

I parked on the landing, and we stood beside the car, throats burning, eyes stung by the acrid air, watching the place go up. The windows were full of dancing yellow light. Every now and then, the smoke parted, and I caught a glimpse of the copper-skinned nude, bubbled and peeling above the bar. Moonshine bottles exploded, adding fuel to the blue fire and bright, crinkled music to the hushed flames. Scorched timbers and splintered shiplap splashed into the river between the pilings as the floor gave way. A cobbled-together cross burned with lopsided fervor, propped up with tables and chairs that had been dragged out and heaped in a pile on the riverbank.

A fire truck was parked down by the river, and volunteer firemen sat on folding lawn chairs beside it, drinking bottles of Coke, observing carefully to make sure no wayward embers caught fire on the covered bridge. Their laughter and easygoing conversation echoed on the water, adding a dissonant edge to the ambient hiss and crackle.

I climbed into the branches of an oak tree to get a better view, and from that elevation, I could see the lace curtains in the upstairs windows, fluttering at first, then sagging into the licking flames, and then disappearing altogether. The shingles on the roof curled and blackened, as did the topiary and flowers in the terra-cotta pots, but Hokey and Pokey remained outside the Dutch door, grinning their agonized white grins, standing their posts to the bitter end.

– 21 –

Another signature of small-town America: a spare key hidden under the plaster-cast St. Francis of Assisi in the flowerbed in 1963 will still be there—same key, same lock, same saint—twenty-five years later.

As the funeral after party rocked on at Mother's house, Poppy let herself in the back door at the law office, climbed the marble stairs without a sound, and knelt in front of Guy's trophy case, shining a penlight across Guy's cache of deadly weapons. When I turned on the desk lamp, she didn't even seem all that surprised. She closed the glass door and came to sit in the client chair across the desk from me, assuming the same stonily erect posture she'd held the day we sat side by side in the courtroom waiting for the jury to decide Othella's fate.

"How did you know I'd be here?" she asked.

"Back in 1963, DNA evidence would have sounded like science fiction." I set the skillet on the tooled-leather desktop between us. "I never thought about it until Red brought it up at my arraignment this morning."

"I thought if I had it, I'd know for good and all if Lucky Winfield was my father."

"Bullshit. You know he wasn't. Your father paid for your education. He put you through law school. It has to be in your mother's financial records. Don't tell me you never looked into it in all these years."

"I looked," she conceded. "About ten years ago. But I already knew."

I wanted to ask, but suddenly my mouth was too dry to speak.

"Your parents were always so good to me," Poppy said. "Like an aunt and uncle. Your daddy had a lot of friends, but I could think of only one man who was really more like a brother."

"*King . . .*"

As his name came out of my mouth, I was wondering how I didn't see it before. The hazel eyes. The barrel chest and straight-legged gait. She belonged to King as surely as I belonged to my father.

"As far as I can tell from Mama's bank records, she made the situation known to him when I was twelve. She must have started thinking about college and put the screws to him. She opened a savings account, and he made the deposits nice and regular."

"He tried to do the right thing."

"Oh! That's rich. The *right thing* for whom?" she flashed in annoyance. "Fuck King Hodges. Anything he did for me was less than a patch on what he owed me—what he owed *Mama*—and you can tell him I said so."

"Tell him yourself. I'm not involved."

"We're off topic." Poppy ticked her chin toward the skillet on the desk. "What's your plan with that?"

"Tatum already took it to Atlanta for the DNA analysis. That's why she wasn't there when Guy passed. Truthfully, she was glad for a reason to not be there. They had a complicated relationship."

"Fathers and daughters," Poppy said bitterly. "What about the DNA?"

"Inconclusive," I shrugged. "But they said the technology is improving, so someday . . . who knows? Anyway, it doesn't matter. After the arraignment this morning, I saw the look on your face, and I realized the evidence was right in front of us back then. Still is, I imagine." I sat forward with my elbows on the desk. "Will you show me, Poppy?"

"What?"

"Your hand."

She presented the back of her hand, wrist arched, fingers fanned gracefully—the way a duchess would offer her hand to be kissed—dark red lips pursed with pride and resistance. I waited without speaking, and after a moment, she turned her palm up, and I saw what I knew

I would. The scar had settled to a webby white stripe that crossed her palm parallel to her lifeline, exactly as wide as the searing hot handle of the cast-iron skillet. The moment had branded her, leaving a mark that told a story of violence and healing, an indelible reminder that we may forgive but dare not forget.

"Walk me through it," I said.

"No."

"He showed up after closing. Angry. He knew she'd set him up for the murder. She tried to calm him down. Offered to make him some food."

"I don't have to listen to this."

"She put the skillet on the grill so it would be hot when she laid sausages in it. But he started beating her. Threw her down on the floor. He got on top of her. Doing what he came there to do. So he didn't hear you come down the stairs."

"You can't prove any of this."

"You took hold of the skillet. With all that adrenaline, all that rage—you didn't even feel it, did you, Poppy? By the time you felt it, he was dead."

She went to the window and stared dry-eyed at the moonlit street.

"Doesn't even seem like something that happened to me," she said. "It was a different lifetime. This is a different world."

"Not yet," I said. "But we have to keep trying."

Tatum tells me the age of secrets has ended, but I tend to agree with Vivvy, who believes that enigma draws us out of our own lives and into the lives of others.

"What would the human experience be without secrets?" Vivvy said to me one day as we cruised beyond Montserrat into the Atlantic.

"Amen to that." I dropped Old Mr. Skillet into the fathomless blue. "And God damn a man who won't commit a felony for a friend."

– 22 –

The summer of 1963 was almost over when Poppy received her letter from the State Bar Association of Georgia. She stood in the foyer at the law office, chin set high, eyes dry.

"I passed," she said.

Mary-Louise and I showed no such decorum. I sprang from the easy chair in the corner, whooped, and threw my arms around her, jubilant.

"I knew you'd pass! I knew it!" I whirled her around, lifting her feet off the ground. "You passed that thing, all right. You kicked its ass and made it cry in a corner."

Poppy swatted my arm and said, "Stop it, fool," but when I set her down, she was laughing.

"Congratulations, honey." Mary-Louise handed her a pink envelope. "A little something for wardrobe. You'll need a new suit and the right pair of shoes for court."

"Thank you, Miss Mary-Louise."

"I think you'd look quite intimidating in aubergine. And I know the seamed stockings have fallen out of favor, but they cut a nice line on the leg, and you've got the right calves for it."

"What's going on down there?" Guy asked from the top of the stairs.

"Mr. Stillwell," Poppy said primly, "I have just received confirmation that I passed the bar exam. In keeping with the long-standing custom, I will be taking you to lunch at Tony's."

She didn't ask him; she informed him. It sounded like she'd practiced it, so I didn't doubt she had an answer for whatever he was about to say. Mary-Louise and I were still as wax figures, waiting to see how Guy would take it. He pondered a moment, hands clasped behind his back, and then said, "Stay put. I got something for you."

He disappeared into his office and, a moment later, came down the stairs and presented Poppy with a small teal gift box tied with a white ribbon.

"On behalf of the partnership," he said. "Congratulations, Miss Sterling."

"Thank you, sir."

"It's from Tiffany's," said Mary-Louise. "In New York City."

"My goodness," said Poppy. She opened the box and found a sterling silver paperweight and matching business card caddy ready to receive a stack of freshly embossed business cards. The paperweight was engraved with the words of Abraham Lincoln, same as a marble one Mother had given Guy when he passed the bar: *May the Almighty grant that the cause of truth, justice, and humanity shall in no wise suffer at my hands.*

"It's beautiful," she said. "Thank you. Thank you for everything you've done for me. I'm grateful. I won't forget."

"Goddamn, we are proud of you, Poppy. All of us," said Guy, and his voice sounded a little husky around the edges. "King, too. I wish he was here to tell you himself."

"I'm kinda proud of my own self." She couldn't quash her broad smile.

"Okay. Well. Lunch is on you, Attorney Sterling. Let's get to it."

"Since King's not available, I'd like to invite Critter to come in his place."

"Good idea," said Guy. "Critter, you'll find a fresh shirt and tie in the closet upstairs."

Seated in Guy's regular booth at Tony's, we waited for a long time. The big dining room, always noisy with conversation, was remarkably quiet. The waiter, a fella about the same age and complexion as Doc, eventually arrived and set a highball glass of rye in front of my father and a Coke in front of me. He glanced nervously at Poppy.

"Mr. Stillwell—"

"Ladies first," said Guy. "What'll it be, Attorney Sterling?"

Poppy closed the menu between her hands. "Clam chowder, please."

"We're out of the chowder," said the waiter.

"Caesar salad, then."

"We don't have any." The waiter leaned in to speak quietly to Guy. "Mr. Stillwell, please, don't put me in an awkward position. I'm just trying to do my job here."

"So do the job, friend. Take the lady's lunch order."

"Sir, I don't make the rules. If you got a problem, might I suggest you take it up with your friend who owns the place?"

"Fair enough," said Guy. "Send him over."

The waiter walked away. The room had fallen utterly silent now. After a minute, Tony appeared beside the booth, wiping his hands on a kitchen towel.

"Is there a problem, Guy?"

"Not as far as I'm concerned," Guy boomed in his stentorian tenor. "Attorney Sterling here, having passed the bar on her first try—unlike many of the lawyers within hearing distance—is sponsoring the traditional partners' lunch, as my law clerks have done every goddamn year since I started being a lawyer. I will have my usual rib eye and whiskey. Thank you."

"Guy, c'mon," said Tony. "We're all friends here. Don't make trouble."

"No trouble here," said Guy. "Attorney Sterling will have the clam chowder. How about you, Critter?"

"Steak sandwich and fries, please."

Tony set his jaw square. "This is America. It's a free country. I got a God-given right to serve whoever I choose, and I choose not to serve coloreds. Nothing against you personally, Miss." He squeezed out a strained smile for Poppy. "It's out of consideration to the other customers. Mixed company makes a lot of folks uncomfortable. And it's not fair to my hardworking Negro staff, asking them to wait on some uppity little girl who don't know her place."

"Tony? A word." Guy got up from the booth, and Tony followed him over to the coat check.

As they walked away, Poppy said, "No disrespect to your daddy, but he doesn't need to fight my battles for me—and he sure as hell doesn't need to order my lunch."

"Why are you mad at Guy?" I said. "He's standing up for you."

"I can stand up for myself. I'd be in a heap of trouble if I couldn't."

"You make trouble for yourself, Poppy. You go around like the whole world is against you."

"And you go around like the whole world is *for* you. Because it *is*." She folded her arms unhappily. "I don't expect you to understand."

Guy and Tony returned to the booth.

Tony said to Poppy, "Would you like oyster crackers or garlic toast with your chowder, Attorney Sterling?"

"Crackers," said Poppy.

He nodded and disappeared into the kitchen again.

"What did you say to him?" I asked Guy.

"I gave him a choice. Either I would represent him in a property dispute he's having with a cousin—or I would represent his wife in the divorce that is sure to be impending when I tell her about his standing appointment at Jeffie's. I know it's not the progress you would like to see in the world, Poppy, but Rome wasn't built in a day."

"Nobody's asking for Rome," she said. "All I want is Athens, Georgia, same as y'all."

"We'll get there," said Guy. "This is a good first step."

"What's the next step?"

"Enjoy your lunch."

"I won't be able to eat it," she said. "They'll have spit in it. Or worse."

"You can have half of mine," I piped up.

"Thanks, little brother." She reached across the table to pat my hand.

Within a few minutes, the room had returned to its usual cacophony. Plea deals being brokered. Land contracts being discussed. Principles being argued across tables and gossip offered between booths. The world did not crack open and spill out its substance until November when JFK was assassinated. In early August, we ate our lunch, and it did seem for a moment that things were getting better.

That night, I sat in the darkened theater, holding the hand of a girl whose name I no longer remember, watching *To Kill a Mockingbird* for the seventh time.

"Scout, do you know what a compromise is?" said Atticus in the plodding, fatherly way so different from Guy's electric delivery. "Bending the law? No. It's an agreement reached by mutual consent."

As the movie droned on to its terrible conclusion, I heard a soft hitch in the girl's breath. Her face was porcelain-white in the shifting light of the silver screen. A single tear slid down her cheek, and with the unbridled desire of a fifteen-year-old, I wanted to taste the salt of that tear, wanted to kiss her, wanted this girl so bad I thought I would die—this girl whose name I no longer recall. That's where my brain was that summer. I had no clue why this movie made girls cry, and I was not curious to know. I was a warm-blooded American male, sitting in the dark, thinking about nothing beyond the reach of my own manhood—as per my birthright. I didn't need Atticus Finch fucking that up, along with Poppy and her haughty talk about changing the world. I didn't want my world to change. I liked my world just fine.

"Of course you did," Vivvy says now. "Why wouldn't you?"

It's a question, candid and curious, not a reproach, and I'm willing to think about it. My conscience is clear. I never did a thing to hurt anybody—not purposely, anyway. I am a magnanimous tipper, courteous to folks of all stations. To the best of my ability, I am self-aware. To the best of my recollection, I'm truthful about what happened back then. And when I'm not able to be truthful with myself, well, then I have Vivvy.

– 23 –

The Ballerini continuance ticked down to its last day, and my opening statement was still at the chicken-scratch stage. My strategy,
flaccid enough to begin with, allowed only a narrow foothold between
twin chasms of damnation. Driving past the undeveloped acreage on
my way to the houseboat, I was deep in thought about the whole tangled
mess, so I didn't even notice the first pair of headlights behind me until
the second pair appeared next to it. Within seconds, precisely as Newt
had described it, a couple of aging Suburbans roared up to flank me
and delivered me with startling efficiency into the ditch that ran alongside the lonely state road. The Suburbans backed out with ease, but my
Thunderbird wallowed, axle-deep in red mud. A hammy fist wrapped
around a .38 Special knocked on the driver's side window.

"Let's go."

I got out, bringing my briefcase with me, and followed him to the
less battered of the two Suburbans. His cohort waved me into the back
seat and slammed the door, which was rigged so it couldn't be opened
from the inside. Like my father and King and most of the other lawyers I
know, I always kept a loaded handgun in the top drawer of my desk and
another in the glove compartment of my car. It seemed excessive to cart
one around in my briefcase as well. Live and learn.

We drove for what felt like a long time and then pulled into the
parking lot of the Open House Café, a twenty-four-hour greasy spoon
on the wrong side of Athens, owned and operated by a stolid widow

named Blanche. Her late husband, the head of the local KKK chapter, had gone to prison in the 1960s for the murder of a black army officer who had unwittingly stopped by the Open House for a bite to eat while traveling from Georgia to Washington, DC. The Klansmen didn't like seeing this fella with his fancy uniform and white aide-de-camp, so Blanche's man and an accomplice followed them down the road until they got onto a bridge, and then they passed by them and blew the black man's head off. King represented the Klansman—the driver, not the shooter, if it makes a difference—because the Klansman was paying the defense lawyer's fee, and they were not about to give one paper dollar to "that fucking nigger-lover Stillwell."

When we arrived at the Open House, Blanche was behind the till, smoking a cigarette and drinking a Coke. The only customer in the place, sitting by herself in a corner booth, was Fernanda DiLippa Ballerini, and she looked singularly unamused. The gentleman with the .38 knuckled me in the back, pushing me toward her, and I headed that direction while he and his sidekick straddled stools at the counter.

"Well, if it ain't the ass-kissin' cousins," said Blanche.

"Let me see a menu," the first cousin said.

"Get your own goddamn menu," said Blanche. "What does this look like, the Ritz?"

They all laughed. This was the routine, apparently.

I sat in the booth across from Fernanda and said, "Good evening."

"August Stillwell," she said. "Look at you. All grown up."

She'd aged well. If anything, she was more beautiful now, in her midsixties, than she ever was as an overdone redhead back in the day. Her naturally black hair was shot with silver, set off by the steely indigo of her tailored suit. She crossed her legs, casually dangling one oxblood stiletto pump on her elegant foot. When she spoke, her dusky Delta drawl was underlaid with a trace of her native Italian accent.

"I was sorry to hear about your father," she said. "My condolences."

"Thank you."

"My own father isn't long for the world, I'm afraid. He's on oxygen. Quite senile. I'm preparing for the inevitable."

"Sorry to hear that," I said. "Is there something I can do for you?"

"Lots of things, I imagine. There's always opportunity for a competent attorney in our organization." She sipped her coffee, leaving a smudge of scarlet lipstick on the white ceramic cup. "First things first, however. There's the matter of my husband."

"You mean your ex-husband."

"Not in the eyes of God," said Fernanda. "It would have been better for me to be a widow. I could have remarried."

"You can remarry. There's nothing stopping you."

"Nothing but faith! Nothing but sacred vows. Clearly, that has no meaning to you. To me, it means eternity. It means the fate of my immortal soul."

Fernanda opened her purse, took out three beefy stacks of cash, and laid them end to end on the table between us.

"Very generous," I said, "but if you're asking me to kill the guy, that's a hard pass. I'm not Tick."

"Tick," she laughed. "There's a blast from the past."

"Look, you were paid two million dollars, you're free to do whatever you like, and I'm due in court tomorrow morning, so if you'll excuse me—"

"Don't get your nuts in a bunch," she said. "I'm not asking you to kill him. There are inmates in general population at Baldwin State Prison who'll take care of that. I just need you to go to court tomorrow and lose."

"That's not going to happen. On purpose."

"It would make everything so simple."

"Nonetheless."

"You're sure I can't change your mind?"

"Positive."

She looked over my shoulder and gestured to the cousins, who shambled away from the counter and hulked over the booth.

"Is that old well still open over on the Ebbot place?" she asked.

"Whoa, whoa, whoa," I said. "Hold on."

"You mean that one on the Carter place?" said Cousin One.

"No, that other one," Cousin Two chimed in. "On the Ebbot place."

"Let's take a breath here," I said. "There's no need for—"

"Oh, the Ebbot place," said Cousin One. "Yeah, we're familiar."

Fernanda nodded and ticked her thumb in my direction. "Make sure you dispose of the car."

"Hey, hey, hey!" I clutched my briefcase to my chest. "Fernanda, don't do this. You don't have to do this. You know anything that passed between you and me just now—that's *privileged*. That is protected by the law of attorney-client privilege, and that means I can never tell anybody, and you can count on that, cradle to grave."

"This gives me no pleasure," she said. "I always thought you were a sweet boy, August. I'm sorry you've chosen the devil's path."

It was a forty-five-minute drive to the Ebbot place, and I used that time trying to talk the cousins out of what they were doing. I made impassioned pleas to their better judgment and wheedling offers of cash and free legal assistance should they ever be arrested or need a divorce. They were unmoved.

The dry well was about twelve feet deep with a spongy layer of weeds and garbage at the bottom, so I was relatively unhurt when they dropped me in, but when they tossed my briefcase in after me, it thumped me painfully on one shoulder. It was as dark as venial sin down there, but I saw the bright ember at the end of the fuse as a blunt stick of dynamite bounced off the stone wall of the cistern. I thrashed through the trash to find it and managed to pinch out the fuse when it was about half an inch from the explosive. There was a minute or so when the only sound was my heavy breathing, and then I heard voices approaching.

"What happened?"

"Dud, maybe."

"Or he pinched it."

"Yeah, probably."

The cousins leaned in, two bucket-head silhouettes in the dappled moonlight, voices echoing.

"Got another one?"

"One, but I need to save it. Self-correcting problem."

"Yeah. Two, three days from now, lawyer, you might wish you hadn't of done that." They laughed like they were back at the diner, yucking it up with the Klan widow. "Have yourself a good evening, now, ya hear?"

"Fuck you!" I bellowed.

As the sound of the Suburban faded into the distance, I located my briefcase, intending to take out the mobile phone and call 911, but when I opened it, my hands were shaking, and the contents spilled out into the knee-deep debris. I spotted the winking blue eye on the back of the phone, dove for it, and dialed 911.

"Sherriff's office. Do you have an emergency?"

"Yes, I'm—"

"Hello?"

"Hello! Can you hear me?"

"Is somebody there?"

"Yes! Hello? Can you hear me now? Can you hear me now?" I shifted the angle of the phone, maneuvering it around the limited space like a model airplane. "Hello! Can you hear me?"

"I hear you. What's your emergency?"

"I'm in a dry well on the Ebbot place. My name is Stillwell. I've been—"

"What's the name?"

"Stillwell," I enunciated. "August. Stillwell. I am down in an old cistern on the Ebbot place off state road—"

"Hello? Are you there?"

"Fucking hell."

"Say now, you watch your language there, Mr. Stillwell."

"I apologize, ma'am, but please—"

"Hello? Mr. Stillwell? Hello?"

I tried to recoup some shred of signal, struggling to maintain my balance on the clattering heap of empty beer cans. A malty stench rose up every time I shuffled my feet. The mouth of the cistern was a good six feet above my head. The concrete walls offered no purchase for hand or foot and were wide enough apart that I couldn't spread-eagle and spider my way up. My fading hopes lay with the 911 operator, who might have gotten enough information to send someone for me, and my mobile phone that might perk up enough to make another call. I tried it intermittently as time passed. Nothing.

Unsuccessful with the phone, I used its meager light to gather up the contents of my briefcase—mostly random deeds and contracts and notes—but I was unable to find the one thing that actually mattered to me: the letter from my father. It occurs to me now that I might have spent that last available thread of light looking around for anything I might have used to save myself. Instead, desperate for a glimpse of the dove gray envelope, I rummaged the stinking refuse until the phone's blue dial pad went black.

Panting and sweating in the darkness, I cursed the phone for its inadequate battery and limp signal and cursed the yokel mobsters for their casual cruelty, but mostly I cursed myself for not opening that letter when King handed it to me. The loss of it rubbed salt in the fresh wound of losing my father. Whatever wisdom was in it disappeared into the truncated void of our unfinished conversation. I was alone at the bottom of a hole, without help, without hope, without the constant hum of energy that had always kept me at the ready and made me feel most alive. My sisters and I grew up with the tightly strung tension created by our father's alcoholism. We hated it. But when it was gone, I longed for it the way a salad fork longs for a light socket.

I leaned against the clammy wall of the cistern and tried not to think about food or water or the need to urinate. After a while, the milk-colored moon peeped over the edge of the black hole overhead. It moved through the naked limbs of a dead tree, marking the passage of an hour or more. I am not good at any sort of stillness, as Vivvy will attest. For the most part, I keep moving and manage to avoid introspection, but on this occasion, the metaphor was too much. If I'd never believed in King's much-ballyhooed "rock bottom" before, I believed in it now.

I won't beleaguer the details, but sitting there among the beer cans, I began to have that "if I get out of this alive" conversation with myself, and as the pale moon disappeared again, I promised God and the ghost of my father that I would fly right, reclaim the path of righteousness, and never touch another drink.

At the sound of a vehicle approaching above, I scrambled to my feet. Footsteps crunched through the dead leaves. A flashlight lanced the darkness.

"Mr. Stillwell?"

"Yes! Down here. Who's there?"

"Deputy DuVernay."

In the awkward silence that followed, I scoured my mind for any thought of what Guy would say.

"Good evening, Deputy."

"Evening."

"I, um . . . I sure appreciate your help," I said. "I wasn't sure the 911 operator got my location."

"What do you mean? Somebody called 911?"

I shifted carefully on my weedy hillock. If the 911 operator had not sent DuVernay, he must have been sent by the only other people who knew where I was: Fernanda and her henchmen.

"Actually, I called 911 just a little while ago," I said. "I've got my mobile phone down here."

"What kind of phone?"

"Mobile. Like a car phone. It's like a—a telephone you can take any-where and call anyone you need to. In case of emergency."

"Who'd you call?"

"Well, 911, of course. And Judge Sterling. Yeah, I let her know exactly where I am, just in case I don't show up for court in the morning. And my sister. My mom. My girlfriend. I'm supposed to meet an asso-ciate at the Regent. He's expecting me. I checked in with everybody. Let them know exactly where to find me if I, um . . . if there's any question."

I heard the soft chirp of DuVernay's radio. "Hey, Enid, did you get a call from a guy that maybe somebody fell down a well? Right. Okay. No, I'll check it out. You don't need to send anybody else."

"Hey, King. Yeah, it's me." I spoke loudly into the dead weight of my lifeless mobile. "You'll never guess who showed up. Deputy DuVernay!

Right, right. From the party. So I'm in good hands. You won't have to alert the FBI after all. Yeah, see you shortly."

Footsteps crunched away and then crunched back to the mouth of the well. A chain ladder dropped down, metal rungs singing against the cistern wall. I tested it for weight and then climbed up, gripping the ladder with one hand and my briefcase with the other. I glanced back to see if I might catch a glimpse of the dove gray envelope in the glow of DuVernay's flashlight, but there was only trash, dead flora, and an appalling population of roaches.

I heaved myself over the lip of the cistern onto the grass, and sat there while Deputy DuVernay hauled the ladder up and collapsed it back into a vinyl bag. He extended a hand and helped me to my feet, and I wobbled toward the waiting cruiser.

"Jeezum crow, you smell like mashed ass," said the deputy. I felt his firm grip on the back of my neck. "You won't be pressing charges. It was all in good humor, right?"

"Sure."

"Next time, it won't be."

"Understood."

"That's the spirit." He laughed and clapped me on my aching shoulder. "You'll find your car at the impound lot tomorrow. I'll give you a lift home."

Not wanting him to see where I lived, I said, "Just drop me at the Regent."

He drove there without speaking. I sat in the back of the police cruiser, as uncomfortable as I had ever been in my life. When we arrived, he opened the door for me and said, "Have a good one."

I went inside and perched on a barstool, sweating and shaking. I pushed my dirty hands in my pockets when Rory and Then Some approached and gingerly slid a cocktail napkin onto the bar in front of me.

"Hey there," she said. "Are you okay? You look kinda rough."

"I'm fine."

She wrinkled her nose. "Critter, you don't smell right."

"I know. A couple of hillbilly mobsters just dropped me down a dry well full of garbage."

"What?"

"It's not a joke. I could have been killed."

Her quizzical smile faded. "My God. Should I call the police?"

"*No.* No. That won't help."

"Should I call King?"

I shook my head. I felt like I didn't know King anymore—had never really known him—and it bothered me more than I thought it would.

"Let me get you a drink," she said.

"No. Just . . . club soda with lime."

"Critter, I'm not judging. If you want a drink—"

"*It's not about you.* Okay? Just shut up and let me think for a minute."

She set up the club soda and left me sitting alone with my head in my hands—and *Christ!* I did smell like Satan's crawl space—weighed down by this fucking irresolvable case and the fact that my father had dumped it on me along with a hundred other cases, not to mention the family, horse farms, beer distributorship, and a mountain of other niggling issues that were my inheritance.

I felt a hot towel on my face.

"Here. Hold still." Rory the Merciful wiped my forehead and jaw and the side of my nose and then scrubbed my grimy palms, pushing the warm, wet cloth between my fingers. She held my wrists, working her thumbs against the heels of my hands, speaking low and calm, saying, "Okay. You're okay." This simple gesture, however platonic, was oddly compelling—which is to say, it was a turn-on—so my intense discomfort was complete. I sat there in sweet misery until some inebriate down the bar said, "Hey, honey, I'll have what he's having."

"Fall in a hole," she shot back.

"I'm fine," I said. "Go do what you need to do."

"Hang tight for a sec. I'll be right back."

She tended to the customers down the bar, disappeared into the back, and returned a few minutes later with a bowl of vegetable beef soup.

"I was raised Methodist," she said. "We douse all spiritual and physical ailments in soup."

"Thank you," I said. "I'm sorry I told you to shut up. I've never told
a woman to shut up. Not once in my life."

"Except your sisters, probably."

"Well, of course, but not—"

"And then this."

"Okay, fine, but I swear to you, I'm not hiding a mean streak."

"I know," she said tenderly. "You're not that clever."

It felt good to laugh, but it made me realize every muscle in my core
was still shaking.

"I think I finally know how my father felt all these years," I said. "He
was at the bottom of a deep hole, and drinking was the only way out."

She listened without letting go of my hand, and I tried to articulate
everything I'd confessed to that milky moon.

"Every lawyer I've ever met is trapped in the profession until they
die," I said, "and most of them wish they were dead long before that.
They live to their limit, surrounded by a bunch of entitled people. They
feel compelled to appear more successful than anybody else in the
room, so they're always throwing money around, taking big trips, buy-
ing fancy cars and big homes. I haven't done any of that. I just worked as
hard as I could and lived close to the vest so I could invest and acquire
income property, because my life—oh, I was going to be different. I was
going to buy myself a yacht and sail off into the sunset. But here I am. I
live on a boat that doesn't go anywhere. And I know that if I don't stop
drinking now, I'll die just like my father did."

I pulled my hand away, uncomfortable at having said too much.

"Anyhoo. Looks like the Dixie Mafia won't let that happen."

She laid her cool palm on the side of my face and said, "August
Stillwell, you listen to me, and you listen hard. You are a good man. You
are a fine lawyer. And you are not your father."

It was too hard to argue around the lump in my throat.

"Critter, what on earth is going on? Why would someone try to kill
you? Does this have to do with the *Unsolved Mysteries* case?"

"Tangentially."

"Can you call the FBI?"

I shook my head.

"How can I help?"

"I don't know. Help me understand why a woman would need her ex-husband dead. Not just wish him dead, but *need* him dead, badly enough to take risks."

"Money."

"No."

"Jealousy?"

"I don't think so."

She considered it and said, "He knows her secrets."

"And now I know them, too." I tried to play it off with an unsteady chuckle. "So, I'm pretty much screwed. Jesus H. Christ. I have to be in court eleven hours from now, and I am so incredibly screwed."

"Dang. Can you get a continuance?"

"No, not again. The judge was very clear about that."

"Okay. You're okay. Reality check and damage control. You're gonna go in there tomorrow and do your voir dire. Run that clock. Drag it out to the end of the day so you have a little more time to sort yourself out. Once you know what you're working with on the jury, you can take a breath and form a strategy."

I nodded. "Yes. I like that. That makes good sense."

"I suspect Redstone will focus on media exposure and sociopolitical leanings," she said. "The first mate who ratted out your client to the TV show—she just did an interview with the *National Enquirer*, claiming he picked her up at a wet T-shirt contest and they had a thing going on, so Redstone might do a little digging in that potato patch. Use your time to connect with the jurors personally."

"How? Specifics. What do I ask them?"

"It doesn't matter what you ask them, Critter. Forget the BELL Curve for now. You need this jury to trust you, and in order to build that trust, you have to show that you trust them. Open doors for them to tell little stories about themselves. Every question is an opportunity for them to show you who they are and for you to demonstrate that you have faith in them."

"Okay. Got it. I can do that."

"You can. You'll be okay."

"May I ask you a personal question?"

"You can ask," she said warily.

"Why are you tending bar instead of doing jury consultation?"

"Why are you living on a boat that doesn't go anywhere?"

"That's the $64,000 question, isn't it?"

She attempted an encouraging smile. "If you go in there tomorrow and let it be a total fishing expedition—who knows? Somebody might say something that inspires you."

"Sure. That could happen."

I didn't actually think it could, but she was right that I could buy myself another day, during which Tatum could shift some money around and find someone to captain the *Rascal* for me, so that if all else failed, I could run.

– 24 –

Court was no longer the hot-ticket entertainment it was back in my father's day, but a good crowd turned up for Newt's trial. In addition to the buzzing media presence, a good number of Newt's old army buddies were there, along with the town's more dedicated busybodies, some jaded gawkers, and a cadre of law students with their professor. Mother and Bootsy were front and center with King, and at the back of the room, Miss Lizzie Mae sat on a folding chair next to Othella's wheelchair.

Sitting beside me at the defense table, Newt nervously drummed his fingers, crossing and uncrossing his legs, eyeing the blank legal pad on the table in front of me. I sat with my hands folded over my roiling gut, trying not to look like a kid with a stomachache.

"Did you bring those Swisher Sweets?" Newt asked.

I set a box of cigarillos on the table. "Enjoy."

"Got a light?"

"You're not allowed to smoke in here."

"Barbarians," Newt grumbled. He placed an unlit cigarillo between his lips and did a little pantomime, pretending to light it with his thumb and relishing a deep imaginary drag. "Ohhhhh, yeaaaaaah."

He leaned back in his chair and stuck his legs out straight, crossing his ankles under the table.

"Well, I'll be damned." Newt elbowed me and pointed to the edge of the table in front of him. "Lookee there."

Sometime in the past—a good while back, from the looks of it—someone had etched small, unevenly blocked letters into the side of the thick tiger oak tabletop: *Guy Stillwell was H*

"Apparently, the jury came back," I said. "Wonder which way it went."

"Probably not great if he was on trial for vandalism," said Newt, and we both roared with laughter.

"As many times as I've sat here at the defense table," I said, "I can't believe I never noticed that."

But of course, I hadn't, because I'd never sat on that side of the table, never spent any time waiting with downcast eyes and trembling hands while strangers debated my fate. At first, it struck me as odd that the defendant had not etched his own name, but then I thought about the men and women I'd seen sitting next to Guy over the years, how they'd looked at him and listened to him during utterly foreign proceedings or gripped his arm during sentencing. Guy was the knobby root they grabbed onto as they went over a cliff; they clung to him, dangling by their last hope, scrambling to right themselves. Whoever that itchy-fingered soul was, he'd found comfort in Guy's stalwart voice and unruffled presence. I ran my thumb across the words and tried to feel that presence now.

Poppy called the proceedings to order and moved briskly through the housekeeping issues: details for the record, instructions for the jury pool, and stern admonitions to Redstone and me about grandstanding and other shenanigans that didn't play as well in the 1980s, after people started watching Judge Wapner on *The People's Court.*

We started voir dire. A.D.A. Chastain covered most of the questions that always come up: Any relatives in law enforcement? Ever been the victim of a crime? Ever been charged with a crime? Ever had a run-in with the cops that might sway you to believe the accused over law enforcement or law enforcement over the accused?

As anticipated, Red went in the direction of media exposure and tabloid innuendo, sussing out who'd seen Newt on TV and read about him in the *National Enquirer* and whether or not that made a difference to them. I don't recall most of their answers. I focused on their faces, reminding myself that the best thing I could do for the moment was gain their trust.

Red asked Juror 1, a Sunday school teacher, "Are you aware of what the Holy Bible says about homosexuality? Would it influence you at all knowing such predilection is an abomination, according to God's word?"

I asked Juror 1, "Have you ever run away from home?"

"When I was five," she said, clearly relishing the memory. "I packed up my lunchbox and walked three blocks to the library, because I wanted to live there. The librarian called my mother. All the librarians knew me."

"That tells me everything I need to know about you," I smiled. "Defense accepts Juror 1."

Chastain asked Juror 2, a lifelong Athenian, "Are you acquainted with the defendant or either of the attorneys?"

"As a matter of fact," she said, "I dated Critter Stillwell a couple of times when we were both at the university. We went to the movies twice, and he took me to a toga party at his fraternity."

Chastain exercised the prosecution's first strike, saying, "I'm sure she'd be fine, but it seems cruel and unusual to make her spend any more time with him."

Red asked Juror 3, the owner of a plumbing supply store, if he remembered seeing Robert Stack as Eliot Ness on *The Untouchables*.

I asked him where he would go, if he could go anywhere in the world. And so it went on. My eyes kept drifting to the edge of the table.

Guy Stillwell was H

While Redstone queried Juror 4 about her family's history with law enforcement—father state trooper, uncle Atlanta PD, grandfather sheriff in the Florida panhandle—I took out the Pollard crime scene photos, recalling Tatum's curiosity about an etched mark on the table in the photograph of Lucky's statement. I scribbled a note on the yellow pad, folded it, and leaned over the rail to hand it to my sister.

"Boots, call Mary-Louise and tell her I need this. Tell her to hurry."

She nodded and went without asking questions, the same way either of us would have hurried off on the errand if our father had asked. Newt looked at me, questioning.

"Prosecution accepts Juror 4," said Chastain.

"You're up, Mr. Stillwell," said Poppy. "If you don't mind directing your attention this way."

"Apologies, Your Honor." I turned to Juror 4. "That's a proud history in your family. I imagine you'd take it hard if this case involved malfeasance on the part of law enforcement. Or maybe on the part of the D.A.?"

"Malfeasance," she said. "Like what?"

"Like creating or coercing a phony murder confession." I purposely didn't look at Redstone, but I heard a small rumble from the prosecution table.

"Defense lawyers always try that angle," she said knowingly. "That never actually happens."

"Because cops are honest."

"Yes."

"And defense lawyers . . . not so much?"

"Present company excepted, I'm *sure*."

She got a laugh from the courtroom and enjoyed it.

"Did you have other plans this week?" I asked. "Seems like maybe you're hoping I'll exercise my first strike."

She shifted in her seat. "My sister is in from Seattle."

"Thank you for your honesty," I said. "Defense accepts Juror 4."

Returning to the defense table, I observed the stony side-eye I was getting from Redstone and Chastain. As voir dire went on, Redstone used his second strike to eliminate Juror 5, who turned out to be one of the Free Newt fanatics, and I eliminated Juror 6, who seemed like he would use up a lot of oxygen, but I was able to get him to gas on and on about ball bearings, which killed a good twelve or thirteen minutes before I cut him loose.

As Chastain went to work on Juror 7, Mary-Louise hurried forward and tapped me on the shoulder.

"Got it," she said, breathless, and fanned herself with the folder before she handed it to me.

The file smelled like basement and old carbon paper. The tab was labeled "GA v. Loebel" with the date—June 1, 1963—and a case number below it.

"Thanks, Mary-Louise."

She nodded and plopped down on the bench next to Bootsy.

"Are you acquainted with the defendant or either of the attorneys?" Chastain asked Juror 7.

"Not exactly," she said, "but I was a year ahead of Critter Stillwell's sister in high school, and I was on the Pancreatic Cancer Society's golf tournament planning committee with his mama three years in a row before my husband passed."

Chastain looked at Red, and Red said, "State accepts Juror 7. Eliminating everyone who's ever served on a committee with Mrs. Stillwell would mean letting half of Athens out of jury duty."

"Defense also accepts Juror 7," I said.

While Red questioned Juror 8, an adjunct physics professor, I flipped through the contents of Mott Loebel's file: a scant few pages of paperwork and the eight-by-ten glossy of the confession offered up for the plea deal:

I am Mott Loebel age 19 years old. Me and my friend Early Simmons who is also a plumber assistant like me robbed the bank in Madison on May 30, 1963 by going in there pretending as if we was there to change out the ball cock on a toilet in the ladies room and Miss Darla the lady who was in charge was familiar with us as we had changed out a ball cock on a toilet this one other time so she let us in there as nice as anything right as the bank was closing and then while Early was having her show him which toilet was the problem stall I went with a blue duffel which we use for tools and quick put money in that and when they came out, I pretended I was on the phone and says to Early how we have to go to an emergency job where water is coming down from a ceiling and Miss Darla said by all means go immediately and come back to the bank tomorrow, so we went out to the car with the tool duffel and drove off like the wind and hid the money under a rusty old Ford pickup behind the barn at the farm of Early's grandmother where we ate supper. I have made this confession by my own free will on the advice of my lawyer Mr. Stillwell. I swear it is truth and will testify in court.

I laid the photo next to the photo of Lucky Winfield's terse confession. Mott's rang true; Lucky's didn't. Even before I knew it was bullshit, I knew it was bullshit. The conundrum was exposing that without turning several worlds upside down.

"Mr. Stillwell?" said Poppy. "Care to join us?"

"Oh. Sorry."

"Do you have any questions for Juror 8?"

"Yes. Sir . . . um . . . you are a professor of . . ."

"Physics. Adjunct professor."

I fumbled with the list in front of me, wishing my current law clerk was worth a damn or that Guy was here instead of me or that there was a shred of hope that someone would say something to inspire me.

"Sir, according to the laws of physics . . . which is worse, the rock or the hard place?"

His blank stare narrowed to suspicion. "Is that a joke?"

"No," I said. "The rock. The hard place. You're familiar with the expression?"

"Of course."

"So . . . what do you think? I'm genuinely asking your opinion."

"I'd say the hard place is worse. The rock is a known quantity. You can measure it, weigh it, form a data-based response. *Hard* is abstruse. Subjective. It could mean different things to different people, so you end up proceeding on assumptions."

"And assumptions are usually based on fear rather than information," I said. "Or so my father always said. Would you agree?"

"I'd agree."

"Defense accepts Juror 8."

Juror 9 was a travel agent. When it was my turn, I asked her, "How far is too far?"

"You do a risk-benefit analysis," she said. "Look at cost, safety factors, time constraints—you know—and ask yourself at what point the value of reaching this destination in no longer worth it."

Juror 10 was a veterinarian.

"Is it better to let sleeping dogs lie?" I asked.

"The health of the dog depends on both sleep and activity," she said, "so you have to base it on which of these is needed at this particular moment."

They were getting the hang of it now. The prospective jurors actually seemed to be enjoying it. Redstone and Chastain were doggedly sticking to their usual modus operandi with declining good humor.

Juror 11 was a housekeeper.

"Ma'am, in your experience," I said, "if the D.A. wanted to avoid airing some dirty laundry—"

"Your Honor," said Red, "defense counsel is making a mockery of this process. We've all seen this tactic before. A shoddy lawyer fails to get a continuance, so he drags out voir dire with a lot of hamster-wheeling to buy himself another day to get his homework done."

"Judge, defense has the right to question prospective jurors," I said.

"Focus on the case at hand," said Poppy, "and be warned—any further innuendo about the integrity of the court, and you'll be in contempt."

"Yes, ma'am."

"Do you have any relevant questions for Juror 11?"

"Ma'am, in your field of expertise," I said, "if the D.A. wanted to sweep something under the rug—"

"That's it." Red slapped his palm on the prosecution table and stood. "What the hell are you playing at?"

"Red, I'm not accusing you of anything. I know you're a good man." I held up Lucky's bogus confession in one hand and Mott Loebel's genuine confession in the other. "You shouldn't have to go into the volcano for this."

"Not everyone was born with a silver spoon in his mouth," Redstone raged. "Some of us had to go along to get along."

"Whoa! Whoa!" Chastain shouted over him. "Move to strike this whole exchange. Your Honor, this is totally inappropriate."

"Sustained," said Judge Sterling. "If you two got something to settle, you settle it somewhere else. This is not the time or place."

"Red," I said, "I know it was Ruckels."

"You don't know a goddamn thing," said Redstone.

"Objection," said Chastain.

"I know he was a drunk."

"Oh!" Red crowed. "You want to open that can o' worms?"

"Objection sustained," said the judge.

"I know he made you sweat bullets, Red, playing fast and loose with rules of evidence. I know he bullied you. I know he dangled this job over your head like a carrot in front of a mule. I know for a fact that this confession is unpasteurized bullshit, as both you and the judge are well aware."

"Objection!" Chastain said sharply. "Badgering the—the—what is happening?"

"Approach, approach." Poppy waved us all in. "Ms. Chastain, get on up here with the rest of the F Troop."

Chastain joined the huddle and hissed, "Your Honor, this is exactly the sort of parlor trick you explicitly cautioned against during pre-trial instructions."

The judge cupped her hand over her microphone and fixed an unsparing gaze on me. "Have you lost your mind?"

"Your Honor, we got a clear mistrial here," said Red. "Certainly, if defense is gonna drag Your Honor's integrity into question, you'll have to recuse yourself."

"Mr. Redstone, please, tell me Ruckels did not leave a trail of peanut shells to that phony confession," Judge Sterling whispered. "Tell me we did not just open the door to retry every case he ever had his stubby little fingers in."

"I've seen zero proof that this confession was falsified," Chastain argued. "He's making this flimsy play for prosecutorial misconduct because he doesn't have jackshit to make his case."

"Throw the statement out," said Red. "We still got the weapon, motive, and opportunity—plenty of rubber on the road."

"Go sit down," said the judge. "I need to think for a minute." She uncovered her mic and brought the gavel down. "Court is in recess. Be back in twenty minutes."

"Your Honor," I said, "may I see you in chambers?"

"No, you may not."

She descended to her office and closed the door. Redstone strode down the aisle, and A.D.A. Chastain followed him out into the hall. I sat down at the defense table. My knees felt like oatmeal. I could feel Mother, Mary-Louise, and Bootsy sitting wide-eyed behind me, but they made not a peep, and I didn't care to look at them.

"Jesus, Critter," said Newt. "I hope to hell you know what you're doing. That seemed pretty buck wild right there."

"I suspect she'll declare a mistrial."

"And then what?"

"You'll end it by pleading guilty."

"Plead guilty?" said Newt. "Why would I do a fool thing like that?"

I took a pencil and paper from my briefcase, and Newt moved aside so I could lean down and place the paper on the edge of the tabletop. I rubbed the side of the pencil lead over the etched letters, taking the sort of imprint you'd collect from a petroglyph or gravestone.

Guy Stillwell was H

It was a fitting epitaph.

"Something I've been meaning to ask you, Newt."

"Shoot."

"How did you know DiLippa ordered the hit on Pollard?"

He placed a Swisher Sweet between his lips and leaned back in his chair.

"You killed him," I said. "That was the actual bargain, wasn't it? The price for the divorce."

"It gave me no joy, Critter. It haunts me."

"Then . . . why?"

"DiLippa needed him removed. He was horning in on the auto parts racket," said Newt. "He was dead whether I did it or not."

"He was your friend."

"Well. There's friends and there's friends."

"Don't I know it."

"It was like in Italy, during the war. I did what I had to do. Justified it as best I could. On those long nights when I can't justify it, I sit on *Rascal*'s fly deck and count stars and say my Hail Marys. We'll see if the saints are watching out for me now that DiLippa knows where I am."

"Let me go to Red and make a deal. Roll over on DiLippa. Go into witness protection."

"Red's not gonna go for that. He and Pollard were like brothers. He's not letting me walk away from this."

"Red doesn't want to kick this hornet's nest any more than I do. He has his campaign to consider. Politics is the art of compromise." I posted my elbows on my knees and tented my fingers, thinking. "You could go to a white-collar prison under a new identity. Life without parole. It's not the Ritz, but it's better than the bottom of a dry well on a horse farm. Trust me. I've seen what's down there."

Newt pondered the forked road before him. "Yeah, that's . . . that's not a bad idea. White-collar prison—that's sort of like a halfway house, isn't it?"

"Sort of."

I put a hand on Newt's shoulder. I wanted to tell him what Guy told Mott Loebel that day. *Be a man. Take responsibility for what got done. You've still got time to build a life on the right side of things.*

But before I could say any of that, Newt said, "Make the deal."

– 25 –

The week after Newt's trial, we gathered in Guy's office—Mother, King, Mary-Louise, my sisters, and me—for the reading of Guy's will, which held only a few surprises. I had assumed that I would be executor of the estate, but in fact, he had named Poppy, so she was there, too. Guy had redone the paperwork recently in preparation for the impending divorce, but the bulk of his estate still went to Mother, including the house, his stock portfolio, and controlling interest in the beer distributorship, for which she already had a buyer.

He left the horse farms and a lump sum of money to Bootsy. I now had controlling interest in the law firm, but the building itself, Guy left to Tatum, and I could see her looking at the big windows in Guy's office, plotting to cover them with yards and yards of aluminum foil. There were charitable and educational donations—the Innocence Project and a special endowment for minorities at UGA law school—and a few cryptic bequests to women who would have to explain these gifts of cash and art to their husbands as they saw fit. He left Mary-Louise a nice chunk of change and strict instructions to retire immediately.

When all was said and done, I realized that I had been left with the one thing he'd never been able to give me when he was living: my freedom. I had money—my own that I had purposefully amassed and a good shot in the arm from my father—and I had *Rascal*. Everyone else headed downstairs, but Tatum strolled over and sat in Guy's chair behind the Chippendale desk.

"You can still have your office here," she said. "I'll help you clear out the storage room behind the kitchen."

"Gee, thanks."

"I found someone to captain your money barge." She tore a sheet from the dot-matrix printer and handed it to me. "I'm running background checks on several candidates for first mate. Seems like these rich fellas mostly use that as a way to install a tax-deductible girlfriend."

I leaned over and kissed the top of her head. "Thank you, Tatum. For everything."

"You'll be invoiced."

Before I left my father's office, I took the empty bottle from the lower left-hand desk drawer and set it in the barrister bookcase between a rusted railroad spike and a ball peen hammer. Downstairs in the foyer, I hugged Mother and Bootsy, extracting myself from tearful embraces and familial bonds as efficiently as possible. I shook King's hand and said, "I'm gonna stop by the Regent before I head down to Thunderbolt Marina. Need a lift?"

"Sure." He nodded, heavy-headed and sad, and followed me to the front door. But at the threshold, he turned back and said, "Judge Sterling, if you're so inclined . . . could I interest you in a cup of coffee?"

"Maybe," said Poppy. "I need a day or two to think about it."

– 26 –

The woman who was never really Rory stood behind the bar at the Regent, puzzling over the daily crossword.

"Someone's waiting for you." She nodded toward a corner booth.

In the shadows under the table, I saw an oxblood stiletto pump dangling from an elegant foot. Posted up at the end of the bar, Fernanda's henchmen followed me with a fixed glare.

I slid into the booth across from her and said, "How did you know I'd be here?"

"Little bird."

"What do you want?"

"Only to wish you well. As long as there's no appeal."

"There won't be. Newt's in protective custody. I don't know where."

"He's been away for twenty-five years. Nothing he knows will bear fruit. They may as well interrogate me about Mussolini." There was a crackled hiss as she took a deep drag on her cigarette. "My father died last night."

"Condolences."

"Same to you."

She drew a dove gray envelope from her purse and laid it on the table. It was smudged and rippled with damp, one end torn open, but I could still see the Stillwell & Hodges logo. My name. My father's handwriting.

"Deputy Duvernay thought it would be prudent to make sure there was no evidence of your sojourn in the netherworld," said Fernanda. "Lo and behold, you'd left this little memento. He was hoping it might contain some deliciously damning information, but it's just a lot of drivel. He goes on at length about his childhood in the sticks and how gaga he was about your mother, and then there's a lot of nitter-natter about legal principle and a final caveat that amounts to 'Don't be like me.' If you were hoping for some outpouring of love and paternal pride, it's not there."

"I prefer to read it myself," I said.

Fernanda was entitled to her opinion, but she didn't speak the secret language in which Guy and I communicated.

"My father. Your father." She sighed heavily. "End of an era."

"Are we through here?"

"The job offer stands."

"I'll pass."

She shrugged and pushed the envelope across the table. I folded it in half, put it in my pocket, and left her to smoke in solitude.

"Bartender," I said, "Sobrietini. Make it a double."

"Yes, sir." She set up a club soda with lime. "Gotta say, I rather like you like this."

"Like what?"

"Bright-eyed and bushy-tailed."

An off-color riff on that crossed my mind, but I resisted it.

"I read about the trial in the newspaper," she said. "I was hoping you'd show up and tell me the rest of the story."

I regaled her with the whole saga, and she reacted with horror and delight in all the right places, interjecting things like, "Oh, my word!" and "Well, dog my cats!" When the tale was all told, she said, "That is one for the textbooks. I can't think of another lawyer who would've thought to play it like that."

"Is that good or bad?"

"Look at the bright side," she said. "You lost a case, but you gained a yacht."

"There ya go." I raised my glass to that. "I'm still figuring out logistics, but it is surprisingly doable to live out on the water like Newt did. The maintenance is a dry well you gotta keep dumping money into. The portside engine is a piece of hammered crap with serious starting issues, and there's a lot of hull corrosion that needs to be addressed. But it's doable. I'll make it work." When I said it out loud, it was real. I was ready.

"So you're leaving," she said. "Sailing off into the sunset. Just like that."

"If I can get the engine started."

"That's wonderful, Critter. I'm glad for you."

"You don't look glad."

"Yeah, well . . . truth is . . . I'll miss you."

"Not if you sail off into the sunset with me."

She laughed and said, "Sure. Let's go."

"I'm serious."

"You are not."

"You'd have your own stateroom with a private head," I said. "I'm not making any assumptions. If I haven't won you over by the time we get to Saint Kitts, I'll buy you a plane ticket back to Savannah. No harm, no foul."

"But what if—I mean, what about—"

She shook her head. Too many questions. Or suspiciously few. I had been falling in love with her for a long time, and I was certain the feeling was mutual, but she wasn't so easily swept off her feet. I could feel her playing with the idea, the same way she always rolled a lime between her hands before she cut into it.

"You are serious," she said.

"As a skull fracture."

"You better not be jerking my chain."

"Never. I promise."

"You don't even know my name."

"Once we get out on the water, we'll have plenty of time to fill in details."

She stood there, lips parted, studying me with her Liz Taylor gaze. I finally understood something Guy had always said about Mother: "I had to believe I was good enough for her, because I could not imagine a world in which I did not have her." The moment, as it is crystallized in my memory, was pregnant with the most optimistic sort of capitalism, the belief that good things do come to those who are willing to imagine something untoward and work their asses off to achieve it.

"I feel obligated to mention there might be Venezuelan pirates after us."

She laughed her unfairly musical laugh. "Well, that makes it a no-brainer."

Without hurrying, she trekked around the end of the long mahogany bar and walked toward me, curvy and athletic. You wouldn't think it's possible to make chinos and sensible shoes look sexy, but somehow, she did. Up close, the white tuxedo shirt smelled starchy and clean. She took my face between her hands and kissed me on the mouth with flagrant intent. I pulled her close and kissed her back, the way a fifteen-year-old dreams of kissing twins.

"Not to be unseemly," she said, "but I think your engine started."

When it felt appropriate to do so, I carefully unpinned the brass nametag from her breast pocket and set it on the bar.

"My name is Vivienne," she said. "Friends call me Vivvy."

ABOUT THE AUTHOR

After thirty years of practicing law in Georgia, Howard T. Scott pivoted from the courtroom to writing fiction inspired by anecdotes from the Southern storytelling tradition he's immersed in. He's one of the founding partners of the Legendary Rhythm & Blues Cruise—the world's only fully chartered blues cruise—and a lover of live music, fitness, nature, historic preservation, and travel. Scott splits his time between the dry land of Athens, Georgia, and the high seas of the Atlantic and the Caribbean aboard *Capricho*. *Rascal on the Run* is his first novel.

Made in the USA
Columbia, SC
07 January 2022

53788815R00143